THE COVEN CONSPIRACY

by

Youngblood Hawke

TELEMACHUS
PRESS

This book is a work of fiction. Names, characters, places and incidents are either the product of the author's imagination or are used fictitiously. Any resemblance to actual persons, living or dead, or to actual events or locales is entirely coincidental.

THE COVEN CONSPIRACY

Edited by: Winslow Eliot

Cover Art:
 Copyright © istockphoto/Skyhobo (4961935)

Visit the author website: http://www.youngbloodhawke1.com

Published by: Telemachus Press, LLC
http: //www.telemachuspress.com

ISBN: 978-1-935670-46-9 (Paperback)
ISBN: 978-1-935670-44-5 (eBook)
2011.05.25
Printed in the United States of America
10 9 8 7 6 5 4 3 2 1

To Katrina

Nightmare Escape

Joanna was running, mile after endless mile of running. Panting. Screaming. The black-robed man was behind her, gaining with every step. It seemed the faster she tried to run, the slower her legs moved. She was now running in slow motion, agonizing minutes passing between each step, and the man was still gaining, until he was only a step behind her! Then his evil hand grabbed her hair, which was blowing behind her in the wind. She heard herself screaming, and it was for real, not just a dream now. Hands were clawing at her face, tearing into her flesh. She jerked away and opened her eyes. She was alone. It was a dream.

But something was wrong ... terribly wrong.

Chapter 1

Had she been looking for signs, that first drive through town would have been taken as a foreboding. The unaccustomed way the skin on the back of her neck seemed to be in the grips of someone's icy fingers. The suspicious, staring-eyed reception she received from the whittler as she drove past his stoop. Even the engine of her shiny red Maverick seemed to whine as she tried to maneuver the dusty ruts in the unpaved street. It was as though the car were aware that it had taken an unwelcome step back through time.

But to Joanna, the foreboding came later. The first signs of her step into terror had been too subtle; her suspicions unaroused. As a stranger, she didn't expect a gracious welcome into a closely-knit mountain community. She was an outsider and would not be accepted, and she knew it.

Even so, Sutters Hamlet had seemed the ideal place to come. Especially if, like Joanna, you wanted to get away from the rush of city life for a year. It was almost at the end of the world. Sutters Hamlet was remote, tucked away in a valley in the mountains of western North Carolina. To Joanna, driving slowly down the dusty main street, and only street for that matter, it seemed that Sutters Hamlet had failed to make the turn of the century along with the rest of the country.

To begin with, there was not one patch of concrete in sight. A precariously old, plank sidewalk looked snaggle-toothed with so many of its boards missing. The dusty street, which ran like a rut between the two dozen or so buildings that were Sutters Hamlet, joined a paved road twenty miles out of town. That twenty miles had taken her over an hour to drive, as it wound along the base of Sutters Mountain and finally dead-ended in a patch of pines about a quarter of a mile the other side of town.

She could see it ahead, the place where the road ran out. She remembered vividly the cattle trail that she would have to force her little Maverick to climb after that. Last summer the trail had been so overgrown that Ted had had to park his car a half a mile away from the bungalow they were headed for. She hoped she could get closer and knew that she should since it was still too early in the spring for the trail to be entirely overgrown.

Curious faces peeked out at her from several shop windows, and an old man sitting on the sidewalk with his chair propped back against the clapboard sides of one of the stores, a pile of shavings around him, stopped his whittling long enough to give her a good once-over. She cringed as she recalled stories of close-knit mountain communities and the way they shunned outsiders. And she was an outsider, no doubt about that. Raised in a New York City orphanage, but a New Yorker all the same, more than her accent set her apart from the mountain folks. In the last few miles on her way into Sutters Hamlet, she had seen several run-down farmhouses with old junk heaps for cars parked outside. With her relatively new 2008 Jeep Cherokee, all shiny and red, she imagined that she was making a splash in Sutters Hamlet. Especially since she was a young woman alone, coming to live for a year in a cabin two miles up the mountain.

Halfway through town she looked in her rear-view mirror and saw the sidewalks behind her suddenly alive. It seemed as though the shops had mysteriously emptied to watch her drive through town. She felt the first gnawing pangs of doubt in the pit of her stomach. She didn't doubt her mission or have misgivings about the career she was giving up in New York. She had already struggled with that decision and knew that she was right. But with this cool and curious reception by the people of Sutters Hamlet (she looked in her rear-view mirror again), she wondered if she couldn't have chosen a friendlier place to hide away for a year. But it was the place, an outpost of the past hidden from the twentieth century by scenic (that was important) mountains, and not the people that had drawn her here, she thought, bolstering her own courage.

She was on the edge of town now, heading toward the mountain, when a small, freshly painted white building at the end of the street caught her eye. It stood out from the rest of the run-down buildings. The sign above the door, printed in large block letters, said very simply: SUTTERS HAMLET

NEWSPAPER. She suddenly felt more at ease. Any town, even one this small, with its own newspaper wasn't completely cut off from the outside. She didn't remember Sutters Hamlet having a newspaper, but for some reason, it made her feel good to know that it did. Involuntarily, she relaxed. She was surprised to find that she had been gripping the wheel with a deathlike hold. After she was out of town, she realized that she had been scared during her drive down Main Street. She began looking for the cattle trail that led to the bungalow and made a point of not looking into her rear-view mirror.

The road abruptly ended at a pine tree. No warning, just . . . suddenly, it wasn't there. The dusty road ran right up to the patch of pines and, about ten feet from the first tree, it gave way to a green patch of saw-bladed Johnson grass. It didn't disappear gradually, with grass and weeds sprinkled along the last few feet as an indication of lack of use: It just ended. Hard packed, tan-colored, little grains of sand and blue-gray gravel one minute, then Johnson grass the next. The almost unnoticeable trail that she had to follow shot off to the left up the mountain.

She forced the Maverick up the side of the mountain, pushing the pedal further into the floorboard when the engine strained in protest at climbing over boulders and skirting logs.

"Sorry, girl," she said between gritted teeth, as she tried to ease over a boulder protruding four inches out of the ground, but heard the rock grinding away sickeningly at the car's undersides. Right then she knew that if she did make it all the way to the bungalow with the car, thereafter, all her trips into Sutters Hamlet for supplies would have to be made on foot. She wasn't going to risk ruining her car by driving over this nontrail unless she absolutely had to.

She inched her way along the trail, glad that she had come this early in the season. Already the trees were beginning to bud, and it wouldn't be long before the bushes and small trees lining this so-called trail would be in full leaf and make it an impossible route to follow except on foot. She remembered last summer. Ted had scratches all over his car after he had gone only three-fourths of the way up the mountain. Maybe she should have packed in to Sutters Hamlet by mule! Not only would she have been able to reach the house with greater ease, she probably would have brought less attention to herself riding through town on the back of a mule than she did in her shiny new car.

Finally. The house, unpainted and weather-beaten like everything else, greeted her with shuttered windows and a padlocked door. It seemed smaller than she remembered, a four-room bungalow sitting in a tiny clearing on the side of the mountain. The view was majestic! The mountain dipped sharply just below the house, giving her a clear view of most of the valley. The valley was a carpet of spotted green below her: evergreens sprinkled among the budding hardwoods, with a patchwork of early spring grays and browns.

Joanna threw open the car door and scrambled out to survey her mountain home for the next year. Already her heart was beating a bit too fast, as it often did when she had just found a promising scene. Her trained eyes were already scrutinizing the landscape for form, color, and play of light and shadow. Her hands ached for a brush and easel, and her soul cried out to be free. She wanted to get to work on the project at hand.

She had come to paint. And as soon as she could get her things unloaded and the house opened and airing, she would make a brief reconnaissance of this part of her mountain, looking for likely scenes for her canvas. Then tomorrow, maybe tomorrow if all went well, or the next day at the very latest, she would begin to paint.

Night fell in the mountains as if someone had suddenly pulled down a black curtain across the sky. With her cabin located on the east slope, the darkness came even more suddenly than she had expected. Joanna was slaving inside the cabin, doors and windows thrown open for airing, the mattress off the bed, and the doors to the cupboards standing open with the shelves freshly scrubbed. She was working madly, trying to do all the cleaning in one afternoon so she would have that unpleasant chore over and done. One minute she could see by the afternoon light; there was a period of brief twilight that she hardly noticed; then she was standing in near blackness.

Without thinking, she stumbled uncertainly across the living room to the front door where she ran her hand along the wall searching for the light switch. With a sinking heart she remembered – the cabin had no electricity. Last summer, which she had spent protected by Ted, the lack of electrical lights in the cabin had added a primitive atmosphere to their week. The final touches of coziness were the shadows dancing against the walls from the dim glow of the kerosene lantern. But now . . . she shuddered in the night. Desperately, she looked around for the lantern, but knew she wouldn't find it among the shadowy forms in the room. The prospect of spending her evenings by lantern light held a foreboding note. Alone in an isolated cabin, facing the darkness for the first time, she was frightened.

Planning her trip back to her well-lighted Manhattan apartment, the thought of spending the year with no electricity had seemed quaint. Not frightening at all. But now…

Grabbing hold of herself, she forced herself to think. Where had Ted found the lantern last year? Without difficulty she remembered, then rushed to the back bedroom that she would occupy and, gratefully, found three lanterns in a corner of the closet. She fumbled among her belongings until she found a book of matches, and when she touched the flame to the wick, gave a grateful sigh.

The living room was bathed in a soft orange-brown glow that sent shadows dancing against the walls with a life of their own. Quaint last year maybe, now she gazed hypnotically at the eerie patterns alive on the walls. An uneasiness crept over her as she watched the shadows spring to the silent tune the lantern played.

Forcefully, she took hold of her emotions lest her imagination run away with her. She pushed aside the lantern's spell and forced herself to remember last summer. A reality of quaint, dancing shadows. Not of living ones.

Her emotions firmly in hand, she looked around her at the nearly clean house and, with the dreaded half day of housework nearly done, viewed the cabin with the same affection she had held for its rustic beauty the week she and Ted spent there.

There was that high-backed rocking chair Ted had liked so much. The bare rafters above, the five-pointed buck's head hanging on the wall above the fireplace, and especially the bearskin rug (Where was the rug?) gave the cabin, especially the living room, a very masculine effect. Involuntarily, she scanned the room for the rug, which she already knew was no longer there, because in cleaning the cabin she had scrubbed every corner of the house.

She missed that furry hide from some large brown bear. Even with its glass eyes and teeth still intact, which had so frightened her when she first entered the room that drizzling, wet day last summer, the bearskin had been her favorite of all the cabin's furnishings.

She and Ted had come in dripping wet after walking the last half mile up the mountain from the parked car; the drizzling rain soaked them and the wet undergrowth finished off the job. The cabin, like today, was shuttered and deserted. The padlock on the front door wouldn't open, so they had to stand there at least five minutes until Ted managed to work the lock, and by the time they opened the door, Joanna was shivering from the wet and the cooler temperatures the rain brought with it. She stepped inside, saw the bear glaring at her from the floor, its jaws open and teeth bared, and screamed.

She felt foolish when she realized it was only a rug, but it had seemed real.

It was summer and was supposed to have been warm, but it was raining and wasn't. The oil heater worked, but there was no oil. The fireplace worked too, but would only burn dry logs-not the soaked-through logs stacked outside the cabin. Ted brought in an armload to begin drying, but in the meantime, Joanna was wet and cold. Right then she had her first and only second thoughts about their stolen week. But Ted, blond, Nordic, and muscular, as usual, had the perfect solution.

He locked the door from the inside, left the cabin shuttered, then with hands accustomed to the hills and valleys of her body, began undressing her. They lay together on the rug, wrapped its thick fur around them, and snuggled until she was warm and dry, then made love. They spent the night wrapped inside the bearskin, then in the morning it was sunny and warm and summer was back. But for the rest of the week, that was their love bed and sometimes their sleeping bed as well.

Now it was gone and she resented it. Futilely, she wondered if it had been stolen, and if so by whom.

She walked to the front door, still open, and looked out into the night. The black sky was sprinkled with specks of light, more stars than she would see in a whole year from her apartment (former apartment) window in New York. Night sounds drifted up the mountain to her. An owl screeched somewhere below, and farther away, she heard the barking of a fox. For a few moments there was silence, then from behind her, and not too far from her cabin, its mate answered. Her skin crawled at hearing these sounds so near her, and she unable to see what was the source. Suddenly she closed the door and bolted it, then dashed into the kitchen and closed the back door. The windows were next. Anything that didn't have a screen was closed and latched. The screened windows were partially closed, left ajar just enough to allow a breeze to circulate. She felt safer now that the night and its cloaked visitors were shut outside the cabin walls.

She pushed her hair back from her face, the long raven-black strands having fallen askew as she rushed about closing windows and slamming doors. She knew her heart was beating too fast, and it wasn't from thinking about all the beautiful scenery the mountains would offer to her canvas.

This fear was one aspect of the next year that she didn't know how well she would cope with. Being on Sutters Mountain with Ted was one thing. But as Ted had been quick to point out when she asked him to see if he could arrange for her to rent the cabin for a year, living there alone would be quite another.

Ted had been right. Already she knew that. She was a city girl, and on this her first night on the mountain she already knew her bravery was not as great as she had imagined. Neither living alone in Manhattan, nor the independence and self-reliance of being raised an orphan had prepared her to live alone in these mountain wilds.

She had always felt a closeness with nature, but only fully realized it during the week she and Ted spent together. Even now she wasn't sure why she felt such a need to be out of the city, such a need to try and paint, and to paint natural beauty. But she had insights, insights that most people never were aware of, or maybe shouldn't be ... She knew, had always known, that it had something to do with her inner self, something more animal than human.

Like the fox. She had never heard a fox before. But as soon as she heard it, she knew it was a fox. She also knew it wouldn't hurt her, but she had closed the doors anyway, because it was somewhere out there unseen in the dark, and she was frightened of things, animals she couldn't see.

There was the time when she was still in the orphanage and she knew that Betty Susan Henderson was going to die. She told Sister Marie, but was told that only God could know when someone was going to die. Betty Susan was ten and Joanna was eleven. They were walking down the sidewalk, and Joanna was holding her hand because she knew it was going to happen. She told Betty Susan that she was feeling ill and asked if she could hold onto her for support, but it was really to protect Betty Susan.

Then it happened. For no reason that Joanna could see, Betty Susan suddenly jerked away and ran into the street! She ran right in front of a huge truck delivering fruit to the orphanage. Joanna screamed after her, tried to grab the tail of her yellow cotton dress, but it was too late! She heard Betty Susan scream just before the truck hit her. Then there was the thud and she was dead.

Sister Marie always looked at her in a strange way after that, and Joanna knew that she was wondering if Joanna had, in some way, killed her.

That was the worst thing she knew. But there were others. Sometimes she could predict when one of the other kids would be adopted, and she also knew who wouldn't. She knew that she never would be adopted, but she didn't know why. And she knew when Sister Teresa would die, but she didn't tell anyone because she knew no one would believe her. And besides, Sister Teresa was old and died of old age. But Joanna knew just the same.

It was mainly because of her inner power that, at the young age of twenty-five, she had illustrated four children's books and was a much sought-after illustrator among the juvenile book publishers and some magazine publishers. She had done well, just happening to be in the right place at the right time. But what she really wanted to do was paint, landscapes mainly, and it was for that reason that she finally decided to take a year away from her illustrating and go into the backwoods and paint. She had sold several of her paintings and had a small exhibition at a very minor downtown art gallery. By devoting a year to painting, she hoped to get together a body of work to sell, which would enable her to devote more of her time to painting and less to commercial illustrating. Perhaps someday she would be able to paint exclusively and would not have to accept any more assignments illustrating children's stories.

She remembered this cabin, and the scenic and almost untouched mountains, and decided this was where she would come. Ted, no longer her lover but still a friend, made the arrangements. Joanna paid a year's rent in advance, and here she was.

Still in a thoughtful mood, she realized she was hungry and remembered that she hadn't eaten since before passing through Sutters Hamlet that morning. She went to a cardboard box still sitting packed atop the kitchen cabinets, threw open the flaps, and looked down on an assortment of canned goods that was meant to see her through until she had the time to go into Sutters Hamlet and stock up. She pulled out a can of pork and beans, and unceremoniously ate them with a glass of water, then crawled wearily into bed.

Again she listened to the night sounds of the mountain, sounds she knew she would have to grow accustomed to. As she drifted off to sleep, she dreamily imagined the screeches and barks of the wild things drawing nearer to her cabin. Once she awoke with a start, after dreaming that a man, cloaked in black, watched her through the window as she slept. She looked at the window. There was no one there. She shoved the frightening thoughts from her mind as she fell back into a fitful sleep.

Chapter 2

What a wonderful sight! The sun peeked its golden orange face over the surface of the earth. The green needles from a million pines glistened like diamonds in the wake of the rising sun, while above a flock of crows played an early morning game of aerial chase over the valley, with the mountain summits rising another thousand feet around them. Standing in front of her cabin, Joanna could watch the crows' game from their own height, halfway up the mountain.

She watched until the birds were too far away for her to enjoy, then turned and, with her sketch pad under her arm, began climbing the mountain. Occasionally, she stopped to sketch a tree or unusual rock outcropping, careful to note the colors and shadows for future reference should she choose that particular sketch as the subject for a painting. She had always found it far easier to make pastel or pencil sketches of her outdoor subjects and do the actual painting at her leisure, sometimes miles away from the subject. In her first efforts at painting landscapes in upstate New York, she had learned it was a mistake to try and carry her easel, brushes, and paints and do her actual painting in the field. For one thing, it was tiring, with her equipment growing both heavy and cumbersome after trekking a few miles. Second, she learned the hard way, after a sudden shower ruined one of her paintings that she could never count on the weather.

By midday her wanderings had taken her in a complete circle of the cabin. She was careful not to get carried away with her drawings and stray too far. That was another thing Ted had cautioned her about. Getting lost.

"You don't know how to find your way around in those mountains," he had warned. "Out there, there's no street guide to help you."

He was right, she knew, and she would have to be extra careful in the beginning as she learned to navigate the mountain. That was why she circled the cabin, always careful to keep her bearings. Each day she went out she would venture a bit farther, and step by step she would learn to fend for herself until she could travel the mountain without fear of getting lost.

The sun was directly overhead, and she knew without looking at her watch that it was noon. For one thing, her stomach was protesting, though she knew that was due in part to the unaccustomed exercise. With sketch pad tucked under her arm, she headed back toward the cabin. Her heart was pounding a bit fast until she saw the clearing ahead and she knew that she had navigated correctly and returned safely.

Another can of tunas soothed her stomach. That was three cans of beans in a row. She had had beans for breakfast as well.

She still hadn't unpacked the boxes of canned foods, sitting on the cabinet top from the day before. She began pulling out cans and was dismayed to find beans, beans, beans! Peas and beans and a few cans of fruit! They had seemed like a good staple when she looked at them from the drawing board of her New York apartment. But after three cans, she suddenly couldn't bear the thought of eating all those beans and nothing else.

She would go back into Sutters Hamlet and buy some more appetizing food. She sat back down at the table and began making a list, careful to list only nonperishables, since there was no refrigerator. Canned goods and vegetables would be easy enough to keep, but there would be no meat unless she could find some cured ham or bacon. When she finished, the grocery list was so long she knew she would have to make several trips if she walked. She cringed at the thought of forcing her car back over that rutty trail, but she knew it was the only way. In the future, she hoped that she could keep her needs down by making frequent trips into town on foot and bringing back smaller loads, and that way use her car only when it was absolutely necessary.

The trip down the mountain, like the trip up the day before, was one long series of grinding metal. Thumps and bumps as the car was slapped in the face by protruding branches and lurched unceremoniously into holes and sudden dips in the trail.

"Goddamn," she cried as a stubby oak branch smashed into the windshield, then scraped along the entire side of the car. She knew the red paint had a white streak in it for sure.

After what seemed like an eternity, she finally emerged at the dead-end outside town. The streets were almost lifeless. The same old man sat in the same place whittling, his chair propped in the same manner against the front of what she now identified as a hardware store. He was wearing the same pair of faded blue overalls. She recognized the patch on one of the knees. It even looked like the same pile of shavings around his chair.

It was eerie how a day made no difference. The town was exactly the same as the day before. She saw the whittler look up and watch her as her car pulled into town, just like yesterday. His unblinking eyes followed her approach; he made no effort to hide his curiosity.

On a snap decision, she whipped her car to the sidewalk in front of him. Grabbing her handbag, the devil in her pumping her blood full of mischief, she jumped from her car, bounded up to the old man and extended her hand.

"I'm Joanna Crawford. I live in that old house up the mountain," she pointed in the general direction, "and I'm glad to meet you."

Her hand went untaken. He nodded his head once, and Joanna took that to be his acknowledgment of her introduction. He didn't speak, but looked steadily into her eyes.

She saw a two or three-day-old growth of salt-and pepper beard, a band of similarly colored hair around a balding head, and kind yet curious, and somewhat distrustful, brown eyes.

When he still had not spoken, she appeared unconcerned and asked, "Can you tell me where I can buy some food?"

After a moment's hesitation he again nodded, indicating a store across the street. Housed next to the Sutters Hamlet Newspaper in a rickety old frame building was the grocery store with a sign above reading, Potter's Food Store.

Joanna thanked him and walked briskly across the brown, dusty street. She entered the store to face a wall of silent stares from two customers and a thin shouldered, bespectacled little man with a white apron whom she assumed was Potter. After a few moments, the three went silently about their business. Finding only shopping baskets and no carts, Joanna rummaged through the store, piling her food into the basket dangling from her arm. By the time she had all that she came for, including some mountain-cured bacon, the other women had paid for their goods and left.

She walked to the counter, purse in hand. The white-aproned man quietly watched her approach.

"Are you Mr. Potter?" she quizzed.

He nodded. He stood without speaking, his face void of emotion. Joanna looked at her pile of food, which he was making no effort to ring up on his antique cash register.

"How much will this come to?" she asked, forcing him into action.

Still without speaking, Potter began to total her bill.

"This is a friendly little town," she said lightly, overcome with the same deviltry that had made her confront the old whittler.

Again he only nodded.

"Have you lived here long?"

This time she was startled to hear him reply with a grunt, that she took to mean yes.

"I just came here yesterday," she said. "I'll be staying about a year."

For some reason unknown to her. Potter stopped suddenly and looked at her, one hand on the cash register ready to ring up a $1.49 purchase. But for a moment his hand hung suspended, like a grotesque ornament hanging from the wall. Blankly he stared at her, making no effort to hide his curiosity or suspicion or whatever it was he felt.

Joanna experienced that same feeling creeping up her spine that she had felt as she drove through town. Uneasiness. She had injected herself into a world where the people were alien. But looking at it from their viewpoint, she was the alien, and not they. This was a small microcosm, a small world unto itself, void of outside influences. She could as well have been from another planet and not been received with more skepticism.

Potter finished totaling her purchase and spoke for the first time when he told her that she had just purchased twenty-seven dollars and nineteen cents worth of groceries, filling three large brown bags.

She paid him, started to ask for help in carrying the groceries to the car, but saw in his eyes that there was no willingness to help, so changed her mind. Choosing the two lightest bags, she lifted them from the counter and walked heavy-footed to the door, which she was relieved to see was standing open. When she stepped onto the sidewalk, downtown Sutters Hamlet stopped to watch. The half-dozen or so people on the street stopped what they were doing and watched her struggle toward her car with the two heavy grocery bags. She noted without surprise that no one made any move to help.

Halfway across the street, the bags suddenly increased in weight. Her arms weakened and she felt her grip loosening. She started to run, half bent over clutching the bags, hoping to reach her car before she dropped everything in the middle of the street. She felt the bag in her left arm begin to slide downward. She stopped it with her knee. The other one began to slip, and just as she felt her grip slipping for good, an unseen arm literally snatched the falling bag from the air. "Saved! She looked up into the first friendly face she had seen.

She straightened up, gaining a secure grip on the one bag she still held.

"Thank you. You just kept dirt off my food," she said, trying to sound light and cheery. "I'm Joanna Crawford."

"You looked like you needed help," the man said.

"I did."

"I'm 0. T. Hanover." He smiled at the proper time, the time you normally should smile in an introduction, and suddenly Joanna knew that he wasn't a native of Sutters Hamlet. Something about that thread of knowledge made her relax.

"You're different from everyone else I've met around here," she said. "You actually talk."

He laughed a deep-throated laugh, revealing facial wrinkles that were not immediately apparent. At first glance, he appeared to be a man in his fifties, but upon closer examination, Joanna guessed him to be close to seventy. With a full head of cotton-white hair, he wore his age well. His eyes were kind and deep brown. They smiled even when the rest of his face was solemn. She sensed that he was her first friend in this small mountain community.

"So you've already noticed that some of our residents aren't particularly friendly to strangers," he joked.

She recognized his statement as the one inalienable truth about Sutters Hamlet.

Hanover set her two bags in the back seat of her Maverick, then with Joanna tagging behind keeping up a breezy conversation, he retrieved the other bag from the counter in Potter's Store. Potter was still behind the counter where she had left him; he couldn't help but have seen her struggle with the groceries outside his door. But he was as taciturn and aloof as before, still making no friendly overtures to Joanna, even though she entered his premises this time in the presence of one of his town folk. He returned Hanover's greeting, but that was all.

"How do you stand it here?" she asked Hanover as he slid the last bag onto the back seat beside the other two. "You don't seem to fit here any more than I do."

Hanover smiled, the wrinkles on his face again becoming pronounced. "Everyone is a misfit to a degree, but some of us are able to disguise the fact and some aren't. I like the simple life here, so I try to fit in as best I can," he said.

He closed the car door, then looked around. She followed his gaze and saw a dozen faces peering at them from the sidewalk, from open doorways, and from behind dark panes of glass in store windows. The skin on the back of her neck crawled again, the tingling spreading through her shoulders and down her arms into her fingertips. She felt like a goldfish, and all those people were on the outside of the bowl looking in at her.

"I believe you're as much a misfit right now as I am," she said, indicating the watchful eyes.

"Don't mind them," Hanover said. "If you stay here long enough, you'll be accepted as one of them."

Joanna shivered. That was one thing she wasn't sure she wanted.

"Did you buy any perishables?" he asked.

Joanna ran her grocery list through her mind, then shook her head. "No, nothing. I don't have a refrigerator."

Hanover seemed pleased.

"Good. Why don't we have a cup of coffee together."

She had no intention of turning down an invitation from her first friend. She accepted.

As she fell in beside him she expected to be led to a cafe, but saw that they were headed directly for the Sutters Hamlet Newspaper office. Hanover caught her look of surprise.

"I run the newspaper," he said in answer to her silent enquiry. "I'm the editor, publisher, reporter, and printer."

As he opened the door and she stepped into the one-typewriter newsroom, she was beginning to realize why Hanover was different and why she had instantly liked him. Like her, he was artistic. He was a writer, if only for a tiny mountain newspaper.

Hanover put a pot of water on to boil on a small gas burner, and she noted that at least one area of civilization was making inroads in Sutters Hamlet. Instant coffee.

Her eyes darted around the room, tracing the course of the news from the old Underwood sitting in the corner by the front window, to the typesetter and finally to a small and very antique hand-powered printing press. The question that she had had upon first seeing the newspaper the day before again popped into her mind.

"How does a place as small as Sutters Hamlet support a newspaper?" she asked.

Hanover had just finished putting instant coffee and Cremora in their cups.

"It doesn't really," he said. "We publish once every other week, and even then it's sometimes hard to fill the paper. The Hamlet isn't the most eventful place I've been. If I didn't have other income I couldn't make it."

Her mouth dropped open for her next question, but the water was boiling and Hanover turned away to finish making their coffee. He carried the two steaming hot cups to the desk by the window and sat them down. He shoved the Underwood back and rearranged some papers, then invited Joanna to sit. He dragged up another chair and sat beside her. Before she could continue with her questioning, he was interrogating her.

"What brought you back to Sutters Hamlet?"

The question came like a slap in the face. What brought her back to Sutters Hamlet? On her visit there with Ted the year before, she had never come into town to shop. She had passed through only twice during the week, and one of those times, when they were leaving, was before dawn.

"How did you know I was here before?" she exclaimed, astonishment showing clearly on her face.

Hanover smiled. "Then it was you who came here with the young man."

She nodded.

"When you drove through town yesterday I thought you looked like the same young lady."

"You must have a fantastic memory," she said, still not quite believing that he could have remembered her face after one brief glance a year before.

"We don't get many visitors here, so there aren't that many new faces to remember," he replied. "But you still haven't told me why you're here. No one comes to Sutters Hamlet without a reason."

"I'm a painter," she explained, "and I came to spend a year here painting the mountains." She went into a brief explanation of her career illustrating children's books and her ambition to paint on a more serious level.

He nodded understandingly as he listened. "I'm sure things will work out to your own benefit." The coffee had cooled and Hanover lifted the cup to his lips. Joanna pounced on that instant to ask a question of her own; there were several things about the man that had aroused her curiosity. For one thing, Hanover was an intellectual, and why would a man like that bury himself away in a tiny mountain village publishing a newspaper every other week?

"What about yourself, Mr. Hanover? There must be an interesting story behind your being here." She hid behind her coffee cup, the steam rising across her face as she took a testing sip.

"Yes, there is, I suppose." A distant look took control of his face, and his voice came out a bit wistfully. "I came here thirty years ago to do much the same as you're doing now, and I never intended to stay. I was a reporter on the Washington Post covering Capitol Hill and the White House. I had begun to have a good many short stories and articles published in several well-known national magazines – Saturday Evening Post and Colliers to name a couple. I came to Sutters Hamlet to research a magazine article, and as you see, I'm still here."

He grew silent. The distant look left his face, and he was again in the present.

Joanna looked at Hanover with renewed interest, but with uncertainty. What was there about him, and about his name, that now seemed familiar?

He must have seen the puzzlement on her face. He smiled and shrugged sheepishly. "Old stories for young hearts," he said, his face curled upward in a fond smile. "I hope I'm not boring you."

"No!" she blurted, her cheeks flushing, embarrassed that her face had mirrored her inner confusion. "I'm not bored at all! It's just that. ..." Her voice trailed off, her words, dangled in silence. His phrase had a familiar ring. " 'Old stories for young hearts' you said?" She thrashed the phrase over in her mind.

She cocked her eyebrows questioningly. "That's it!" she nearly shouted, and spilled coffee over both of them as she too quickly placed her cup on the desk. "You're that 0. T. Hanover. The writer!"

She looked into his face expectantly, searching for confirmation. When she saw that same fond smile she knew she was right.

"You've guessed my secret," he said beaming, obviously pleased that he had been recognized. "We don't get many visitors from the outside here in Sutters Hamlet. And very few of them know who I am. Not that it matters," he said shrugging. "If I had wanted the worldly rewards of fame and fortune, I would have remained in Washington, or maybe even New York. But even for a recluse like me, it does the spirit good to meet a stranger familiar with my work."

"I'm more than just familiar with your work," she said, "I studied you in a college lit course. The literature of American folklore, and one of your books was our major text."

"Which one?" he asked, his eyes beaming their satisfaction.

"Your last remark! 'Old stories for young hearts.' That was the title of the book!"

"Oh, yes," he said, and chuckled to himself. "I suppose I did use that expression, didn't I? Old Stories for Young Hearts was one of my first books."

"It was one of your best," Joanna said.

"It was my best," he corrected. He wrinkled his brow questioningly. "Have you read the others?"

"Not all of them," she confessed. "1 got pretty interested in folklore during that course, and I read a couple of your other books."

She looked at him now with a new understanding, with admiration. Her questions, most of them at least, had been answered. Hanover, the intellectual, the writer on American folklore, would naturally live in a place like Sutters Hamlet. A mirror to a past way of life, the tiny mountain community would be a logical place of residence. But still, he was different from the others. He was still an intellectual, an outsider like herself. And it was that, along with the fact that he was a writer, which drew her to him. They were kindred spirits, both artists, both from an outside world.

"You're required reading, did you know that?" she asked, admiringly.

"Enough," he said uneasily, and dismissed her with a wave of his hand. He shifted his eyes away from her to the sandy street outside.

And he was indeed modest about his professional stature, she thought. Another reason for choosing Sutters Hamlet over New York. "I didn't mean to get personal," she said apologetically.

He smiled. "You didn't. I guess I'm an old man who's not accustomed to such attention and particularly not from one as young and pretty as you."

He lifted his shoulders and his whole body seemed to shrug, wistfully she thought. "I guess I'm really not suited for the life of an author in the big city. That's one of the reasons I left Washington and came here. I grew up in these mountains."

"In Sutters Hamlet?" she asked.

"No. Asheville. Tom Wolfe's town. I knew him."

Joanna detected a trace of pride in his voice, and she imagined that Wolfe might have been one of his boyhood idols.

"You actually knew Tom Wolfe?" She was no particular fan of Wolfe's, but she was fully aware of the legacy he had carved for himself in the literary world several decades before.

"Not well," Hanover admitted. "I was just a young reporter working in Asheville at the time. I interviewed him once, then ran into him several times afterwards. We had a few drinks together."

Joanna was impressed, and her face must have showed her admiration. Hanover now seemed comfortable talking about himself.

"But then I made the mistake of thinking I wanted to go to the big city, and I found myself in Washington, making a lot of money, becoming well-known, and generally making myself miserable."

He stopped talking and again brought the cup of coffee to his lips. His mouth wrinkled into a frown. "Cold. That's what I get for talking so much. See what I mean," he said, his eyes twinkling. "I'm no extrovert. A true extrovert could talk and drink at the same time." He chuckled at his own joke, then sat the cup on the desk and shoved it aside. "Anyway," he said, continuing his story, "I finally decided the city wasn't the place for me. I came back to the mountains and finally ended up here where I can write in peace and publish the newspaper as something of a side interest."

"But Sutters Hamlet is quite a ways from Asheville," she said. "How did you end up in such a secluded place? You said you first came here to research a magazine article?"

"That's right," he nodded. "But it was several years later that I eventually came here to live."

"That's interesting," she said introspectively. "I mean, we have another thing in common. We both visited here and later decided it would be a good place to come and work. Odd too, now that I think of it. At least in my case it is."

"How so?" he asked.

"Ted, the man I vacationed with last summer, just by chance met the man who owns the cabin I'm renting. It was a snap decision to get away for that week, and this cabin just happened to be available. It would have made more sense had we rented a cabin nearer home in the Catskills, but we took potluck and drove six hundred miles to a place neither of us had ever seen. Don't you think it's odd?" she asked. "I mean coming all the way here? And now here I am again."

"Maybe so," he said, his face contemplative. "But who knows what makes us do these things?"

He again shrugged his shoulders in his distinctive way, his whole body arching upward to place the question mark at the end of his sentence. "But I think you've come to a good place. These mountains are very scenic. If I were a painter, I think I would have come here too. How do you like your cabin?" he asked suddenly, changing the subject.

"Fine, so far," she said. "I've never tried to live without electricity, but I guess I'll get used to it. Do many of the houses around here lack electricity?"

"Only a few," he said. "As a matter of fact, yours is one of the very few I can think of, and that's only because it's rarely used. The mountains around here are still pretty primitive, but electricity is something everyone now takes for granted."

"I wish the man who owns the cabin would have taken it more for granted." she complained. "It will definitely take some getting used to."

"Look," Hanover said impulsively, "if you need any help up there I'm just down the mountain. So don't be shy about letting me know of any way I can be of help."

"Thanks," she said and honestly meant it. "I'm sure I'll be calling on you."

"And I'll look in on you from time to time," he said. "Sometimes I like to get out and walk just to be alone, so when I'm up your way I'll check on you."

"Would you?" she asked, surprising herself at her enthusiasm for his promised visits. She felt a sudden relief, a relief from tension she didn't know had existed. The prospect of sharing the mountain with the unknown was not comforting. She knew that. But she hadn't known what tension had already begun to build up inside her. It was, she supposed, the thought of being alone on the mountain in a shadowy cabin that was so relieved at the promise of having an occasional visit from a friend. "I'd like that," she said.

"Then it's settled. For the next year I'll be your guardian and friend. Oh, and let me know if you need paints or canvas or anything of that nature brought in from the outside. I make occasional trips out and would be glad to buy anything you can't get here."

"Thanks," she said. "I'll keep that in mind."

A shuffling of feet and the rattle of a door opening behind them ended their conversation. Joanna looked over her shoulder and saw a frail little woman walk in off the street.

"Mr. Hanover, and how are ye today?"

Hanover was rising, smiling, going to greet her.

"Fine, Mrs. Johnson. And how are you?" His voice was warm.

"Fair to middlin'."

Hanover turned to Joanna. "Mrs. Johnson, I'd like you to meet Miss Crawford. She's come here to paint the mountains."

Mrs. Johnson's face dropped in astonishment. "Paint the mountains, ye say?" Her voice was a high-pitched whine, almost a screech. "What in heaven's name do ye mean? They turn pretty colors in the fall!"

Hanover was laughing. "No, no! Miss Crawford has come to paint pictures of the mountains."

Mrs. Johnson flushed. "Oh! Silly me! You're an artist then."

Joanna nodded, barely able to conceal her amusement.

"Mrs. Johnson is one of my birddogs," Hanover said. "When she hears something that might make an interesting news story, she tells me. You got something for me today?"

Mrs. Johnson smiled. "Just a little story."

Their voices were fading as Joanna again looked out the window and saw that the sun was getting dangerously low. "I must go. It's getting late." She excused herself, making over Mrs. Johnson's dress, her freshly styled hair, striving to make a good impression on the second person who had greeted her without hostility. She was a bit lightheaded with her good fortune at finding two friendly souls after such an unfriendly beginning.

She stepped onto the dusty street ignoring the unfriendly looks from the townspeople. The dirt road felt good under her feet. The air felt good to breathe. Fresh. No exhaust fumes. No blaring horns. No crowds of people rushing past, clawing their way ahead. Peaceful. Serene. Close to nature. It all felt good.

She looked at the mountain, now long in shadows. She wanted to get back while there was still plenty of light, prepare a decent meal, and go to bed early. Tomorrow was a new day, under a new sky, with a brand-new mountain, which she had come to paint.

Chapter 3

A thump on the door woke her up. She lay in the darkness, her mind trying to determine if she had actually heard a noise at the front door of her cabin or if she had just dreamed it. There it was again. A thud at the front door, a dull thud as though someone had kicked it. Terror gripped her like an icy hand. She lay motionless, her heart pounding wildly in the protection the darkness gave. There was a rustling of clothes, then footsteps disappearing into the night, then silence.

For several minutes she listened. Her heart was a knot in her throat. Satisfied that the intruder was gone, she eased herself out of bed. The hardwood floor was rough and cold beneath her bare feet. A splinter pricked her foot, and she stepped more gently. She crept into the living room, stopped in the middle of the room, and listened again. There was only the black of the cabin and the stillness of the night. Her eyes were fixed on the door. There was not a sound outside.

Against her better judgment, she crept to the front window by the door. Cautiously, she parted the curtains just enough to allow one eye to peer out. She was met with a wall of black. She tried to see the front door, but the cabin walls obscured her vision.

She dropped the curtain back in place. Curiosity shoved her fear aside. She stepped to the door and unfastened the inside latch. She hesitated a few moments before cracking the door. A gust of night air struck her in the face. She stuck her face in the gap of the opened door and peered into the night. She saw nothing. Her ears were tuned to the outside. At the slightest sound out of place, she was prepared to slam shut the door. There was nothing. Not a sound.

She was about to close the door and wait until morning for a closer inspection when she glanced up the mountain. Above her cabin, the mountain became even steeper, then appeared to level off again to a gentler climb to the summit. Through the trees she saw a light flickering in the darkness. The way it danced about and changed intensity she knew it was a burning fire and not an artificial light.

A chill ran up her spine. She had dreamed she saw a face in the window last night. Another intruder tonight. And now a fire burning not far from her cabin! She wondered if the evening's intruder and the fire were in any way connected? It could have just been a prankster. Some teenagers out for fun. A peeping tom. A burglar. Her mind ran down a list of possibilities.

While she watched, the fire on the mountain suddenly died. It happened too fast for it to have burned out naturally. It was extinguished. She slammed the door and bolted it in one swift motion.

Terror gripped her – terror brought by precognition. She knew that whoever extinguished the fire was now on his way to her cabin. But any knowledge was agonizingly incomplete! She did not know, had no idea, of the purpose of the coming visit. But reason told her that the intent of middle-of-the-night visitors could not be good.

She wanted to flee, but she was trapped. Trapped by the darkness and the mountain that she hardly knew. To flee and get lost on the mountain was no salvation. But here in the cabin she was a target. The cabin's windows and doors could easily be bashed in, and she would be trapped by her very refuge.

Her only protection was the night. The same darkness that cloaked her visitors could also cloak her. Her mind was made. She raced into the bedroom, ripping off her white nightgown. She pulled on her jeans and a dark pullover sweater, then grabbing her shoes in her hands, she raced out the back door into the night.

She ran to the edge of the clearing and disappeared into the trees. With the forest serving as her protection, she quietly navigated around the edge of the clearing to a point beside the cabin that gave her a clear view of both the front and rear doors. She was located slightly down the mountain from the cabin and across the clearing from the point where she expected her visitors to appear. She found a spot sheltered on three sides by bushes, and sat down to wait.

She didn't have to wait long.

First she heard their footsteps, a snapping of dried branches and twigs across the clearing. The sound was faint, and it happened only once. Her eyes ached in their sockets as she tried to see through the night.

Suddenly, it was there, whatever or whoever it was. A dark figure stood ghostlike just inside the clearing, hardly more than a shadow. A black robe hung from its shoulders, falling nearly to the ground. The face was hidden deep in the hood, which was peaked at the back like an ancient monk's robe.

Joanna could feel her heart pounding as the figure remained motionless, looking intently at the cabin while the minutes dragged agonizingly by. At any moment, she expected the figure to advance on the cabin and crash inside in search of her. Or (and she gasped so loud at the second possibility that she was afraid she had been heard) go to her bedroom window and peer in.

This was the cloaked visitor from her dream of the night before! It had been no dream at all! The face in her window had been real. The realization sent shivers of fear quaking through her. Was this an exact repeat of last night? Had this same vigil occurred? Had this man, or this thing, silently watched her cabin from that exact same spot, then quietly walked to her window and watched her as she slept?

She was rigid with fear. Riveted to the ground, too numb to run had she any place to run. She was afraid to breathe, lest her hiding place be discovered.

The minutes dragged by. Agonizingly slow. And still the black thing waited, standing like a black post at the edge of the clearing. The night was silent. It was as though the mountain had died. No barking of foxes. No breeze rustling the leaves. Nothing. The mountain, like herself, was holding its breath to see what the black thing did.

Finally, it moved. In a slow, almost ghostlike motion, two arms draped in flowing black sleeves raised to the sky. They remained fixed there for a moment, then snapped in a circular movement as though signaling.

Joanna tensed, hardly daring to breathe, hoping that she was wrong. But then she heard the others and she knew ... the black-robed figure across the clearing was not alone. There were others hidden by the night, and on signal from their leader, they were circling her cabin.

She fought the panic that gripped her, the panic that wanted to rip her from her hiding place and send her crashing blindly down the mountain to ... to what? To reveal her location, surely.

The mountain was no longer cloaked in silence. She heard their movements as they circled the edge of the clearing, the crisp undergrowth tracking their progress as the group drew steadily nearer to her hiding place.

Suddenly, there were two black, silhouettes in the clearing, then farther along another stepped from the forest. Listening, she followed the progress of the band – there were many of them – and at intervals others stepped out of the trees, and like their leader, motionlessly watched her cabin. The remainder of the troupe drew closer, and she knew that when the mountain again grew silent, her cabin would be circled by the figures in the black, hooded robes.

They were drawing closer, nearly upon her now. Twenty feet away from her hiding place, another stepped into view. They were heading directly for her, their feet making muffled thuds on the ground. They would see her! They must see her! They were on a collision course! Her body tensed, ready for action, ready to run if she was spotted. But she froze. Blended into the dark foliage as another dark bush. Shoved herself as far as possible into the bush for hiding. They were upon her! She heard their breathing, short gasps of breath as though they were tired. Or excited like herself. Her bush trembled as they pushed past its outer branches. Three of them, then four crept past. She listened, but there were no others. Their footsteps were moving away, the bushes around her still trembling from their passage.

Suddenly without thinking, she stood, exposing herself to the night. But the night hid them, and it would hide her. She knew the deathly silence that would fall when they all found their positions. Silence so dense that any movement would be detected. But now. . . ! Her movement would be lost in their own. She followed them, staying close enough so that her sounds blended with theirs, but hidden behind them in the night. One of them pulled away and took his position in the clearing, and she moved a little closer. When another took position, she knew that her chances of detection had increased with only two of them hiding her movement. Quickly she took her bearings. It was only a little farther. She moved ahead with crossed fingers.

The ground dipped suddenly, and she stumbled and nearly fell. She instantly froze. She had made it! At least this far. She listened to the two ahead of her, and they moved steadily away. Her stumble had not alerted them. She detected a change, and knew that another of them had stopped. Only one of them left, and he would soon be in position. She quickly moved ahead a half dozen steps and found herself on solid ground. No undergrowth to give away her movements if she were careful.

She hesitated briefly and looked through the break in the forest into the clearing. Her cabin squatted forlorn against the forest, the clearing washed in a sudden spurt of moonlight as the silver ball above played hide-and-seek among the clouds. The black-hooded figures now ringed her cabin, though she could see only a few of them. Though her heart pounded from fright, and her mind was muddled as to her next move, she could not stop the smile that creased her lips. The black silhouettes watched her cabin, thinking she was inside, while she watched them.

Silently, she turned away, pleased that she had outwitted them and particularly pleased that she had not panicked. With eyes accustomed to the darkness and with the aid of hopscotch patches of moonlight, she moved silently down the rocky trail her Maverick had found so demanding. Along the car path the undergrowth was still sparse, and by moving cautiously she could move silently.

She knew that by following the established trail, she ran the risk of being spotted if there were other hooded figures roaming the mountain. But she felt reasonably certain the black figures, whoever they were, had but one purpose this night to ring her cabin, for whatever reason they might have. And she knew that she had left them all behind. And the trail offered the only silent means of escape. But escape to where?

By moonlight she kept to the trail, not a difficult task when the moon was out. But increasingly it dipped behind clouds to throw her into a world of total darkness, only to emerge moments later to again act as guide. When it disappeared and did not return, Joanna had to feel her way. She had to let her feet and hands tell her where the trail was. Once she stumbled and fell. Inch by inch she continued down the mountain, the foliage growing thicker with each passing yard. When the moon finally emerged, sending splinters of light down through the trees, she looked around her in dismay. There was no trail, only a tangle of undergrowth in all directions. With a sinking heart she realized she was lost.

She had only the mountain's topography to guide her, knowing that somewhere down below was the town. So letting the downward slope help pull her ahead, she forged headlong into the unseen thickets before her. Branches reached out of the darkness to tap her shoulder, to slice across her face, and tug mercilessly at her sweater. But she pushed ahead, cautiously picking her way and trying to avoid the thickest undergrowth.

Unlike the deathly silence surrounding her cabin, this part of the mountain was alive with the sounds of night creatures. Again she heard the bark of a fox nearby, and the icy hand of fear chilled the back of her neck, then immodestly slid inside her sweater and down her spine. She had no cabin walls to hide behind this time, and the sound brought her to a halt. She attuned her ears to the mountain, and soon there was another bark, then another. For a moment her bounding imagination pictured a dozen foxes hidden in the foliage around her. But she knew it was just that – her imagination.

She pushed ahead, trying to ignore the sound that, for some unexplained reason, struck such fear into her heart. The undergrowth became thicker, and her progress became even more difficult. To her right the fox barked again. To Joanna it seemed that the fox had descended the mountain with her, its bark remaining at a constant point of reference off her right shoulder. Even amid the thick undergrowth, her pace quickened. The realization that the fox was still there, somewhere out in the darkness, had sent a fleeting chord of panic through her mind.

The fox grew silent, so she stopped and listened. There was no sound. The silence was as dense as it had been earlier around her cabin. She crept ahead, apprehensive now that the mountain had grown silent. Her animal instincts were at work, activating the same sense of preknowledge that had warned her of Betty Susan Henderson. She suddenly knew that she was not alone. She grew as rigid as a monument. There was nothing to give away the location of whatever waited in the dark. She knew she must keep moving, make it move, force it to make a sound that she could run from.

Once again she crept ahead, making as little noise as possible. She heard a faint sound, too faint to identify or locate. A dark clump of bushes loomed ahead and she veered away from it, afraid of what might be beyond. Halfway past she stopped abruptly. She had seen a movement ahead; Attaint, almost undetectable movement. Her eyes locked onto the spot, and it came again, then again. Relieved, she knew it was too consistent to be anything but the swaying of some weak stemmed weed. She started to move forward again, but was stopped in midstride!

Suddenly, a hand shot out of the darkness, crossed her left shoulder, and clamped itself around her mouth. A second hand locked her arm into a merciless, viselike grip. She tried to struggle, tried to scream, but could do neither. She threw her head back and looked into a shadowy face, the features indistinct in the fleeting moonlight. Frozen by terror, but still in control of her wits, she knew that struggle was futile. Her captor's grip was too strong, too powerful. She grew rigid, her eyes wide with fear, but she did not struggle, did not give him cause to harm her. She felt an immediate slackening of his grip.

"Don't be afraid," a voice croaked in her ear. "I ain't gonna hurt ye."

Again she looked into the face. The moon emerged from behind a cloud, shedding light on her captor. She gasped. It was the whittler!

"Don't scream," he said, loosening his grip still more, "or they'll know we're here."

Joanna nodded her assent, and he set her free.

"Ye see 'em too?" The whittler's raspy voice again croaked its question in hardly more than a whisper.

She nodded affirmatively. So she was not the only one harassed by the black-hooded figures!

"I thought ye was one of 'em when I heard ye coming. I thought they was after me for sure."

"Who are they?" Joanna finally gasped, her heart pounding not quite so fast, but still recovering from being grabbed in the night.

The whittler didn't answer immediately. His moonlit face seemed to twitch as he stood gazing at her through the darkness. He seemed to be sizing her up, trying to decide some uncertain matter. He opened his mouth as though to speak, then clamped it shut. "Don't ye know who they are?" he finally asked.

"No," she shook her head.

"They're witches!" He flung the words at her. Set them free as though freeing a man-eating tiger, afraid of what the animal would do with its freedom. He recoiled at the sound of his own words, and unmasked fear pervaded his voice and body.

"Witches!" she echoed him. An ominous fear gripped her, sending a wave of shivers through her body. Her knees grew weak, and for the first time that night the fear seemed too much, almost sickening in its clarity. She was suddenly sick at her stomach. "What would they be doing at my house?" she asked feebly.

"They was at your place, ye say?" The whittler's voice held an excited edge, a quality of near disbelief.

She nodded.

The moon had again disappeared, and the whittler was only a dark shadow across from her. Only his breathing told her that he was alive. His body was motionless.

"Do ye live in that little cabin in the clearing up the mountain?"

"Yes."

"Then that's where they was going when I saw 'em. It's been a long time since they been seen 'round and about. And let me tell ye, they're up to no good. Yessiree, when a body sees them people on the mountain, you know they's a fox in the hen house." He paused, then leaned forward as he peered at her through the darkness. "Where ye headed, anyway?"

She was taken aback, uncertain of the meaning of his mountain dialect. "Do you mean, where am I going?"

He nodded silently.

"I'm lost."

"Lost?"

"I had to sneak away from them, and I lost that trail that goes into town."

"Ye goin' to town, then?"

"I was," she replied.

"Go back that-a-way." He pointed into the darkness. "Ye'll find the trail about two hundred yards."

He abruptly turned his back on her and walked away, the darkness closing in around him like a shrouded mist. Joanna was taken by surprise, not expecting him to leave her to fend for herself. Again she was clutched by fear and she called after him.

"Wait!"

He stopped and turned, but remained silent.

"Can you help me?" she asked.

He didn't reply.

"Can't you please help me? Can I come with you?" She took a stumbling step toward him, but he offered no encouragement so she stopped.

Out of the darkness his voice reached her. "Ye a stranger here 'bouts. Ye oughtn't to be here."

Resolutely, she squared her shoulders to his coldness. For a few moments she had held a fleeting ray of hope that he might help her, but he had reverted to the taciturn whittler who had begrudgingly directed her to Potter's Store earlier in the day.

With an air of aloofness she spun away, heading in the direction he had pointed. At least she would be headed in the right direction. She had taken half a dozen steps when the call of his voice from behind stopped her.

"Ye could help me, if ye want to," his voice croaked at her.

She turned but could not see him in the darkness. She retraced her steps until she saw him standing in the same spot. "How could I help you?" she asked, the puzzlement on her face lost in the darkness.

"I was a-carrying some things home," he said. "Ye could help me."

His voice was softer, not so harsh and uninviting as before, but still not friendly. For only an instant did she wonder about her personal safety with him, a man who obviously was offering his companionship against his will. But pitted against the black watchers, or witches, he had said, from whom she had just escaped, she chose to follow the whittler.

"Over here," he said, turning away and leading her through the darkness. He walked to the far side of the bush that she had veered away from in fear earlier. He knelt beside it, and from within the protection of its branches began pulling out an assortment of small necked jugs. He gave her three to carry, one in each hand and one cradled in her arms, took three himself and led her into the undergrowth.

He offered no explanations as he led her silently across the mountain, but Joanna knew that she carried three jugs of bootleg whiskey. The thought that she was helping a bootlegger didn't bother her. She was too relieved at finding herself rescued, even though unwillingly so, to be concerned about the illegality of the man's profession.

She followed him as he weaved his way across the mountain, and after the first few minutes of blind navigating, she had totally lost all sense of direction. His dark shadow was her guide as silently she followed him, keeping half a dozen steps behind. When at last he ended their journey she was weary, her arms aching from carrying the jugs – and she had no idea at all where she was.

Chapter 4

It was the uncomfortable morning chill, not the daylight, that dragged her from her sleep. Her shoulder ached. She rolled over and rubbed it, her eyes still closed, her mind as foggy as the mist that rolled down the mountain. Her body ached and her groggy mind would not explain why. Forcing her eyes open, her first sight was a jolt – a dirty plank floor beneath her cheek.

She sat up with a start! Where was she? She remembered. But it looked different in the daylight, not so cozy now that she could see it clearly. Four clapboard walls with one room leading off – his bedroom. The kitchen was at one end of the room she had slept in, the living room at the other. Her feet were warm, and she realized that the wood-burning stove was blazing, a hot skillet of grease crackling on top. The smoky aroma of cured ham floated down to her, and immediately she was anticipating the meal to come.

But she was cold! She looked around and discovered why. The living room door, not two feet from her head, stood open. The morning fog swirled in pools as it cascaded down the mountainside, a virtual wave of gray that drifted past the open doorway. She could see dimly the darker gray that was the shadowy forest beyond. She heard the first morning sounds, the crows that played somewhere above, surely beyond the murky fog. Then she heard him, moving nearly noiselessly across the wet grass and twigs. The footsteps were coming toward her, so she jumped to her feet, anticipating his return. The doorway darkened and the whittler stood before her.

"Thought ye was going to sleep the day away," he said, shoving past her with a fresh armload of firewood, which he placed in a wide-brimmed bucket beside the stove.

She stifled a yawn, covering her mouth with her hand. "What time is it?" she finally managed.

"Don't rightly know." He threw another split log into the stove. "Gotta keep it hot." He turned the sizzling ham, the exposed sides now a crisp golden brown. She eyed the meat. Remembering her last meal from a can, her tongue slid involuntarily across her lips.

"Imagine it's close to five, though," he said. "Ye always sleep this late?"

She shrugged, glancing outside at the fog that told that the morning was barely born. "Not always."

He looked past her into the gloomy morning. "Gonna be a right pretty day."

"It is?" she asked skeptically, again casting an untrusting glance at the fog.

"Shore is. Fog in the morning generally means the sun'll come out. Ye can usually count on it."

Now more nearly awake, she glanced around the room again, more observant than on her earlier sleepy appraisal. On a stool shoved offhandedly into a corner, she spotted several tiny wooden animals, products, she assumed, of his days spent working at his namesake. She picked one up, a carving of a pig, and was impressed at the quality of the man's handiwork.

"Like the piggy?" he mumbled.

"It's very nice." She turned it over in her hands and felt its smoothly finished surface, then exchanged it for a carving of a dog, equally as good. Out of the corner of her eye she saw him watching her.

"Ye from the city, ain't ye?" he finally asked.

"Yes," she nodded, replacing the dog.   '

"Can ye cook?" His voice held a challenge, not totally friendly, and he stared belligerently at her.

"I can cook."

"Then cook us up some eggs," he said, sliding the ham out of the pan. He shoved the pan to her, then set a full box of eggs beside it. "Give me four, and make 'em nice and runny."

Her brow wrinkled. "Runny?" She stared at him questioningly. "Oh! You mean over easy." She couldn't keep away the smile that slid onto her face.

"No! I mean I want 'em runny," he declared.

"The way you want it is called 'over easy,'" she said, wishing she had never mentioned it.

"I don't give a damn if you throw 'em down and stomp on 'em! Just make 'em runny."

Without further conversation, she began breaking the eggs, careful not to break the yolks.

"Did ye sleep okay?" he asked, as he watched her crack an egg and drop it in the hot grease.

Her shoulder ached from the hard floor, and involuntarily she rubbed it. "Fine."

"I imagine the floor's a mite hard for a city girl."

"It wasn't bad."

She glanced at him and his eyes were dancing, evidently enjoying his harassment. She found him likable in a strange sort of way, yet somewhat cold and detached. The untrusting way he watched her, the way he deliberately challenged her almost at every turn, made her uneasy. But she shrugged it off to his clannish mountain ways.

"Ye shoulda slept in the chair like I said," his voice reproached her.

She glanced at the rocking chair, far too cramped for her to spread out and sleep comfortably.

"The floor was fine."

She dished up the eggs, and without ceremony he took his portion of eggs and ham and moved silently to the table. A moment later she was sitting across from him, staring into his unshaven face. He ignored her as he shoved one bite after another into his mouth, his unkempt face expressionless. They ate in silence.

"I want to thank you for helping me last night."

"Tweren't nothing," he said, not bothering to look at her.

"It meant a great deal to me. I was frightened out of my wits."

His eyes suddenly bore into her, his piercing glare again making her uncomfortable. Ever so slightly, he leaned toward her.

"Like I said, tweren't nothing," he said coldly, the edge on his voice sending shivers along her spine. "If I'd a found a dog trapped on the mountain, I'd a set it loose. Either that or killed it. But I'd a got it out of its misery. That's all I did for you – put you out o' your misery."

His eyes glared so fiercely at her that she dropped her gaze into her lap. His words had shaken her, so callous was his disregard for her feelings. She composed herself and finally lifted her eyes to challenge his.

"I appreciate what you did, anyway," she said, sliding away from the table. "I'll leave now so I won't be any further bother to you."

She crossed the room to the front door and stopped. Outside the fog was beginning to lift, but farther down the mountain, the trees were still obscured by the gray sea. Joanna looked back over her shoulder at him as he meticulously cleaned the last bit of food from his plate. "And thanks for the breakfast."

"Umm," he grunted, not bothering to turn to face her. "Ye leaving now?" he asked casually, still not looking at her.

"Yes."

"Ye know where ye are?"

She glanced out the front door for a familiar landmark, but saw none. Somewhere down the mountain, she imagined, was Sutters Hamlet . . . though they had traveled for seeming ages last night and she could easily be wrong.

"I don't know exactly where I am," she admitted, "but I'll find my way."

"I doubt it." He swung out of his chair and crossed the floor to her side. "Which way would ye reckon is town?"

She pointed down the mountain, then looked hopefully into his face.

"All ye'd find off in that direction is nothing," he said triumphantly. "Ye'd be lost again."

He returned to the table, where he began clearing away their dirty dishes. "If ye'll wait a while, I'll take ye home." His voice was softer, lacking its belligerence, but still not friendly. Joanna felt the warm, tingling fingers of affection caress her body. He was not as hard and callous as he would have her believe. He had strange, stern ways perhaps, but occasionally she spotted a break in his tough rhinoceros skin.

"I'll do the dishes," she said, crossing the room on impulse and taking the dirty plates from his hands.

His face scowled. "There ain't no need for that."

"I'll do it."

"Then do it! Lordy me, if ye ain't jest like a woman!" he growled and stalked out of the house.

Joanna finished the dishes in short time, found a raggle-taggle broom standing in a corner and began sweeping at the dirt that was caught in the unwaxed plank floor. After finishing the living-room-kitchen, she entered his bedroom and stopped short at the sight before her. Wood carvings, dozens of them, dominated the room. Sitting on shelves, two bedside tables, and stacked three-deep along the floor lining the walls, the carvings occupied virtually every inch of unused space. She stared at them, dumbfounded, for several moments, stepping to a nearby shelf nailed to the wall and running her fingers lightly over a delicately carved deer and fawn. In the New York galleries, she had seen some of the best art and sculpture available, but never had she seen a better collection of wood carvings than these. The sheer numbers staggered her. Looking at the tiny statues before her and appreciating the time that must have gone into each one, she realized she was looking at the man's life work.

Finally, she pulled her eyes away and finished sweeping. As she swept the pile of dirt out the front door, she saw the whittler sitting against the front wall, knife and a cube of wood in hand, with shavings dropping around him. She propped the broom in the doorway and approached him. "Mr. . . ." she stopped, unable to finish. "You know, I don't even know your name."

"Umm," the whittler grunted.

"My name's Joanna."

He nodded his head, never looking up from his carving. Joanna decided not to pursue the issue.

"I saw the carvings in your bedroom, and they're very good," she said, hoping to flatter him.

At the mention of his carvings, he suddenly looked at her, the scowl once again distorting his face. "What ye doing in there!" he demanded.

"I was just sweeping," she explained, pointing to the broom leaning against the door.

His eyes followed her finger, then dropped from the broom to the pile of dirt still visible on the ground. Satisfied, his eyes lost their hardness and he resumed his whittling.

"I particularly like the mother deer with her fawn sitting on the shelf just inside the door," she said. "How long did it take you to finish them?"

His nose twitched and he seemed to be thinking, but he continued his carving. "A week, I reckon. I don't rightly remember."

"I've never tried any carving," she said, admiring the speed and precision with which he sent the chips flying. She dropped to the ground and sat cross-legged at his feet. He would make an interesting subject, she thought, for a portrait. "How long have you been carving?"

"I been a whittlin' most my life," he said, emphasizing the word whittling.

"You're very creative."

He glanced up at her without stopping his work. "Ye think so? And what would ye know about that?"

"Well I paint! And I know something about good artwork, including sculpture."

"Ye paint, do ye? And what do ye paint?"

"Pictures," she blurted, remembering Mrs. Johnson's first reaction to learning that she had come to paint the mountains. "I'm an artist, and I came here to paint landscapes."

The whittler had stopped his work and was looking at her, interest clearly shown in his eyes. He seemed to be considering something, and finally spoke.

"I thought painters was usually men."

"Not always," she replied, not knowing how else to answer. On impulse she continued, "I have a few pictures I brought with me from New York. You can see them if you like when you take me home."

He nodded his head silently and resumed his carving. In a few moments he looked at her again. "I reckon it's about time to get you back." He started to stand, but she stopped him.

"Can you tell me something first?"

"Tell ye what?"

Joanna hesitated. She had forced herself not to think of it since the night before. But suddenly her thoughts were filled with the foreboding she had felt then, the fear at seeing the black figures ring her cabin, at realizing that she had seen the hooded face of one of them in her window on her first night on the mountain. And with a chilling reminder, she remembered what the whittler had called them.

"Tell me about the witches," she said, apprehensive at his reaction.

His face turned pale, and again grew stern and unpleasant. His eyes were set on her in a cold stare, his lips a firm line zipped shut. "What ye wanna know about them for?" he demanded.

"Are they really witches?" she asked with a quaver in her voice. She waited for his reaction, and it was quick in coming.

"Well, ye seen 'em, didn't ye? Ye seen 'em with your own eyes! Running around the mountain all covered up in black like that?"

The way his eyes bore into her demanded that she reply. He sat propped against the wall amid his shavings, his whittling hands still, and looked searchingly into her face.

"I don't know. I didn't know what to think. It's just that . . . that I didn't know that some people still believed in witches."

Joanna felt her hands trembling, and she clasped one with the other and forced them to stop. She was in control of herself, though frightened at the mention of something so unknown and sinister. Frightened at the thought of being alone on the mountain with them roaming about. Yet she was curious enough to want to know more. Darkness and fear were hours away, and she knew that if she had to cope with fear, she would prefer to cope with it knowledgeably.

The whistler's mention of witches had triggered something inside of her. It was as though the mere mention of the word had unlocked a mysterious vault of knowledge that she could only tap at certain times. A vault that told her to listen, listen to what the whittler had to say. Listen, because all that he said was not fantasy. As much as her New York instincts told her that it should be only a fairy tale, she knew that for Sutters Hamlet it was reality. And their reality was hers.

Why that word had triggered her, she didn't know. She was never able to determine why she had these visions of truth, these experiences in ESP; she knew only she had them. She could not predict their occurrence, nor could she call for them at will. They happened when they chose, and they happened in the manner they chose.

The whittler was watching her intently. The rising sun cast long shadows around them and played grotesque games with the lines on the man's face. His facial wrinkles seemed so deep, so much like open scars and made him appear older and more battle-torn than he actually was.

Joanna looked away, up the mountain where the world seemed fresh and peaceful. She could see its sides rising gently upward, the green pine-covered slopes hiding her cabin somewhere among them. Looking at them there was no hint, not a whisper, that they might also hide something so sinister as witches. But did they? Or was it just one man's imagination? Or the medieval beliefs of an entire community?

Still gazing up the mountain, she asked, "What makes you think those people we saw last night were witches?"

"Oh, they was witches all right," he said emphatically, peeling a shaving off the piece of wood in his hands. "Ye ask anybody. What ye saw was the witches." He stopped and gazed intently at her, and almost undetectably his eyes seemed to change. It was as though he had come to an understanding. When he resumed speaking, his voice was less stem. "I guess ye don't have this sort of thing in the city. Witches and such. I reckon that's why it's so hard for you to believe that they was witches."

"It is hard to believe."

"These is the mountains," he said sweeping his gaze around him. "The mountains don't change its ways none too easy. Some folks hereabouts still does things the same as they was done hundreds of years ago. And them folks ye saw last night – them in the black robes – they been roaming the mountains hereabouts for nigh on two hundred years." His eyes seemed out of focus, a distant, cloudy film covering them as his mind wandered from the present. "But they was the witches, all right. And it worries me," he said in a near whisper. "Yes, sir, it worries me a lot. They ain't been seen around here in twenty-five years, not since the bitch was killed." He paused. "I wonder what in hell they was doing on the mountain last night?"

His eyes were fixed on infinity. Silence deepened between them, a trough that grew so wide that she was afraid to cross it. His words were hissed whispers that still rang in her ears. They held a foreboding, voicing a question that she had already asked herself, one that was becoming more sinister by daylight than it had been the night before. I wonder what in hell they was doing on the mountain last night? His words chilled her.

But one thought was even more chilling. Last night was not their first night on the mountain in twenty-five years. They had been at her cabin before. One of them had gazed in her window.

"What do ye reckon they was doing at your place?" the whittler asked, drawing her away from her thoughts. He was looking at her with interest, like one would stare at a rare animal in a zoo.

"I wish I knew." She turned on him. "Do you know why they were there?"

He shrugged. "Nope. Can't say that I do. Except it ain't very often anybody stays at that old place you're living at." His eyes again fixed on infinity, the film obscuring his vision. He gazed past her, over her head into the mountain. "But it do seem strange that they'd come back all of a sudden. Somethin' must have brought 'em back." He bore down on her with his gaze. "Do ye reckon it had anything to do with your moving into that old house?"

Joanna shivered. She shifted her gaze so that she did not have to see his accusing face. But accusing her of what? "Why would my moving into the cabin have anything to do with it?"

He shrugged, started to speak, then stopped himself. His mind seemed to visibly shift gear, and when he spoke, Joanna had an uneasy knowledge that he did not say what he had originally intended. That the unspoken words had something to do with her or the cabin, something sinister, something obvious to others but unknown to her.

"They was up there last night, wasn't they? There must be somethin' about that place, or about you coming here, that made 'em come up there. They ain't been seen in twenty-five years ... till now."

"What happened twenty-five years ago to drive them away?" she asked, curious, but also wanting to steer the conversation away from herself.

"Hell, I don't know!" he declared. "It ain't important noway."

She knew from his defensiveness that she had struck upon some sour point. That he did know but didn't want to say.

"Did it have anything to do with killing the bitch?" she asked, using the expression he had used minutes before. She thought he was going to fall from his propped chair. His startled look changed into a scowl.

"What do ye know about the bitch?" he demanded.

"Only that she was killed. You just told me that." Joanna was taken aback by the fierceness of his voice.

"That's all ye need to know," he said with finality, closing the subject. He was out of his chair and tramping into the house. Joanna remained seated, undecided what she should do. In a moment, he reappeared at the door.

"Come on," he said stalking past her and heading into the forest. "I'm taking ye home now." He disappeared into the trees without looking back to see if she was following.

She jumped up and ran after, then fell into step behind him. He was in no talking mood, she could tell. His pace was a bit too quick for a man of his years, and not once did he acknowledge her presence behind him.

He led her along a winding trail that maintained a constant level on the mountainside, neither climbing nor dropping: When finally he left the trail and began to climb through the unchartered undergrowth, she realized that they must be approaching her cabin. She dropped back several paces to stay clear of the flying tree limbs that he released without regard to her. The denseness of the undergrowth caused him to slow his pace, and she could hear him cursing to himself as he fought his way through the tangled greenery. The cawing of the tattletale crows above tracked their progress up the mountain, and something about their presence made her feel more at ease.

The undergrowth began to thin, but the whittler maintained his slower pace. She was unprepared for their journey's end when 'suddenly the forest broke away and she found herself standing in a clearing at the rear of a small cabin. For a moment she was puzzled, then realized that it was her cabin. Instead of the greater expanse of clearing that she had expected, the whittler had led her to the cabin's rear door, only a few feet away from the forest's edge.

Without speaking, he turned to leave, and was partway into the trees before she spoke.

"Wait!" she cried, running after him. "I thought you wanted to see some of my paintings."

He looked at her, then glanced at the cabin. Then still without speaking he let her lead him inside.

She led him into the tiny front bedroom where she had stored all her painting equipment along with the few finished paintings she had brought with her. She sat the three best against the wall, leaving two others still hidden. He squatted down to get a better view, and for several minutes silently appraised her work: two landscapes of Upstate New York and a Greenwich Village street scene. When finally he rose, his eyes viewed her admiringly.

"Them's plumb good," he said, nodding toward the pictures, a twinkle of satisfaction in his eyes. "You paint good."

"Thank you."

His gaze dropped to the pictures again, and she saw his eyes come to rest on one of the landscapes. She impulsively picked it up. "Here. I'd like you to have this."

He stepped away, seemingly embarrassed at her gesture.

"It's for helping me," she said and shoved it into his hands.

He held the picture before him. Then he seemed to once again become aware of her presence, and again became distant, uneasy at the friendship gesture of a stranger. He dipped his head in a nod of thanks, then turned and left, passing through the kitchen and out the back door as he had come.

Joanna took a few steps after him, but stopped. She had hoped that he would remain for a while. She had hoped to better establish a friendship with him. But he was a man of the mountain, a loner unaccustomed to friendliness from strangers. As she watched him disappear out the rear door, protectively holding the painting, she knew that the groundwork had been laid. In time, they would be friends.

She walked into the kitchen to wave goodbye from the door should he turn and look back. But as she stepped into the kitchen she stopped, her heart swelling with warmth. Sitting on the edge of the table were two tiny figures. She crossed quickly to the table and looked down on the doe and fawn, the carvings she had admired from the whittler's collection.

She scooped them up and dashed to the door, but he was gone, only the crackling undergrowth telling his whereabouts as he descended the mountain. She listened until there was no more sound, then walked into the living room to find a place for her new acquisitions.

Chapter 5

With the whittler gone, Joanna found herself alone again up against the mountain and the secrets it held. She felt uneasy. She moved uncertainly about the cabin, then in a flash of inspiration stalked to the front door, still closed from the night before, and flung it open. The morning sun bathed the living room, sweeping away some of the foreboding that the cabin now seemed to hold.

She stepped through the door and into the shimmering morning brightness. Forgotten was the fog of an hour before, and she noted that the whittler's weather prediction had been accurate. She squinted against the sky's pale blue and watched the aerial stunts of the half-dozen crows that seemed to live there. This morning her yearning was to paint, and she knew that she must.

As she returned to the cabin for her paints, she glanced at the ground. She dropped to her knees and scooped up a fistful of dirt with her fingers. Small white flecks of something resembling salt was sprinkled across the earth in front of her door. She picked up one of the granules, smelled it, then placed it on her tongue. It had no taste.

She stood and looked around, but found the white specks only in front of the door. A chilling thought raced across her mind, sending goose bumps sweeping like a wave over her body. The white flecks . . . the witches had sprinkled them there!

The realization made her react. As though touched by an electrical rod, she suddenly jumped backwards, landing on ground untainted by the mysterious white flecks. From her safe distance she gazed at them, her dreaded preknowledge telling her things she wished had been left unsaid. The mysterious knock at her door last night that had jerked her awake ...

it was made as one of the witches spread the white flecks. She was certain. And it was intended that she step on them, as she had done. But why?

Suddenly, all that she wanted was that those white specks disappear. She looked frantically around her. When finally she saw a broken tree limb lying at the forest's edge, she dashed to retrieve it. Using it as a broom, she began sweeping clean the ground in front of the cabin door.. She swept until not one speck of white was visible.

Breathing heavily, more from fright than exertion, she stood propped against the cabin wall, eyeing the area she had just swept clean. Her mind kept asking the frightening question – why had the witches wanted her to step on those white granules? What were they doing? Then, even in the face of her fear, she couldn't keep from smiling. It was ludicrous. Here she was, a cynical New Yorker. Accepting even the possibility that witches might exist would have been impossible for her a week ago. Now she wondered if they were really witches – witches with power?

Her wandering mind had drifted. But then a voice startled her, and she swung to face it, brandishing the branch she still held.

"Hey!" A shout pierced her ears.

A man stumbled backward, arms flung up defensively across his face to ward off the branch that stopped inches from his temple. Joanna remained on guard.

"All I said was hello," the man said, attempting a smile, "and I nearly got my head knocked off." He was out of range of her branch, and he dropped his arms to his side. "I didn't know you were lethal," he joked.

"You shouldn't sneak up on people like that," Joanna asserted, still shaking from the sudden fright he had given her.

"I didn't try to sneak up on you," he said. "You looked miles away and just didn't hear me coming."

She knew he was right. "Who are you?"

"Peter Tillary." He flashed a beguiling grin that would have set her at ease under other circumstances. He was tall and muscular, with sandy hair that the wind had blown down across his forehead. His shirt stood open at the collar exposing a bit too much of his chest, and she wondered if he had noticed her eyes linger there. She felt a warm surge of attraction rush through her body, and she relaxed her vigil.

"I'm sorry if I frightened you," he said. "I suppose I should have spoken when I first came into the clearing. But I thought you would have heard me approach."

She shook her head.

"I didn't hear a thing until you spoke, and that scared me out of my wits," she said a bit sheepishly. "I didn't know there was anyone for miles around."

"Do you think that's necessary," he said lightly, pointing at the branch she still held at the ready.

Embarrassed, she felt herself flush. She threw the branch several yards away, then faced him empty-handed. "All right?"

"I feel safer now," he said. "Less likely to get my head bashed in. You know, you scared me as much as I must have you."

"You deserved it," she shot back.

They faced each other for a moment in silence, and she was the first to speak. "What are you doing here?"

"I was looking for Mr. Pembroke, but I gather he's not here?"

"Mr. Pembroke?"

"Jim Pembroke. He owns this little cabin."

"Oh." With his prompting, the name held a meaning. Pembroke was the name of Ted's friend who had rented her the cabin. "He's not here. I'm renting the cabin for the next year."

"There goes my trout," Peter said smiling.

"I beg your pardon?"

Peter laughed at her puzzlement. "Mr. Pembroke usually comes here for a few weeks about this time every year, and we go trout fishing together. But evidently he's not coming this year."

"Evidently not. You have me instead, and I don't trout fish," she said impishly.

"Then what do you do? And who are you?"

"I'm Joanna Crawford." Then deliberately copying her response to Mrs. Johnson, she added, "and I came here to paint the mountains."

He hesitated a moment, seeming to study her. "Do I take that to mean that you're an artist?"

"You take it right," she smiled. "More than I can say for some around here."

"What?"

"Oh, nothing."

Peter looked past her at the cabin door. She anticipated his next question.

"Could I see some of your paintings?"

Joanna smiled. "For the backwoods. Sutters Hamlet certainly has its share of art appreciators," she observed.

"What do you mean?"

She shrugged her shoulders casually. "I just wouldn't have thought that the people here, being so cut off from the outside, would have known or cared much about art. But you're the third I've met who seems at least mildly interested."

Peter was grinning ear to ear. "Thought we're just a bunch of country hicks, huh?"

"No!" she declared defensively.

"It's all right," Peter said, stopping her with a wave of his hand. "I was just making a joke." His voice took on a more confidential tone. "Actually, I sketch a bit. Just black-and-white line drawings. I've never tried oils or watercolors. I'd like to though."

Joanna gazed at him questioningly. Something about him just didn't mesh with the rest of the characters in Sutters Hamlet. He stood apart. Like Hanover, he was different.

He must have detected her inquisitive gaze.

"Am I that strange?" he asked. "You're looking at me as though you'd never seen one of me before."

"Oh," she said blushing, "I didn't mean to stare. It's just that I somehow have trouble picturing you as a mountain man. Your speech. It's too refined."

"It comes from practice. I'm an English teacher."

"You're kidding!" she blurted. "Who do you teach? The squirrels?"

Peter laughed a deep-throated laugh. "Hardly. Actually I'm an English instructor at a junior college in Asheiville. I have this term off and don't have to go back until August."

"That's a nice long vacation," she said.

"It is," he agreed. "That's why I teach."

"Lazy?" she asked.

"That's part of it, I suppose. But mainly I just like these mountains and want to spend my free time here." He jerked his thumb over his shoulder, pointing higher up the mountain. "I grew up about a half mile above you.

My mother lives there alone except when I'm here between terms and during the summer."

Joanna nodded understandingly.

"So, to answer your question, I do appreciate good art. Mainly because I would like to give it a try, but I sketch so poorly that I suppose there's no need even trying."

"If you want to paint, you really should try your hand at it," Joanna said. "Painting is much easier than drawing. Did you know that?"

"I assumed it would be the other way around."

"No." She turned to enter the cabin. "I'll show you some of my paintings, if you like."

He followed her, studying her few exhibits approvingly. They returned to the morning's brightness outside, and when they once again stood facing each other, she noticed a new glint in his eyes, something that had not been there a few moments before. He seemed to be toying with some new thought, and she waited for him to voice it.

"Do you paint mainly landscapes?" he asked. Upon her affirmative reply, he continued. "Then naturally you'd want to find the most scenic spots around, and I could help you. I'll be your guide."

"My guide?"

"Yes," he said, "at least until you learn your way around. You might get lost otherwise. Some of the nicer spots require some traveling, and I don't think it wise that you should go traipsing about the mountain until you learn your way."

She eyed him cautiously. He seemed sincere, trustworthy. But the thought of traveling the remote reaches of the mountain with a just-met stranger put her ill at ease. It was her New Yorker's caution, she knew, that worked on her now. She stood facing him without answering, debating the matter.

"But maybe you'd prefer to wait until we get to know each other before trusting your fate to a strange man," he said, reading her thoughts.

She smiled sheepishly at him. "Am I that easy to read?"

"Just cautious, I imagine," he said. "And rightfully so."

His suggestion that they first get to know each other decided the matter for her. She recognized the savings in time that having someone show her the way around would mean. It could be a great help to her, and she knew that she could not afford to turn down his offer.

"I'd like that," she said.

"Are you sure? Sure you don't want to wait until you've known me for a while?" he asked.

"Well, we're not leaving right this minute, are we?" she smiled.

"No, I guess not," he acknowledged.

"Then we're getting to know each other better right now, aren't we?"

"I suppose we are," he said good-naturedly. He threw his head back and laughed again, and Joanna felt the same crimson glow of attraction sweep over her. Then his expression turned serious. "There is one condition."

Her senses were alerted. "What's that?"

"In payment for my acting as your guide, you agree to give me a few pointers on painting."

She breathed a relieved sigh. "Lessons?"

"You could call it that."

"Agreed," she said, extending her hand in a businesslike manner. They shook on it.

"When do we begin?" he asked.

"How about tomorrow morning?"

"Fine."

She was about to invite him inside for coffee, but he spoke first.

"I suppose rd better be going. I was on my way down the mountain to get some things for my mother. Spring planting time, and she wants some new seeds for the garden."

Turning to leave, he called back over his shoulder. "See you in the morning."

"All right. Goodbye."

She watched him walk noiselessly across the clearing and disappear into the forest. She watched the trees until she could no longer hear the sound of his footsteps breaking twigs and crushing leaves. She knew that a guide could be very beneficial in her first days on the mountain. Even though she had laughed at Ted's suggestion that she may get lost wandering about the forest, she felt more confident now that she would not have to learn the mountain alone.

But there was one worry gnawing away at the back of her mind. Peter was a stranger, and should he not be what he seemed, she would be at his mercy. But there was something about him, some openness that made her trust him. Even though her past two nights had made her wary of people, she knew that she must trust her judgment and trust some of them as friends.

She went back inside and got her sketch pad and spent the rest of the afternoon sketching scenes near her cabin.

As night drew near, so did her fears. She bolted the doors and windows and sat in the living room trying to read, but found that she couldn't concentrate. Abandoning her book she decided to face the darkness and went to bed. Sleep was slow in coming, since she kept her senses attuned to the outdoor sounds. Finally, she drifted away into an uneventful sleep.

She awoke in the morning refreshed and ready to get on with the business of learning her way about the mountain. She fixed a bag of sandwiches and was waiting when Peter arrived.

By noon she was convinced of the wisdom of allowing Peter to act as guide. He showed her unmistakable landmarks she could use as navigation tools, but more important, he took her to many places of unparalleled beauty. He seemed to have an artist's eye, showing her not only majestic overlooks, but places of quaint beauty, a rippling brook and a solitary tree that would go unnoticed by most people. Some scenes she sketched on her pad, others she made a mental note to return to later. By the end of the day her fingers were itching to put brush to canvas and recreate some of the day's scenes.

Another uneventful night left her calm and in the proper frame of mind to begin her work. The sky was a spotless blue, so she took her easel into the front yard and, using one of her sketches from the day before, began to rough in a scene.

Hanover stopped by at midday to check on her. He spent an hour chatting as she painted and seemed pleased that she was doing well. He expressed concern for her, living alone as she did, and left with a reavowed promise to look in on her periodically. As she watched him start his homeward journey back down the mountain, Joanna felt an affectionate warmth for the old man. It made her feel better to know that someone was concerned for her welfare.

Another uneventful night, and Joanna found herself halfway convinced that there would be no more disturbances in the night. She sat reading with the door ajar to allow a breeze to circulate before going to bed.

Over the following week she completed two oils. Peter came by for his first lesson, and she found that her judgment was correct – he did have an artist's eye. Even in his first painting attempt, she saw promise in his use of color and his handling of form. On another occasion, they spent the day again on the mountain, this time going in another direction and covering new territory. Peter brought along some poems that he had written and let Joanna read them as they sat on some rocks by a stream eating their sandwiches. His poems were simple, yet beautifully described his love for the mountains. .

Her days were filled splashing a rainbow of color on canvas, her nights spent reading by the lantern's flickering light. After those first two nights, there were no more incidents. A week after the dark figure had stood in the clearing watching her cabin, there had been no more visitors in the night. The absence of night visitors gave Joanna a growing sense of security – which proved to be false.

On her thirteenth night on the mountain, the terror began …

Chapter 6

She had spent the day alone, painting. It was not Peter's day for lessons. It was one of those beautiful spring mountain days. Endless blue sky, the singing of birds returning north after the winter, and air so fresh and cool that it stung her lungs when she took in large gulps.

Dressed in her habitual jeans and sweater, Joanna had set up her easel near the front of her cabin and was painting a mountain scene. When the evening's chill began to sweep down the mountain, she packed her brushes and went inside. The temperature dropped sharply, and she knew it was going to be a cold night, so she fired up the oil heater and shut all the windows and doors.

The last room she secured was her bedroom. Over the past few warm nights, she had grown accustomed to sleeping with her bedroom window wide open. Only in the very early morning did it get so cool as to be uncomfortable, and on two occasions she had gotten up in the middle of the night to shut out the cold.

She closed and bolted the open window.

Thinking back on the incident later, after her mind was free enough from fear to be able to think logically, she was certain, absolutely certain, that there was nothing out of place or wrong in the room at the time.

She returned to the living room, made a sandwich for dinner, then settled in a chair beside the oil heater to read. She remained there, unmoving, until ten-thirty, when she closed her book and decided to go to bed in order to get an early morning's start on her painting.

Carrying a lantern, she went into her bedroom. Tongues of orange light licked against the walls as the lantern flame danced a merry jig.

Stopping short in the middle of the room, she gave a sharp scream.

As the flame danced erratically across her bed, her eyes locked onto an object lying there, a tiny black object that stared back at her. She heard herself screaming, unable to stop, almost as though she were distant and detached from reality. She heard her screams piercing the night and willed them to stop, knowing they were totally useless. Her will was weak, and only after what seemed an eternity, though she knew it was only a few seconds, did the night once again return to its former deathly silence.

Her knees were trembling, every muscle in her body weak and limp from fear as she stared into the face of the strange doll lying on her bed. It was a tiny doll, no more than six inches tall, sitting in the spot where she went to sleep. Its tiny head rested on her pillow. But the thing that horrified her was its clothing. It was dressed in a tiny black robe with a hood pulled around its face.

She could barely see the speck of white face staring lifelessly at her.

It was a miniature replica of one of the dark-robed witches who had visited her cabin her first two nights on the mountain!

The meaning was not lost on her either. Somewhere in the past she had read of the voodoo rites where a doll is created in the image of a person upon whom a spell is to be cast. By sticking pins in the doll, pain supposedly was felt by the victim. Or by casting a spell on the doll, the spell would also hold the victim. But to achieve the most potent spells, a possession of the victim was used as the thought object upon which the spell was cast. Lacking a personal belonging, then an object such as the doll would be substituted. Suddenly, her mind raced back to the white specks outside the door, and she wondered if that too had been intended as a spell.

She stared in numb terror at the tiny black doll in front of her. She was not as afraid of the doll as she was concerned with how it got there. Her eyes shifted to the window. Still locked. That left only one other entrance through which a person could have entered her bedroom and deposited the doll, and that was the door. But she knew that was impossible! By the greatest stretch of the imagination, the cabin was small, with small rooms. Sitting by the heater, reading, she had been no more than ten feet from the door, and she was turned in such a way that she would have had to see anyone trying to enter her bedroom door!

On impulse, she ran into the kitchen. The door was locked. From the inside! So were the kitchen windows! She checked every door, every window leading to the outside, and as she knew she would, found each of them securely fastened from the inside. In desperation she looked overhead. The loft! But only high-beamed rafters met her searching gaze. There was no loft.

She returned to her bedroom, deliberately diverting her eyes from the bed. If someone entered, as they must have or else the doll would not be there, she knew they must have entered her bedroom directly. She searched the walls inch by inch, and when she found no secret passage she felt somewhat foolish. After all, she was in a small cabin on a mountain and not some medieval castle.

Finally, after searching the entire cabin for possible entrances, she was convinced that there was no way a person could have entered her bedroom undetected.

Fear sprang at her from every shadowy corner, from behind every door. Every creak of the rafters above made her jump. She wanted to rush to a corner and cower there. That way she would only have her front to watch. She was in a box of terror. The pitch-black from her bedroom window was suddenly more than she could bear, so she rushed to the window and drew the curtain to shut out any eyes from the night beyond.

She turned and looked at the doll, both hating and fearing it. It was a black scar on her gold bedspread.

"How did you get there?" she heard herself screaming. It was motionless, still staring into space. She followed the path of its gaze, through the door and into the living room. She trembled in fear, her knees nearly betraying her. The doll's gaze was on the chair where she had sat and read. It had watched her as she sat there; she had been unaware that she was not alone in the cabin.

From across the room she studied the doll, which she knew was meant to symbolize her. Else, why would it be on her bed? But why the black witch's robe? She numbly asked herself these questions over and over, but found no answers.

She knew that something had to be done. The doll could not remain on her bed. The thought of touching it frightened her, but she knew she must. She would put it in the living room, then tomorrow she would dispose of it some way. But how? If the doll symbolized her, could it be that the doll's fate would be symbolic of her own?

She shoved that thought aside and walked over to her bed. The doll looked like a corpse. Of the two of them, its will was the stronger. She started to grab it to quickly toss it into the living room, but for some unknown reason she didn't.

Instead, she gently picked it up. Some deadly curiosity inside her wanted to see the doll's face with the hood shoved back. The doll was limp and soft in her hand, and she knew from its feel that it was made from cloth stuffed with hay or grass. The face was still buried in shadows as her trembling hand pushed back the tiny hood. She was afraid that she would see her own face, but she had to know.

The hood fell back and she gasped. It had no face! No eyes, no mouth, no nose. Its face was a plain piece of white cotton cloth. But from its head fell long, straight strands of black hair, falling nearly to its ankles. Joanna gently touched the doll's hair and it felt ... real!

She had a sudden sickening fear. Her hands went rigid and she dropped the doll! It landed face-down on the bed.

She stumbled to the dresser and sat down, staring in the mirror at her face contorted with fear. She fought the hysteria that she felt creeping over her as she leaned closer to the mirror and, grabbing a handful of hair at a time, examined her own head. Soon she found what she hoped she would not.

At the nape of her neck, where her hair was the longest and thickest, there was a gap where the end of her hair had been cut. The missing length was the same as the hair length on the doll's head.

The hair on the doll was her own!

Someone! Somehow! Something! Someone had cut her hair and put it on that curse doll! The image of a black-hooded figure bending over her while she slept flashed through her mind.

She sprang from the dresser, grabbed the doll from the bed, and ran crying to the front door. More afraid of the doll now than the dark outside, she flung open the door and tossed the doll into the night. She slammed the door and bolted it, then fell sobbing to her knees.

In spite of the fact that something evil had access to the inside of her cabin, she felt safer inside with the lantern light than with the dark and unseen on the other side of the walls.

Still sobbing and trembling in fear, she crawled to the chair by the heater, where she was determined to keep an all-night vigil. She sat listening to the night sounds and the house sounds and strange sounds she had never before heard.

Halfway through the night she fell asleep, and when she awoke it was morning.

She jerked awake still terrified, but when she saw that it was daylight her racing heart slowed to a normal pace. She looked into her bedroom, half expecting to see the doll back on her bed staring at her with no eyes. She snuffed out the still-burning lantern that had stood guard while she slept, then threw open the front door to let in the morning air.

Instinctively, her eyes shot off in the direction she had tossed the doll, expecting to see it on the ground in front of her cabin. But it wasn't there. She was tempted to run into the yard and search for the doll, but she knew it would be useless. The yard sloped softly until it met the forest, and she knew that she couldn't have thrown a doll that light into the forest. Someone had retrieved the doll after she threw it out.

Either that, or the doll had disappeared of its own power, in the same mysterious way it had appeared.

With the morning's incident, Joanna made up her mind that she would not spend another night facing this thing alone. She would go to the local authorities, whatever Sutters Hamlet had in the way of law enforcement, and tell them about her night prowlers.

She ran inside and got her keys, then scrambled into her red Cherokee and rumbled down the mountain. She decided to see Hanover first. To tell him everything that had happened, omitting nothing. Let him decide if he thought it was just a prankster trying to frighten her.

Even though she was still weak from fear, she was determined not to give up, not to be driven out of her mountain cabin without a fight. One fact had not escaped her. Whoever was doing this seemed more intent on frightening her than in physically harming her. If it was fear alone they were planning to use against her, she knew she was equipped for the fight. Just as she had always sat through the late-night horror movies on television, terrified but determined to see the end, she would sit through this one – if she must. She had already plonked down all her savings on the cabin, and if for no other reason, she was not going to lose her money. But more important, she was determined not to give up on her painting career that she so desired. For that she would fight. Prowlers or witches or whatever, she would fight!

But the one thing that she could not push from her mind was why? Why was this being done to her?

As she drove into Sutters Hamlet, she saw the traditional handful of people on the sidewalk and had grown to expect their curious stares. But she was surprised this time to see everyone scurry inside as she drove into town. She looked for the whittler, but he was not in sight.

She stopped her car across from the newspaper and walked briskly into Hanover's office.

Hanover wasn't there, at least at first she thought he wasn't. She heard a stirring behind a door to the rear of the office in the part of the building that she assumed was his living quarters. In a few moments, Hanover appeared. He saw Joanna and beamed.

"You're an awfully pretty sight to greet an old man first thing in the morning," he said. He ran his fingers through his uncombed hair, trying to push it in place. "I had intended to come up the mountain this morning and see how you were making it. Hadn't seen you in nearly a week and was getting a bit worried."

He put his hand over his mouth to stifle a yawn, then began tucking in his shirt tail that hung like a wrinkled rag around his waist. She knew he wasn't long out of bed and hoped that she hadn't come too early. His eyes were still clouded with sleep, but even so they beamed his satisfaction at seeing her.

"And to what do I owe this pleasure?" he said, as he began preparing his habitual pot of coffee.

"I need some advice," Joanna said, deciding to ease into the subject. Her wits were about her, and in Hanover's presence she felt at ease, not so much in need of rushing headlong into the topic of the frightening incidents at her cabin. "I need to talk to someone who's not a native of this place."

Hanover's brow wrinkled in apparent concern, but he didn't look up from the fixings of the coffee. "I don't like the way you refer to 'this place.' It sounds as though something's the matter. Is there?"

He had finished spooning coffee into the pot and looked at her. His eyes were wrinkled and worried.

She nodded.

"I'm scared." She hesitated, uncertain as to how to continue. "Something's happening up there. They're after me!"

She burst into tears and Hanover rushed to her. She buried her head in his shoulder and he held her gently as she cried. She felt him stroking her hair, giving her soft reassurances that she was safe. When finally she regained control of her emotions, he led her gently to the same chair by his desk. He took his seat across from her, and without prodding waited patiently until she felt like talking. She dried her eyes and gathered her courage, then in a quavering voice, she began, telling about the incidents at her cabin.

Hanover listened uneasily to her story, his face growing pale, mouth gaping from the shock of her tale. He listened without comment to her account of each incident, speaking only when she grew silent. His voice rolled out hoarsely from his throat, as though forced over a great distance..

"I thought all that had ended years ago," he murmured.

She barely heard him, so low was his reply. His eyes held a faraway look, gazing without seeing. His face was contorted, his concern clearly showing through. Suddenly, the distance left his eyes and he turned on her.

"I want you to leave that cabin!" he commanded. "Either go back to New York and forget all about Sutters Hamlet, or if you insist on staying to paint, I'll find you somewhere else to stay, someone to stay with."

She was taken aback by his forcefulness. "I don't know," she said in confusion. "I can't leave. I've got too much at stake. My career!" She turned to him. "You can understand that, can't you, Mr. Hanover? How I've got to stay and paint?"

He nodded. "I know," he said. "I was young once and full of ambition." His eyes turned softly upon her. "I can understand that you feel you must stay, but if these things are starting to happen again on the mountain, it's no place for a young woman alone."

Deep inside she agreed with what he said. Her rational self knew he was right. Already too much had happened to her, too many frightening moments to allow her to question the wisdom of advice. But to abide by those same feelings and be controlled by her fears would be a compromise – a compromise of her painting. And if she did that, if she did not allow herself to paint with all her feelings, if she held back at all, then her painting would suffer. And she would never accomplish what she had set out to achieve. She could not be confined to living with people! She had to be alone.

She reconsidered his suggestions and realized that she had not three choices, but two. She must discard the suggestion that she move in with someone else. To do so would stifle her creative energies. She knew herself this well. That left her with only two alternatives – either leave the mountain altogether or stay as she was. Alone.

He was waiting on her answer.

"I won't leave," she said. "I won't be run off. I've got too much at stake. And it would affect my painting if I moved in and lived with someone else. So I have to stay as I am."

She saw the disapproval in his expression.

"I'm not sure that's wise," he said. "Not in view of what you've told me."

"Maybe not," she agreed. "But after all," she injected, searching for justification, as much for her own peace of mind as his, "there's been no real attempt to harm me."

He sat staring at her without comment. After a moment he spoke. "You're a very brave and determined young lady."

Joanna laughed half-heartedly. "I don't know about that," she said. "I came into town for help. I'm going to the police."

The sound of her own declaration gave her a sense of safety. Just knowing that she would not be alone in her struggle against whatever there was at her cabin. But then Hanover shattered her hopes.

"There aren't any police in Sutters Hamlet," he said. "There's only the sheriff's department. But they're over twenty miles away, and we very rarely see anything of them. I'm afraid you really can't expect help from the authorities in a matter like this."

He shrugged his shoulders helplessly, and she cringed at the implications. "This thing about the witches is considered a joke outside the Hamlet. No one from the outside will take you seriously."

He looked at her unblinkingly, his face in unmasked concern. He made no further move to continue talking, and she realized that he was waiting for her reaction. She sat staring at him, uncertain now just what to do. She realized that if what he said were true, if she remained in her cabin, she was truly alone against the witches. He seemed to tune into her indecision.

"I certainly don't want you to think that I'm trying to get you to leave the mountain simply because I want you to," he said, finally breaking the silence. "It's just that I'm sincerely concerned about your safety. I don't think you should be alone!" he said emphatically.

"But my work!" she wailed. "I've got every penny I could scrape together tied up in this year, and most of it is invested in renting that cabin. Can't you see – I can't just leave!"

His head finally began to nod slowly up and down, as though moving against his will.

"I know," he said slowly. "I suppose only someone who has had that same burning desire to create could understand. I've had it... and I do understand."

His eyes settled upon her, and for the first time she saw they held admiration. All trace of his concern was gone, and in its place she saw approval. She knew they had found a common ground.

"It's been said that most artists, whether writers or painters or whatever, recognize whether or not they have the ability to succeed with their art," he said. "But sad to say that some refuse to abide by their own judgment when it tells them they're not good enough to be a professional. They keep knocking their heads against the wall even after they have realized there's no use. But on the other hand, an artist who knows he's got it, who knows that given time and the right turn of events he can make it, must never give up. No matter what the obstacles, he mustn't give in."

She was at once comfortable and ill-at-ease in his presence.

"Is that the way it is with you, Joanna? Do you know within yourself you have the talent?"

She gave a positive nod.

"Then I can't fault your decision to remain," he said. "You'll never again hear me suggest you pack it in and leave. You have to do what you have to do. Just remember, I'll help you however I can."

His face changed in an instant from the solemn lecturer to a smiling comrade-in-arms. "I don't know just how much help an old man can be to you on the mountain. But for what it's worth, all you have to do is ask, and I'll do what I can."

"Thank you," she said gratefully, glad indeed that Hanover was her friend.

"There is something you can do for me," she said, her mind flipping back several days before to her meeting with the whittler. "Tell me something. What or who was the bitch?"

At his puzzled expression, she recounted her meeting with the whittler the night the witches had circled her cabin and told him what the mountaineer had told her about the witches, including his mention of the bitch. Hanover's head began to nod understandingly.

"The bitch," he said, "was a woman named Isadora. She was supposed to have been the last high priestess of the coven."

He rose abruptly from his chair and crossed the room to a bookcase standing against a far wall. He withdrew a hard-bound volume and returned to Joanna.

"Here," he said handing it to her. "When you have a chance, read this. It might explain a lot."

She looked at the title. Tales from the Southern Mountains, by O. T. Hanover.

"I've seen this one," she said with interest, flipping through the pages. "But it's one of your books I've never read."

"That's too bad," he said. "If you had, you might have chosen some other place to do your painting. A place where you could paint in peace."

"This is about Sutters Hamlet?" she quizzed.

"Yes," he confirmed. "One chapter is about the legend of the witches who are supposed to reside on Sutters Mountain. I was working on the book during the heyday of the witch stories arising out of this village. Isadora was killed while I was writing it, and I ended that particular story with her death."

"Isadora was killed?" she asked, her heart pounding too hard. "How?"

He carefully considered her question. "Before getting onto that topic, you really should have some background on what had been going on before her death. It's all there in the book," he said pointing to the volume in her lap. "I imagine it's explained better there than I could begin to recall."

"I don't know," she said with a sudden shiver. "I get the feeling I'd rather hear it from you than read about it alone in my cabin."

She set the book on his desk and slid it away from her with a sudden shove.

"Would you mind telling me?"

"All right," he said. "But let me tell you something about the mountains first. Not just these mountains, but all mountains.

"You know I've made my living for much of my adult life writing about the folklore and legends of the American mountains. And there's one thing I've learned about legends. Most of them are just that – legends. Tall tales that someone made up one night while he was sitting on his front porch telling bedtime stories to his kids."

Hanover shifted gear.

"Even though the modern world is just a few minutes away from most any spot in the mountains of the eastern United States, there's still something inaccessible about them, something shrouded in mystery. Mountain people are a different breed, still willing, or maybe wanting, to repeat and believe the stories handed down by their forefathers. And mountains are ideally suited to perpetrate this sort of believing. Mountains are inhabited, yet at the same time the forests are so vast and dense they're virtually desolate. Though our logic may tell us that something is untrue, it is almost impossible to physically disprove some of the stories that come out of the mountains."

"Do you see what I'm saying?" he asked, stopping his monolog. "Do you see how the mountains are different from the streets of your New York? In the mountains there's always an unknown and mysterious quantity. And where there's an unknown, there are always stories of the supernatural."

"I understand what you're saying," Joanna said.

Satisfied, Hanover continued.

"Back in the 1950s there was a story about a place not too far from here where there was an animal called the 'vampire beast.'"

He saw her look at him, and he paused. "No, it's true," he said. "You can check some of the old newspapers from this area and read about it. There was such an animal in these mountains. It mainly attacked dogs, killed them, and drank their blood. Once it attacked a woman, but her scream and a shotgun blast from her husband drove it off.

"People thought there was a genuine vampire, some sort of deadly and unknown creature loose in the mountains. But do you know what the vampire beast turned out to be? A bobcat. But because it was loose in the wilds of the mountains, the tales about it were truly terrifying. So it was the mountains more than the animal itself that created the legend.

"Now as to witches," he continued, "I imagine that every mountain range in the world has stories about people with supernatural powers who live somewhere alone in the woods. Everyone knows someone who knows about one of these mystery people. But, oddly enough, few people will ever admit that they themselves know. It's always one person removed. Someone had told them a story, and they believe the story. But they never know first-hand. Hearsay – this is what legends are made of.

"In the Ozarks, for instance, there is the fairly common practice of herb medicine, passed down from generation to generation. There's nothing supernatural about it at all, simply that these herb-doctors have passed along their knowledge of their ancient science to others, knowledge dealing with nothing more strange than the natural healing properties found in certain plants. Modern medicine is well aware of the medicinal properties of some plants, and in fact many of the medicines that we have today come from extensive research into plants. But to the people of the mountains, these herb doctors are considered witches.

"Now," Hanover shifted in his chair, "the thing that is different about the witches that supposedly inhabit the mountains around Sutters Hamlet is that, according to legend, they possess uncanny powers. And the people around here believed in the power of the witches to the point that, for all practical purposes, Sutters Hamlet was virtually ruled by the coven for nearly two hundred years. But they are no longer."

Joanna was not as unwilling to believe in people with power to control others as she appeared. She knew that she had some sort of power or knowledge that others lacked. It stood to reason that if she had this one form of power, another person could have another form.

Hanover was speaking again.

"To be absolutely truthful, I suppose it must be said that the coven's rule was a rule by fear. Just as in ancient times, the people were afraid of the witches. They feared their power. When someone died an unexplained death, it was attributed to a curse of the witches."

Joanna was spellbound, captivated with an uneasy interest. She sat silently, listening intently as Hanover unraveled the tale of the witches at Sutters Hamlet.

"The people led normal lives for the most part. But when the witches beckoned, they complied. Each order came in the form of writing, usually written on parchment and tacked to the front door of the church. This way the witches were able to remain anonymous. So far as anyone knows, the witches have been here for several hundred years, having their way with the community."

Hanover paused. When he resumed, his speech became more clipped, more emphatic.

"It's rather interesting that the people here still practice an ancient custom, a sort of ritual designed to protect themselves from the witches. On Midsummer Night, June 21," he added as Joanna's eyebrows rose in question, "many people around here keep an all-night vigil to protect their crops and livestock against the witches."

"Why that night?" Joanna asked.

"Midsummer Night is traditionally the night all witches hold their unholy revelry. This custom," Hanover continued his narrative, "of keeping a vigil on Midsummer Night dates back for centuries in Europe. So far as I know, there are only two places where it is still practiced. Sutters Hamlet and among certain groups of peasants in northern Italy."

"That's spooky!" Joanna shivered. It was as though an icy hand had touched the back of her neck. "Coming here is like moving backwards in time. I feel like I've suddenly been told that I'm in Transylvania and Count Dracula lives next door!"

"Am I frightening you?" Hanover asked. "You wanted to know about the witches, but I didn't intend to make it frightening."

"You're darn right it's frightening!" She had a sudden recollection of the face in her window. "But I asked for it, so go on," she said more bravely than she felt.

Hanover didn't continue immediately. He seemed to be weighing his words.

"That's pretty much the story of the coven up to about twenty-four years ago. Since then things have been different. Oh, the people still keep their Midsummer vigil. Occasionally, someone will stumble across a remote clearing somewhere on the mountain and find a makeshift altar and some week-old ashes where it appears that the witches have held their rituals. Occasionally, but very rarely now, some farmer will miss a sheep, and there will be some evidence that the witches took it for their ceremony. As a matter of fact, about a year ago a sheep went missing, and a few days later some young boys found one of those clearings and there was a sheep's head resting on top of a rock altar."

"How horrible!" Joanna exclaimed.

"But that sort of thing doesn't happen much anymore," Hanover said. "It's been twenty-four years since anyone found a parchment tacked to the church door. And oddly enough," he said quizzically, "there have been very few if any unexplained deaths in that time. The witches, and all acts attributed to them, have been keeping a very low profile."

"But why?" Joanna asked.

Hanover was pensive for several moments, his eyes staring out the window. The orange sun was climbing higher in the midmorning sky.

"It's not very nice," he said softly. "Not very nice at all."

"What?" Her voice was a bare whisper. Her eyes were glued to the man.

"Isadora's death," he said quietly. He grew silent before continuing.

"In any witches lore you care to study, you'll find that covens are dominated by either a man or a woman. High priest or high priestess. Traditionally, a coven consists of thirteen witches. The high priest or priestess is, essentially, a monarch, an absolute dictator over the members of the coven."

"Incidentally," he cracked a faint smile, "witchcraft is probably the only religion in existence where women aren't discriminated against as leaders."

"I didn't know that," Joanna said offhandedly. "I didn't know there was any religion that didn't discriminate against women."

"Women's lib?" his eyebrow arched up in humor.

"Yes. Who isn't to a degree nowadays?" she smiled impishly. "But I'm no militant. Don't burn bras. Can't afford to."

Silence. She waited for Hanover to continue.

"The legend says that the coven in these mountains has been ruled by a high priestess for two centuries. Each high priestess has been a direct descendant, a daughter, of the one before, or so the legend goes. A sort of royal line of witches."

"The high priestesses of this coven have been attributed with unusually strong powers. Many of the people in these mountains believe that in addition to the normal powers witches supposedly have, the high priestess even had the power to change herself into a fox."

"You're kidding!" Joanna had to interrupt. The tension! The icy hand that played with her neck! She had to relieve the tension, to interrupt the flow of the story.

Hanover's face was serious. "I think you've had enough. You're frightened. I think you've had enough of this story."

"Oh, no!" she nearly shouted, fear overriding fear. Her hands were trembling, but she would not let him stop. She had to know! Her instincts, her ESP or whatever, drove her forward. After all, she reasoned, trying to calm herself, it's only a story. It would not frighten her so if she were not living alone, and if she had not had visitors in the night.

"You can't stop in the middle of a story this exciting," she said.

"You sure?" He was concerned.

She nodded.

"Maybe I lay it on too thick because I've written about so many legends."

"Well, don't leave out anything!" She didn't often watch the late-night horror movies from her Manhattan apartment, but when she did she always stayed with it until the end, and then made it through the night the best she could.

"All right," he said a bit skeptically. "But you tell me if you want me to stop. After all, you do live alone on the mountain, and thinking about this could be frightening if you're not accustomed to it."

He went back to his story.

"The last high priestess the coven had was Isadora. At least the people around here decided that Isadora was the coven's high priestess, and she was killed twenty-four years ago. She was just a young woman. Beautiful. Dark and mysterious, come to think of it. She lived alone a good ways up the mountain with her daughter. The child was only about a year old when Isadora died.

"Story has it that one evening about dusk some youngster was on his way across the mountain to join in on a coon hunt. He was somewhere near Isadora's house when he saw her. He said that she stepped into a small clearing and began changing into a fox. Her fingernails began changing into claws, her nose began growing longer, and she began bending to the ground ... as if to walk on all fours."

"You're kidding! You don't believe that!" The story, though eerie, was too far-out to be frightening. Joanna suddenly wanted to laugh out loud. This thing about the witches was a joke, a medieval joke. It had to be!

"Suggestion," Hanover said in explanation. "It was nearly dark. The boy was alone on the mountain, and his imagination just ran away with him. . . . That's what happened, I'm sure. No one can change themselves into a fox – or anything else."

"But the people around here believe that the boy really saw her turn into a fox?" Joanna asked.

"Well, the boy said he ran before she finished her transformation. But, yes, people here believed, and mostly still believe, what he said."

"A few days later Isadora was dead." Hanover spoke grimly, with regret.

"How?" Her heart pounded against the walls of her chest. She knew his answer was going to be unpleasant.

"The traditional witch's death." His voice croaked with emotion. "She was burned at the stake."

"Oh, my God!"

A shocking stillness filled the room. For the first time, Joanna heard a clock ticking somewhere against a far wall.

"Did you know her?" she whispered.

Hanover nodded. "I had met her. I was in Sutters Hamlet doing research for that book," he pointed at the volume on his desk. "In doing my research, I imagine I talked to nearly everyone in Sutters Hamlet. I met Isadora two or three times, I suppose, and she was just an ordinary young woman. Bright and inquisitive, though not very well educated. She was just as afraid of whoever these people are that call themselves witches as everyone else on the mountain.

"I didn't know her very well. In fact, at that time I didn't know anyone around here very well. But I would bet my reputation that that girl wasn't involved in this madness."

"Then you think that's what it is?" Joanna asked. "Madness?"

Hanover paused, the look on his face an unanswered question mark.

"I honestly don't know," he finally said. "I've been here all these years trying to pry loose possibly the best story I've ever run across, and I honestly don't know. I'm no closer to knowing now than the first day I arrived in Sutters Hamlet. When Isadora was killed, everything stopped. The coven seemed to vanish without a trace, except for an occasional altar found every now and then."

Joanna looked at the old man across from her and saw only bafflement on his face.

"Is that why you stayed here, Mr. Hanover?" she asked. "To try and find out the truth about this legend?"

Hanover nodded slowly. "I suppose so," he admitted. "I've written a dozen books since then, but the one I really want to write always eludes me. The chapter in that book you were just looking at tells about the legend, but I want to know the truth behind that legend. That's the one story I haven't been able to get.

"So far as I know, the people calling themselves the coven have this entire community hoodwinked into believing they're real witches," he said. "But I don't know that. I don't know what the truth is."

"Evidently, the people here must believe it without question if they went so far as to kill Isadora," Joanna said.

"Oh, that they do," he replied. "I know what I've told you isn't very pleasant. It can be downright frightening. I hope you can see why I was concerned for you when you told me about your visitors. No one has actually seen the witches in all these years, and I don't know why they should suddenly turn up now. It worries me."

"It is spooky," she said.

She knew the story was over, that the next step was up to her, whether to remain or leave, but she had already decided. She could not leave, at least not unless she knew with certainty that remaining would endanger her personal safety.

She had chosen her course, and she would stick to it, for the time being at least. She slid from her seat, thanked Hanover for his time, then walked uncertainly out the door.

She looked at the mountain towering above her, hiding what secrets she didn't know. The sharp fangs of fear gnawed at her insides as she returned to her car and drove it into the unknown.

Chapter 7

Peter was sitting on the grass in front of the cabin when Joanna returned to the cabin. She had forgotten that today he was scheduled for painting lessons. When she stopped the car, he casually threw his arm up and waved, then pushed himself off the grass and onto his feet.

"I thought you'd forgotten," he said. "I'm glad I waited."

She saw his eyes drift down her body, and once again she blushed; she was attracted to him. She experienced a sudden quickening of her breath and wondered if it had gone undetected. Her cheeks felt flushed, and she knew that was one telltale sign she could not conceal. Her eyes darted to his shirt standing open at the collar, and wondered if he was aware of the effect he sometimes had on her.

She turned away suddenly, walking briskly to the front door.

"I hadn't forgotten," she lied. "I had to go down the mountain."

She found herself already beginning to use some mountain vocabulary. Inserting the key in the lock, she asked, "Are you ready to paint?"

She tried to keep her voice light and cheery.

"Ummm," he said affirmatively.

She felt his arm lightly brush against her side as she rumbled with the rusty lock and realized that his nearness was having a devastating effect upon her. A thought briefly entered her mind. Had she really agreed to allow Peter to act as her guide because he could help her learn her way about the mountain, or had there been other reasons? Reasons known only to her subconscious at the time? Perhaps she had been more attracted to him at their first meeting than she had been willing to admit.

Under her breath she cursed the lock that would not work, but which forced her to stand there fumbling with it, experiencing the uncertainty of her own feelings. She had had trouble with the lock since the first day, and normally didn't lock it when leaving the cabin. But the appearance of the doll had prompted her to lock the door when she went in to see Hanover. The key turned and the door opened.

With a relieved sigh she stepped inside. Apprehensively, she looked around, hoping that everything was as she left it. She wanted no more surprises like last night. A thought suddenly occurred to her. She tried to dismiss it, but decided to see if she could learn anything.

"Did you find anything in the yard this morning while you were waiting for me?" she asked, standing in the open doorway and pointing in the general direction she had thrown the doll. She purposely diverted her eyes from his face.

"No," Peter answered. "What did you lose?"

She felt guilty at trying to trap him, particularly since he was a friend and she had no reason to suspect him. But was there, in fact, no reason? As she chastised herself for suspecting Peter for no cause, she suddenly realized that he had first come to her cabin the morning after the witches had sprinkled their white powder and circled her cabin. Now he was here the morning after the appearance of the doll. It could be coincidence. After all, his painting lesson this morning was planned several days ago.

"Oh, I don't suppose I lost anything," she said. "Come on in and let's have some coffee before we start."

Normally, if she were in the mood to paint, she would have begun painting immediately without the interruption of coffee. That had been her plan when she left Hanover. But when she left Hanover, she had not remembered she had promised Peter a lesson. She was keyed up from last night and wanted to paint to ease the tension and bitterly regretted that she must now spend the next few hours with Peter. She regretted it, yet she looked forward to it. Looked forward to being in his company.

"Is there anything wrong?" he asked as he helped her throw wood into the stove, then put a match to it as she set a pot of coffee water on top.

"What makes you think anything's wrong?" she replied distantly. She busied herself in the kitchen, first setting out two cups, then pretending that the table needed wiping.

"Because you're trying to act so normal."

He covered the distance between them in three giant strides, took her by the shoulders, and spun her around. She looked uncertainly into his face, not knowing what to expect.

"What's wrong?" he demanded. His eyes gazed sternly into hers. "I know that I don't know you very well, Joanna. But you seem like a very frightened young lady. You seemed that way the first time I met you, and you seem that way now."

He let go of her shoulders, but still stood challenging her.

"There's nothing wrong," she said. She ached to tell him, to tell anyone who might help her. But more than help, right then she wanted to clear her mind of the recent events on the mountain. She wanted to forget. She wanted to spend a carefree day, to relax, to relieve the tension that the appearance of the doll had instilled in her. And she didn't want to relive again, for the second time that morning, the events that had driven her to tell her tale to Hanover.

"There's nothing wrong," she repeated.

Peter pursued the matter no further. Their conversation shifted to small talk as they waited for the water to boil, and it continued in that vein during coffee.

An hour later they were trekking through the forest, heading around and slightly down the mountain. Peter did not tell her where they were going, saying only that it was one of his favorite spots, and that he wanted to try to capture it on canvas.

After fifteen minutes of travel through dense foliage, they followed a game trail that wove its way around the mountain. Several times she spotted something, some bush or tree or a sudden twist in the trail that seemed vaguely familiar to her. Puzzled at first, she finally realized when she had seen these same sights before.

"How much longer do we stay on this path?" she asked Peter.

"Not much longer," he shot back over his shoulder. He was carrying the painting box and lightweight easel slung across his shoulders and did not look back.

"Where does this path eventually go?" she asked, but almost certain she knew the answer.

"It ends at a house," he said, "not far from here."

"Let's go there. Do you mind?"

Peter stopped and stood facing her. The legs of the easel protruding toward her kept her at a distance.

"It's the whittler's house, isn't it?" she asked.

Peter cocked an eyebrow. "Yeh. Old Silas would be the whittler."

"Silas," she repeated to herself. "I didn't know his name."

"I didn't know you knew him!" Peter said incredulously. "He's the meanest old bootlegger in these parts. You want to watch yourself around him."

"Why?"

"Why!" He faced her belligerently, then he mellowed. His voice lost its edge. "I don't know," he admitted. "You hear all sorts of stories about Old Silas. When I was a kid, everyone always said to stay away from him, and I did. He's a loner and keeps pretty much to himself. Supposed to be a mean old buzzard."

"So the English teacher's afraid of the bootlegger," she taunted good-naturedly.

"Not afraid," Peter denied sheepishly, embarrassment on his face. "Just ingrained into me from childhood. Even English teachers don't lose all their childhood prejudices."

He laughed, and she knew that he was trying to save face, trying to come across as a sophisticate and not a mountaineer to this New Yorker he was dealing with.

"He's not so mean," she said smiling devilishly. "I helped him carry some of his moonshine across the mountain the other night."

The same deviltry that had forced her to confront the whittler on that first day in town now forced her to chide Peter, and she watched with glee as the look of bewilderment enveloped his face.

"He's a friend of mine," she said, pushing the matter still further.

"I'll be damned!" Peter exclaimed. He looked at her, shaking his head. A faint smile crept onto his face, then broke into a broad grin. "You're gutsy as hell. You know that?"

"Yeh. I've been told that before."

He looked at her admiringly and she knew that, if there had been a contest between them, she had won. She was at her best when sparring verbally with people.

"Let's go visit him. Do you mind?" she asked, more demurely now.

Peter shrugged. "It's all right with me."

He turned and once again led the way.

They followed the trail until the forest broke away to reveal the whittler's tiny cabin, smaller even than Joanna's own. It was as she last remembered it. The door stood open, and the chair still leaned against the wall where she had sat at his feet talking. Only the whittler was missing. As they approached the cabin she began looking for signs of activity. With Peter now following behind, she walked to the door and peered inside, but saw no one. She tapped the door several times and called his name, thinking that he may be in his bedroom with his carvings, but again she was met with silence.

"He must not be here," Joanna said shrugging.

"Then let's leave," Peter said a bit too quickly. "We can come back some other time."

Joanna turned to face him.

"You are afraid of him, aren't you?" she asked, surprised.

Peter's face flushed.

"He has the reputation of not being too kind to strangers who drop by unexpectedly. He's taken potshots at people who came around and surprised him," Peter said.   '

"I'm not a stranger," she declared. She stuck her head inside the door again, knowing the gesture was useless since the cabin was too small to hide the man inside, but she didn't know what else to do.

A gruff voice from behind made her turn around with a start.

"I ain't in there!" the voice bellowed.

She turned to find the whittler watching them from only a few yards behind, a rifle held like a shield across his chest. His eyes were focused menacingly on Peter, who shifted uncomfortably under the older man's gaze. He dropped the rifle to his side, muzzle pointing at the ground, and stepped toward them. He glided silently across the grass, and she could easily see how he had gotten so near them undetected. He moved like a ghost.

He walked up to Peter and stopped.

Peter faced him, their eyes locking together when they were only a yard apart.

"Who ye be?" the whittler demanded. "I seen your face round and 'bout."

"My name's Peter Tillary."

"Ye the widow Tillary's boy?"

Peter nodded.

Seemingly satisfied, the whittler turned away, focusing his attention on Joanna. She felt apprehensive at first as his eyes settled upon her, but then she saw them soften. She had seen that change in him before, as he changed from the brusque old mountaineer to a likable old man. When he spoke, his voice had softened as well, and his words rolled from him with an affectionate warmth.

' "Well if it ain't the picture girl," he said, and his eyes seemed to dance as he spoke. "Ye ain't lost again, are ye?"

"Not this time. We were near here, and I thought it would be nice to drop in for a visit."

The whittler's face cracked a cynical smile.

"I didn't know who ye might be when I heard ye coming," he declared, netting the rifle to waist level. "So I took this here gun and went to see."

He paused and his eyes sparkled, as though hiding some dark secret.

"I was out on the mountain again last night, so I had to be right careful when I heard ye coming. But I figured if it was the law, they'd a been a bit quieter than ye were."

He grinned and winked at her, and she knew that he had made another night run to his cabin with his moonshine.

"I halfway thought I might run into ye again," he joked, "but I reckon I didn't."

His face clouded over and he cast a suspicious glance at Peter. He dropped his voice to a conspiring level, and she knew the conversation was taking a twist.

"They was out again last night," he said. "I nearly run right into one of 'em."

Her breath caught in her throat, and she felt the goose bumps prick her flesh. There was no question in her mind who they were. She knew it was the witches! And she knew where they had been headed. She hadn't seen them, but there was no doubt in her mind that they had someway put the doll on her bed.

"They been back to your place?" the whittler asked curiously.

She shook her head, not wanting to talk about last night's incident.

"I haven't seen them since that night on the mountain," she said, knowing that she had not told a lie, but neither had she told the complete and entire truth.

"I wonder what they was up to last night?" The whittler's face was wrinkled in thought.

Joanna noticed that Peter was intently following their conversation but remained silent. Obviously, he didn't know what they were discussing, but she knew that when he got her alone he would most .likely ask. The concern in the whittler's voice was apparent.

Joanna asked, "Has anyone else seen them? Other than you and me?"

"Dunno," he replied. "I ain't been down the mountain lately. But I reckon if they been out on the mountain, we ain't the only ones that seen 'em."

"Probably not," Joanna said thoughtfully.

Silence fell between them, and she saw their conversation fizzling. After a moment, she remembered why she had wanted to see the whittler again.

"I wanted to thank you for the two carvings you left me," she said.

The whittler's voice turned gruff from embarrassment. "Tweren't nothin'. Them was the ones you liked, wasn't they?"

"Yes," Joanna said. "I put them on a little table beside my bed."

She wanted to question him about the painting she had given him, but out of politeness did not. When he mentioned the picture, she was delighted.

"I got your picture in there with all the little whittlin's," he said. "Ye can see it if ye want to."

"I'd like that," Joanna said, and followed him into his bedroom, with Peter right behind.

He had hung the painting on his bedroom wall above a shelf full of carvings. The landscape went well with the rustic log walls of his cabin, and he had arranged the wooden figures below to accentuate the picture. Upon seeing the arrangement, Joanna realized with renewed fascination that the old mountain man had an artist's eye for arrangement. But remembering their earlier talk about creativity, she knew that to make such an observation in front of Peter would unnecessarily embarrass him. So she remained quiet, though she was pleased at the prominent place he had given her painting among his own carvings.

The whittler led them back outside, leaning his rifle against a wall as he walked back through the cabin.

"Your friend here don't have much to say," he said to her as he stepped through the door. His eyes drifted to Peter, who grinned sheepishly.

"It's your reunion," Peter said to the two of them. "I guess I feel like the intruder."

The whittler solemnly nodded his head. "I reckon ye are at that."

Five minutes later the reunion was over, and Joanna was again following Peter through the forest as he led her to the place that he wanted to capture on canvas.

They walked in silence, with only an occasional word passed between them. Joanna could tell from the forced silence that something was bothering Peter, but she decided to let him broach the subject, whatever it might be.

When finally he ended their journey, she found herself at the base of a sheer cliff that dropped off the side of the mountain. The cliff began two hundred feet above them, dropped vertically to their feet, then the mountain continued to drop sharply beneath them, unveiling an unobstructed view of the valley and the surrounding mountains. The sight was majestic, and she quickly understood why Peter would choose this spot for a landscape.

"It's beautiful!" she gasped.

Peter put down the easel, grunting affirmatively. The panoramic view sent her mind off on a trip of the imagination, but even so, she recognized the abruptness of Peter's reply. Shifting back to him, she realized that the sudden change in Peter must be related to their visit to the whittler.

"What's the matter?" she asked casually. "You seem like something's bothering you."

Peter began setting up the easel as he seemed to consider her question. He set up the stretched canvas, then brought out several tubes of oils before finally replying.

"Who did you see on the mountain?" he finally asked, facing her with the question.

Joanna understood. Her suspicions at the whittler's cabin had been correct. Peter had tuned into their conversation about the witches; she knew this was what he was referring to.

Hesitating only a moment she replied, "The witches."

Peter's face grew pale. He had some brushes in his hand and absently he placed them on the easel ledge.

"That's what I thought," he said. "The last time I was down the mountain I learned that several people have seen them lately."

His voice trailed off and he looked at her with worried eyes. When finally he resumed speaking his voice was tense.

"Did I hear Old Silas say that they had been at your cabin?" he asked. She nodded.

"Then I wasn't imagining things," he said. "You are frightened, aren't you?"

She knew that he was referring to his earlier remark that she had seemed like a very frightened young lady on several occasions. Restraining herself, remaining very much the sophisticate, she primly nodded her head. Tears welled up in her eyes and she fought them back. But suddenly she felt them rolling down her cheeks and she tried no more to stop them. She let them flow freely.

In an instant Peter crossed the distance between them. She threw herself into his arms and felt protected as he closed them around her. She buried her head in his chest, expecting to cry as she had with Hanover, but she did not. In Peter's arms she felt totally safe.

The fear was gone, and in its place she felt the red torch of passion overcoming her. The same flush she experienced when she first met him returned, amplified a thousand times with his arms about her. He held her tightly, and in an instant she felt his hand lifting her chin, tilting her head upwards to his. He placed his lips gently on hers and she responded. The moment was over too quickly, the magic broken when she found the strength to stand alone. She took a step backwards, looking into his eyes, and she knew that their relationship had changed.

"Do you want to tell me about it?" he gently asked, their fingertips still entwined.

He led her to a patch of grass where they sat. She told him, beginning with the face she had seen in the window and ending with the doll last night, of the incidents since she had arrived on the mountain.

"Why me?" she ended. "Why am I being singled out, do you know? It does seem that I'm being singled out, doesn't it? Or are these things happening to others, too?"

She looked questioningly into his face, which showed his utter bewilderment. "I don't know. It's strange though. All my life I've heard about the witches, but except for a few isolated incidents . . . you would almost think they weren't here anymore." He looked her squarely in the eyes, his face a mirror of his concern. "But now they seem active again. Because of what's happening to you . . . and some other things. Mainly animals gone missing. And it all seems to have started again just in the past few weeks."

"Just since I've been here," she said hollowly.

"I don't know," he said, shaking his head in confusion. "But it does seem that way."

"But why me!" she nearly shouted at him. "I want to know why I'm being singled out!"

He clasped her hand tightly in his own. "I just don't know," he said. "But there must be a reason."

He lay back on the grass, shoving a blade of grass between his teeth and falling silent. Suddenly, he turned toward her. "Maybe you shouldn't be living alone. Wouldn't you feel better living with people?"

"I can't if I'm going to paint."

He nodded understandingly. "Is there any way I can help?"

"Yes, there is," she said resolutely, but with a forced smile. "When you're near my cabin, stop by and see if I'm all right."

She started to say more. She started to tell him to tell any witches that he might run into to leave her alone! But she didn't. If there was one thing she knew, it was that whatever was going on at her cabin was something she had to face alone. She either had to face it alone and beat it – or leave.

She knew that terror was something you don't invite your friends to share, particularly not if you're the one who's being singled out. It was hard for her not to say these things, knowing that night lay in wait for her at the end of the day. Once again, the night was her enemy. And as Peter finally began to work on his painting and the shadows grew longer, she saw the enemy coming.

Chapter 8

She was running, mile after endless mile of running. Panting! Screaming! The black-robed man was behind her, gaining with every step! It seemed the faster she tried to run, the slower her legs moved. She was now running in slow motion, agonizing minutes passing between each step, and the man was still gaining. He was only a step behind her! He was reaching for her! His evil hand grabbed her hair, which was flowing behind her in the wind. She screamed! She heard herself screaming and it was for real, not just a dream now. Hands were clawing at her face! Tearing into her flesh! She jerked away! Opened her eyes! She was alone.

Fear gripped her, sucking her breath from her lungs in huge, uneven gulps. She looked around. She was alone in her bedroom. The morning sun shone in the east window. She was groggy. Something was wrong, terribly wrong.

Her head was spinning; she was trying to bring herself back into reality. She couldn't think. She was muddled, but she didn't know immediately if it was from the terror of the dream or something else. But what? She could still see the black faceless figure chasing her. She vividly remembered looking around in her dream and trying to peer into the face hidden deep in the dark, hooded opening. But there was no face. Only black. She remembered the doll. It was like the doll she thought had been staring at her, but it had had no eyes. No face at all. She was still trembling. She was glad it was morning.

But there was something wrong. She sat up in bed and saw it. Blood! There was blood on the sheets! On her body! There was a streak of blood smeared from her neck running between her breasts to her stomach. She threw back the sheets and her vaginal area and pubic hairs were matted with dried blood. Mutely, and without understanding, she stared at the story her body told. But what story she didn't know!

The terror of her dream was now a reality. Something – something horrible had happened. Something her mind wanted to block out. She remembered being with Peter. She remembered their talk. She remembered waiting as he finished his painting of the cliff. She remembered walking home. But she didn't recall arriving at her cabin. She didn't remember just where her recollection of events stopped. It just stopped somewhere.

The room was eerie in its silence. She listened, but there was no sound throughout the cabin. The silence was both a relief and another point of terror jabbing her in the side. It was like death.

She looked at the blood smeared between her breasts, and for the first time it struck her that she had never before slept in the nude when she was alone. She had slept in the nude, but when she did she had not slept alone.

The fear, brought first by the dream and then by the mystery of her bloody body, had dulled her mind. She could see but she couldn't think. As the first shocking moments passed, her senses began to return.

She needed to go to the bathroom. It was the call of nature that focused her attention on the lower part of her body and brought with it the realization that she had been used. She felt violated and abused. Her vagina had that sticky feeling it always had after she had had sex. She touched the lip and it was sore. There was a dull ache inside her, a soreness reminding her of her first sexual experience. She ran her finger along the outside, testing, but jerked it away quickly when pain shot up into her abdomen.

At once a thought entered and was dismissed from her mind. The blood on her was not from her own body. Never in her own sexual experience had she bled this much from normal intercourse, even repeated intercourse. Her vagina showed no trace of bleeding, just pain. She could remember several weekends when she had had sex repeatedly, maybe even excessively, with Ted or other lovers. But never had the experiences left her this sore. She realized that whatever had happened, it had occurred repeatedly.

If she had been raped, it had been many times, judging by her soreness, the aching all over her. If this were tomorrow, the day she thought it was, the day after her painting trip with Peter, she doubted that one man could get an erection that many times in the sixteen or so hours that had elapsed. That left the possibility of several men having violated her.

One horror entered her mind. The coven!

She was overcome with the need to react, to do something, to protest or fight back, but to calm her frayed nerves. To ease her frightened mind. She got up out of bed as fast as she was able. But she was in pain. She had to do something. Anything! Instinctively, yet filled with fear, she walked to the dresser to better view her blood-covered body in the mirror.

The first look into the mirror sent her reeling. Not from the blood spattered all over her body but from ... the other!

The reflection in the mirror wasn't her!

She jerked away, stumbled, nearly tripped and fell as she reeled in the middle of the room. Trembling first, then her entire body shaking, she embraced herself, fearing what she had just seen. She forced herself to go back, forced herself to look again, and when she did she nearly retched. The image she saw was of herself, but not her! The thing she saw in the mirror was someone she had never seen before! It was her own image, she knew, but it was a portrait of herself she had never before seen or could have imagined. A wretched, scrawny face stared back at her. Sunken cheeks. Blue shadows under her eyes. Her hair was matted and tangled as though it had been left uncombed for weeks, and the brown stubby ends of two snarled twigs protruded from the snarls.

She stared in disbelief and horror. "Oh my God!" She ran her fingers over the weather-beaten skin of her face. The skin was coarse, chafed by the wind. She couldn't make her mind function properly. What had happened? Again her memory gave her no explanation. Her face, like her body, told some horrible story. But the meaning of the lines was lost with her memory.

How much time had really passed to make her look like this?

And what had really happened?

She remembered the screams that had jolted her out of the nightmare of being chased into the nightmare of reality. She remembered the chase dream and wondered if it had been more than a dream. She trembled. She was crying, tears running down her sunken cheeks.

"My God! It looks like I've been outside for days!"

Sitting in front of the dresser, Joanna had a realization, a thought that sent uneasiness washing over her body like a tide.

"Why in hell don't I leave?"

She looked at her face in the mirror, and she knew that she shouldn't be there. She should be packing her bags, ready to return to New York. But, by God, she had spent her savings on this place and she wasn't going to be run off. Even after these last dreadful events, she was still intent on staying. It made no sense to her. She looked at the room, and it calmed her. It was as though the cabin had some hold on her. It promised her protection, but her rational self knew it lied. How could she dare stay?

A voice inside of her told her to stop this silliness, that she had work to do, as yet unimagined paintings still to be put to canvas. She recognized it as the voice of her artistic self, telling her to remain against all odds . . . even rape. But fleetingly she wondered if it might be some other voice – some alien voice hiding inside her – disguised as the artist.

Shoving aside her terror, she drew water and washed away the blood all over her body. She used washrag after washrag to wipe it away. Once cleaned, she began wondering what she would do next. How was she going to protect herself. She returned to the dresser, sat down in front of the mirror, and began applying moisturizing cream, then makeup to hide the blue shadows under her eyes. Her sunken cheeks couldn't be disguised. Neither could her fear.

It took her nearly half an hour to comb and untangle her hair. Finally, it hung from her shoulders, halfway resembling normal. Her face in the mirror now was not so wretched after all. The mess of her hair had made her slender face appear even more so, creating the sunken effect in her cheeks. She now appeared almost normal. She ran her fingers over her cheeks testingly. Several days of constant application of moisturizing cream would have her skin back to normal.

Puzzled and frightened, she sat staring at her restored face. The first shock of seeing herself, bloodstained in bed, and then her face in the mirror, had worn off as she realized that her face was not as bad as it had appeared after that first frightened glance. But the return to normalcy did not remove her confusion. What had happened? And how long had it been since she was first taken with this amnesia? She knew without having to reason that her face could not have become so weatherworn in just one day. How much time really had passed since her painting trip with Peter?

She looked around, but there was nothing to tell her today's date. She knew there was nothing anywhere in the cabin that could tell her what day it was. She had deliberately cut herself off from such modern conveniences as the radio, and there were no issues of the New York Times lying around.

She still sat before the mirror, her doctored face nearly itself again. Her telltale body now clothed, she walked to the bedroom window and looked out. Early morning dew still coated the grass. The forest beyond looked fresh and innocent. But she knew it was deceiving. Hidden by its walls was something unexplained.

Her mind was tormented by the demons of doubt. What had happened? What story did her body tell? Inwardly she was outraged that she could have been violated – without remembering – but outwardly she was muddled. She wanted to strike out, but against what? The cabin? The mountain?

Anger streamed through her body like a current. Rationally, she should leave. Now! Irrationally, and she knew it was irrational, she would not be pushed about. She would not be run off the mountain!

If she were to maintain her sanity this morning, she knew she had to be active, had to be doing something to get her mind off the rape. She knew she must or she would lose her courage and run,

The cabin was stuffy, the air stale, as though it had been breathed and recycled. She walked to the front of the cabin, looked out the front window, and found the clearing empty. She opened the front door. The cold rush of air refreshed her, and she breathed it deeply. But uneasiness crept into her, a fear of opening her cabin to whatever may be hidden outside. The fear of allowing in whatever had been there, whatever had had her, whatever had used her. Afraid of being trapped inside should it return, she went quickly to the kitchen and opened the rear door. Should anything or anyone come, she now had an escape route.

Still uneasy, not knowing if danger might come from within or without, she made a painstaking search of her tiny cabin. Looking in every crevice, every dark place for anything – anything at all. A doll. A person. A thing. But there was none.

In her bedroom she returned to the mirror and looked at herself. Clothed now. Her body clean. Her face fixed. Hardly anything out of place.

But looking at her reflection in the mirror and remembering the condition of her body upon awakening, she knew that her initial judgment had been wrong. After two bouts with the night visitors, the white powder at her door, and the doll, she was convinced that whoever was doing these things meant her harm. Someone had violated her body, and she knew, was almost certain, that whoever had done it had done so without her consent. But she couldn't be sure. She didn't remember! She wanted to run, to leave the mountain, but some insane part of her would not let her.

Right now, the most frightening thing was what had happened to make her unable to remember. Was it a shock so unpleasant that her subconscious mind had deemed it necessary to obliterate all recollection from her conscious mind? If so, the subconscious had failed dismally by leaving the physical evidence, and in doing so had created a grisly puzzle for her conscious mind to unravel. Or had something else robbed her of her memory?

She had an uneasy feeling – no, not a feeling at all – just a slight glimmer of suspicion that the latter was the case. The feeling that something else had robbed her of her memory, something out of her control. Looking at the reflection of herself that had only minutes ago been so unladylike, she had a fleeting sense of being a puppet, of being manipulated.

Her contemplation was suddenly interrupted by a sound from outside.

She was deep in thought when she heard a shuffling noise at the front of her cabin. Her mind and body reacted as one. Fear clutched her in its viselike grip. Her front door was standing open! She jumped and dashed from the bedroom to slam the door against whoever was outside. Heavy on her mind was the thought that whatever had just happened to her was about to be reenacted.

As she rushed across the living room, Peter appeared smiling in the open doorway. She stopped abruptly. Too late! On impulse, she started to turn and run for the back door and make a dash down the mountain. She had begun to turn when his voice stopped her.

"Good morning," he said jovially. "I hope you don't run me off again today."

She saw a cardboard-backed canvas under one arm, while his free hand held brushes (her brushes!) and an assortment of fifty-cent tubes of oils. He was smiling openly at her. What had he meant when he said he hoped she didn't run him off again today?

She eyed him with suspicion. He was the last person she remembered before her memory left her. She was with him when her memory left! But here he was speaking to her as though he knew nothing of what had happened.

She didn't run.

"Do you mind if I come in?" He made no move to enter, apparently awaiting her invitation.

She took a step back. Swept her arm out in a welcoming gesture, and he took one step into the cabin. He was watching her curiously, and seemed uncertain as to whether he should come any farther or not. His nervousness made Joanna feel a bit more at ease.

"Is anything wrong?" he asked.

"What appears to be wrong?" she replied cautiously.

"You seemed frightened when you saw me," he said.

She shrugged, trying to appear unconcerned. "I wasn't expecting anyone, and it startled me when I heard you moving around outside."

Peter's face showed its surprise. "You don't mean that you've forgotten?"

"Forgotten what?"

"That I was supposed to come by today to show you this." He held up the canvas, a painting of a mountain stream. "And to return your paint and brushes. Don't you remember? You said you wouldn't be needing your brushes again until today. I got here as early as I could so you wouldn't have to wait for your brushes. You said you had a very important picture that you wanted to start on."

Her face must have showed her disbelief.

"Don't you remember?"

She shook her head. She had no idea what he was talking about. She didn't remember lending him her paint and brushes or giving him the canvas. She didn't remember any of it. She had never lent her brushes to anyone. She had never before been asked to lend them, but she knew it was something she just wouldn't do. Particularly here, where she knew there was no place to buy others should hers be lost. No, she thought resolutely, I know I wouldn't let them out of my sight.

"Are you sure you're all right?" he asked when she still hadn't spoken.

She wasn't sure. She wasn't sure of anything. Peter seemed so concerned, so innocent and concerned for her. She found herself wanting to believe that he was who he said he was. But he had been the last person with her before she lost her memory. And here he was again the morning after something horrible had happened. Just like the morning after those other things. She didn't know what to believe.

But there was one thing she realized immediately Peter knew something of her activities since her memory loss. He knew, and she wanted to know. Still not sure of him, she decided to remain cautious.

"Yes, I'm all right," she said.

Her voice wasn't particularly friendly, but neither was it unfriendly. She wanted to bait him. She wanted to use him, for good or bad, to try and learn what had happened. This seemed to her to be a morning of uncertainties, and once again she was uncertain. Now she was uncertain as to how to go about getting the information she needed from Peter. It seemed impossible to do it without letting him know that there was something terribly wrong. She couldn't just start asking him detailed questions about their last meeting without arousing his suspicion, and she saw no way around it.

Peter was either a friend, as innocent as he seemed, and concerned for her, or he was involved in what had been happening to her. If he was involved, if he was a member of the coven, then he already knew what was wrong with her. But if he was a friend, and God how she needed a friend, then she needed him. She needed someone to confide in, someone who could trust and who would possibly help her.

Either way, she could see nothing to be lost by confiding in him. He either already knew, or he was a person she could trust. Anyway, she remembered telling him about the other incidents when they talked by the cliff, so why not now?

"What are you doing here, Peter?" As soon as she heard her words come out, she knew she had phrased them wrong.

"What do you mean?" He seemed startled at the abruptness of her question.

She was in tears. She buried her face in her hands and sobbed, shaking her head in despair. "I don't know! I don't know! I don't know!"

He stepped to her side and took her in his arms, letting her bury her tear-stained face on his shoulder. She sobbed silently. She felt his hand on her back patting her gently, and she remembered the kiss they had shared the last time he held her like this.

"Don't cry," he said.

When the tears stopped, she stepped away and tried to smile but couldn't. She brushed a tear from her eye with the back of her hand.

"Something is the matter," he stated matter-of-factly.

She nodded. "Yes." Her black hair bounced on her shoulders as she admitted the truth.

"Do you want to tell me about it?"

"Yes." She looked past him into the yard. "Let's go outside and sit in the grass."

He followed her to a patch of grass halfway between the cabin and the trees where she began her story.

"I don't remember anything that has happened since the day you painted the cliff," she said, letting it all out at once as they dropped onto the green carpet of grass. "I've lost my memory."

His forehead wrinkled in concern. "That was four days ago!"

So now she knew!

"Will you tell me everything you know that has happened to me since then?"

"Okay," he said skeptically, his hand reaching out to gently touch hers. "But what happened to make you forget?"

"I don't know. I was hoping that maybe you could help me try to remember."

She saw his deep-blue eyes looking warmly at her. They openly showed their concern. When he was like this, she couldn't believe that he might be a member of the coven. But she knew that looks could be deceiving. And she couldn't erase the fact that the last events she could recall were in his presence. She couldn't erase it even though she again felt that same glow of arousal around him.

"I'll do anything I can to help you," he said. "Where do you want me to begin?"

"The last thing I remember is starting back home after you finished your picture."

He looked into the distance as though he were pulling together his thoughts.

"Well, I walked back here with you," he said, nodding to the cabin. "I don't remember exactly what we talked about, just things in general, I think. We had been talking about the witches. Do you remember that?"

He looked questioningly at her.

"Yes," she said, "there at the cliff."

"Right. I don't believe we talked about that anymore after we left the cliff. I remember when walking back you asked me if I would come inside for some coffee. You said you didn't want to be alone. It was getting late, and you said you wanted me to stay with you for a few minutes. It was the day after you had found the doll in your bedroom, and you wanted me to check out the cabin to make certain there was nothing else like that inside."

Joanna was listening with interest. She didn't remember asking him in for coffee.

"But when we got back, it seemed as though you had forgotten you asked me in," he continued. "You opened the door and turned around and said good-bye. Then you started to go inside and close the door. I remember I reached out and stopped the door closing, because you had said you wanted me to come in with you until we checked the house out."

"I blocked the door and said, 'Hey, don't you want me to come in?'"

"You looked at me like you were sort of mad and scared both, and said, 'Let go!'"

"I asked you if you didn't still want me to come inside and look around, and you said no. You said you weren't scared anymore. I asked you when you wanted me to come back, and you said to come back the next day." '

He paused, looking thoughtfully at her.

"You know, I should have realized something was wrong. I mean –" He seemed at a loss for words. "I did realize it, but I didn't realize it was so serious. You didn't act like yourself, but I didn't want to force my way in if you had changed your mind."

"Did you come back the next day?" Joanna asked.

"Yes, that's when you gave me your brushes and canvas and told me to go paint something on my own."

"Did I seem odd that day?"

"Well, not really. You seemed pretty normal. You were sitting here when I came."

"What was I doing?"

"Nothing," he said. "Just sitting here in the grass doing nothing. You seemed sort of glad to see me, but you said you wouldn't have time to work with me. That's when you gave me the canvas and told me to go off and paint by myself."

"I hope I wasn't nasty."

"No, you just said you didn't have time. You said you had an appointment later and would have to leave."

"An appointment? What kind of appointment?" She was getting excited. This appointment that she didn't remember, following a day when she had acted so strange, could very well be linked to whatever had happened. Inside, deep down in her animal instincts, she knew there was a link. But Peter's response dulled the excitement's edge and abruptly dashed her hopes of finding out.

"You didn't say anything about the appointment, and I didn't ask," he confessed. "You just said you had one. Then you went inside and got the canvas, brushes, and paint and gave them to me. You said to take care of your brushes, because you didn't normally lend them to anyone."

That sounded more like her normal self, she thought.

"And then you left?"

He pondered the question for a moment. "You told me to be certain to return the paint and brushes today, because you said you had a very important picture to paint. Then I left."

"What sort of picture? Did I say?"

"No," he shrugged. "You didn't say anything about anything."

Her hopes were again shattered, and she was again as much in the dark about what had happened to her as she was before Peter came. Only now there were some added pieces to the puzzle. There were more unexplained ends to try to tie into some sort of coherent explanation of four lost days. But where to begin?

From Peter's account, there was one clue. It may be a clue. Could it be that she had some idea beforehand that something was going to happen to her. Could her ESP have been at work, and she knew without knowing how that something was going to happen. Could that explain the appointment?

"Did I seem upset when I told you I had an appointment?" She shot the question at him suddenly.

"No."

No help. Then it could be that she had either sensed what was going to happen, or she actually had some sort of prearranged appointment, one that she had willingly set. If that was the case, could she have consented to whatever she had had a part in?

"No!" The word shot out without her knowing it, catching both her and Peter unawares.

He eyed her with even more concern, but said nothing. He seemed aware that she was very upset and was content to let the conversation progress at her selected speed.

The thought that she may have consented to something so horrible as that which had happened to her was disturbing. It was a possibility that she couldn't accept. But it was only a thought, only an idea. Just an outside possibility, the sort of far-out grappling for truth that a puzzled and frightened mind could put forward. There was no basis for believing it. She knew there was no basis for believing it. But the thought was still there. She had had an appointment that she knew about, but one which she didn't remember keeping. And her next conscious knowledge was one of waking up to terror.

She shook her head as though trying to dislodge the thought from her brain and toss it outside.

"Have you been back since then? Or have you seen me since then?" she asked hopefully.

Peter shook his head. "I was a bit afraid to come back today because of the way you didn't seem to want me around the last two times."

"I'm sorry," she said. "I don't know what's wrong with me. I don't know what's been happening. It just doesn't sound like me to be rude like that."

He reached to her and patted the back of her hand affectionately. "You don't have to apologize. Something's wrong, and I want to help. You'll never find anyone you can trust more than me, and I mean it. I want to help you if I can."

He stopped talking and looked at her as though trying to determine what effect his words had had.

"Do you want to tell me what happened?" he asked.

"Yes," she said softly, shuddering as she remembered the terror she had faced when she awoke.

In spite of the way circumstances always seemed to point toward Peter, when she was with him she felt she could trust him. Even though she had decided earlier that he must be in the coven and involved in what was happening to her, she now had serious doubts. He always seemed to be around when something unpleasant happened, but Joanna kept telling herself that that could be coincidence. She only had three friends in Sutters Hamlet, and Peter was one of them. She wanted to give him every chance to be a friend before accusing him of anything else.

It was easy enough to place an accusing finger when she was alone and unsure, but now that she was with him it was different. Her womanly instincts told her that he was sincere in his concern for her, that she could trust him. She wanted to believe him, and did, up to a point. She believed what he said. She believed that he was as sincerely concerned for her as he said he was, but she didn't know that he was. She had always distinguished between believing and knowing. She could believe that Peter was being truthful, as she did now want to believe. But she didn't know that he was.

She didn't know who was involved in this madness. Until she knew who, everyone would be suspect, including Peter.

She knew she had to look to someone for help, and Peter was one of the only ones she could turn to.

"When I woke up this morning, I was naked and there was blood smeared all over me," she said, beginning her story cautiously.

She saw Peter's expression change when she mentioned the blood, and as she continued her story and told of her suspicion of rape, the lines in his face were set in a deep frown. He didn't speak, but sat with his eyes piercing her soul.

"What in hell's going on around here?" be finally shouted in desperation.

Joanna shook her head.

"I don't know. But do you know, sometimes I feel I'm not really me."

Peter's eyes narrowed. "What do you mean?"

"Well, after all this happened this morning, I was calmly sitting in front of the dresser putting on makeup. And I know damned well that what I should have been doing was getting the hell off this mountain!"

"Then why don't you?"

"I don't know! Because of my painting, I suppose," she sobbed. Tears streaked down her face again, and she fought to control them. "I tell myself that I stay because of my painting, and the fact that I invested all my savings in this trip. But I don't know. Sometimes I think that's not the reason at all."

Peter's voice was serious. "Then what do you think is the reason?"

Joanna looked past him into the forest, trying to collect her thoughts and put them into words that he would understand.

"When I was sitting in front of the mirror I had a strange feeling," she said. "It's as though one side of me, my rational self, wants me to leave. But some other part of myself, some part deep down within, keeps telling me to stay."

She looked at him hopefully. "Does that make any sense?"

"None." He was looking at her sternly, his eyes accusing her. "You're a very silly young lady, Joanna. No career should be so important."

She saw Peter's eyes growing angry. Suddenly a rush of angry words nearly stumbled over each other.

"That does it! I want you to pack your things and come and live with Mother and me! You shouldn't be here alone anyway!"

His eyes were ablaze. His breath was short and choppy. Joanna had never before seen Peter like this. It was more than an invitation; it was an order! At first she was frightened of him. She had an urge to jump up and run. But the same instant that brought her fear also made her realize that he was not angry at her. He was angry at whoever had done this to her.

He reached to her face and gingerly ran a finger over her chafed cheeks.

"You must have been outside for the past several nights," he said. "Last night was cool and windy. So was the night before. The night air could have done this to you if you were out in it for very long with no protection.

"I would like you to come and stay with us for a while," he said, this time gently. "At least for a few days. Give yourself a chance to rest."

She was opening her mouth to speak when he held up his hand and stopped her.

"I know you have to paint, and you need to be alone," he said. "But with everything that's happened to you, I think you shouldn't be alone. You need to be around people where you can be watched. Just for a few days. Look, today's Saturday. Come stay with us until Monday. I'll be good for you."

The prospect of being with other people at night, even if only for a few nights, suddenly seemed like just the thing she needed. She didn't want to face the night in her cabin wondering what hell awaited her next. She didn't even feel like painting anymore. Maybe a few day's rest at Peter's would put her back in a frame of mind more agreeable to continuing her painting.

"But do you have room for me?" she asked.

"We have two bedrooms," he said. "You can sleep in my room, and I'll sleep in the living room."

"I wouldn't want to do it unless I knew it was all right with your mother."

"It's fine with her," he said. "I've told her about meeting you, and she said you shouldn't be staying by yourself on the mountain. She said to tell you that if you're ever painting near our house to just stay with us at night and you won't have to come all the way back here."

"She said that?" Joanna asked surprised. Yet another person from Sutters Hamlet would accept her as a friend?

"Yes. She won't mind, so why don't you come for a few days?"

"All right," Joanna said. "Will you help me get some things together?"

Chapter 9

Mrs. Tillary was one of those rare people who Joanna met and liked instantly. As if there were some sort of natural bond between them, Joanna sensed that Peter's mother felt the same about her. Right away she knew she had made the right decision in accepting Peter's invitation. She had been apprehensive at first, fearing Mrs. Tillary would resent the sudden intrusion into her household. But the instant the two women met, the way Mrs. Tillary grabbed her hand in her own stout one and nearly pumped it off, smiling broadly all the while, Joanna knew she was genuinely welcome.

"I'm pleased to meet ye," she said as she greeted Joanna. Her half-gray hair was twisted into an old-fashioned ball and rested precariously on the back of her head. Her big frame and homey ways immediately endeared her to Joanna, who was reminded of the Ma and Pa Kettle movies she had so enjoyed as a child. To Joanna, Mrs. Tillary was Ma Kettle personified. Not even Marjorie Main looked more the part. She even noticed a similarity in the way Mrs. Tillary and the character from fiction talked.

Joanna was soon made to feel a member of the household. Aside from Peter and his mother, there was HD, the dog, and Tom, the black-and-white tomcat that came and went as he pleased and was out carousing much of the time. As she and Peter had first drawn near to his home, HD's howling was her first hint they were nearing the end of their climb up the mountain. Peter had told her that no one got within a hundred yards of his home without HD setting off the alarm.

It was late morning when they had arrived. The climb up the mountain had grown steep as they neared Peter's home, and when the pine forest broke and they emerged in a clearing, she saw the house. She was tired from the climb and glad the journey was over. She had had to struggle to keep up with Peter, who, unaccustomed to city women, hadn't stopped for a rest.

Mrs. Tillary had been at the side of the house, hanging out a fresh wash on a rope clothesline strung between a hook on the side of the clapboard house and a nearby tree. She saw them approaching and hurried to finish hanging the last of her wash.

"Ye caught me a real mess," she said, after they had been introduced, motioning to her plain, un-pressed dress. Several strands of hair had pulled out of the ball on her head and hung askew against her cheek. Beads of sweat spotted her forehead, which was wrinkled and weather-beaten from a life of hard work. But she was smiling. That was when Joanna first knew that she had found a person she really liked. With lunch, or dinner as Mrs. Tillary called it, barely an hour away, Joanna soon found that she was an expert cook. With all the canned foods and quickie meals that Joanna had been eating, she knew that any home-cooked meal would have tasted good. But Mrs. Tillary's cooking was equal to that of any chef in New York, and the large quantity of food that she placed on the table would have cost a fortune in any New York restaurant.

When Joanna complimented her cooking, Mrs. Tillary modestly brushed it aside, replying, "It's only ordinary country cooking. But I'll try to fancy it up come suppertime. This here's jest leftovers," she said pointing to the table. "Supper's when we eat high on the hog."

HD and Tom were fed from the table. HD sat by Mrs. Tillary's chair and waited expectantly for each morsel she or Peter tossed him. Tom was less conspicuous and walked about under the table beating a steady path between the three of them begging for handouts. When someone slipped him a piece of meat, he immediately went off by himself to eat, but he was soon back begging. Joanna gave him some ham, which placed her chair permanently on his list of must-stops.

"I expect Tom'll be around for a few days," Mrs. Tillary said. "He's been gone the past few nights, and by the looks of him I doubt he ate a thing since he left."

"There must have been a female in heat," Peter said matter-of-factly, as he gnawed the last of his ham from the bone.

"Must have been," his mother agreed.

Turning to Joanna, Mrs. Tillary said. "Tom only comes back here to fatten up so he can go chase women. Then he's off again for a spell and he comes back skinny as a bean pole. Just like a man," she said disdainfully.

Peter was smiling.

"Don't take her wrong," he said to Joanna. "She loves that old cat. Both these animals are hers. They follow her around everywhere."

"Yep," she said nodding her head. "I love 'um like they was my own young 'uns. But I do wish Tom wouldn't chase women so much and stay gone so long."

Tom seemed to sense he was being talked about. He suddenly stopped begging and jumped into Mrs. Tillary's lap. He sat there purring and looking affectionately into her face. She stroked him, his back arching to better receive the affection. "As ancient as he is, you'd think he'd be gettin' too old for woman-chasing and that sort of thing," she said.

"Cats don't get too old, Mom," Peter said. "Animals don't have hang-ups like that."

"That's my son the poet talking," she said to Joanna, but her eyes were warmly watching Peter. "Did you know my boy writes poetry?"

Joanna was resting her elbows on the table, enjoying being with a family. This was a part of life she hadn't experienced. At times like this, seeing Peter and his mother teasing each other, she missed family life. Sometimes she wondered about her own parents.

"Yes, I knew," she said. "Peter let me read some of them."

"What!" Mrs. Tillary turned on Peter. "Ye never let me read a one of your poems!"

She was teasing, but at the same time seemed hurt.

Peter smiled and patted his mother's hand,

"Joanna's an artist and she understand these things," he said appeasingly.

"I can understand things, too."

Joanna had had enough. It was her offhand comment that had started this, and now she wanted the conversation to return to a subject that didn't make her the center of controversy.

"I was wondering," Joanna said. They stopped arguing and both of them fixed on her. "What does HD stand for?"

Peter grinned and patted the old dog on the head.

"Hound dog," he said. "It stands for hound dog."

"Yep," Mrs. Tillary said. "Peter named him that when he was jest a puppy. I remember he said he wanted a dog with a different sort of name. With them old droopy ears, he has a lot of hound in him."

HD wagged his tail and seemed to bask in the sudden attention. He opened his mouth and yawned, emitting a high-pitched squeak. It seemed too small a sound to come from a dog so large. Then he turned back to Peter for more petting.

Joanna insisted on helping Mrs. Tillary with the washing up. She washed while the older woman dried. Peter left them alone, and as they worked together cleaning the kitchen, Joanna told Mrs. Tillary of her artwork. She told her of the books she had illustrated and how she wanted to work in oils and watercolors.

"I'm glad Peter had a chance to get the learnin' he needs," Mrs. Tillary said. "I was born and raised 'round here, and I ain't very educated. But I always wished I could have learned more. There's so much to learn these days. They're puttin' men on the moon, and I have trouble writin' my own name. That ain't right! It ain't right that some folks knows so much, and ones like me knows so little. I don't mind so much, though," she said wistfully. "Not anymore. I'm gettin' old, and things that ye never had ye don't miss at my age."

Joanna was moved by the woman's insight into human needs.

"I'm glad Peter brought ye here," she said, suddenly changing the subject. "You're a nice girl. He told me about ye and how ye was helpin' him learn to paint, but he didn't tell me how nice ye are."

Joanna flashed her a smile. "Thank you. I almost didn't come this morning when he asked me here for the weekend. I was afraid you would think I was intruding. Now I'm glad I came."

"I'm glad ye did too."

The afternoon was lazy and warm. Joanna helped weed the flowers. She enjoyed the exercise. HD sat in the shade with Tom nearby. Peter disappeared for an hour doing chores in the back yard.

As the sun began to drop, Mrs. Tillary made a move toward the kitchen. Joanna started to help her prepare supper but was stopped.

"Ye just relax," she said. "I'll do the cookin' and ye do the enjoying."

Mrs. Tillary stood firm. While she prepared the meal, Joanna and Peter sat on the front steps and watched the sun sink into the mountain.

"I like your mother," she said, breaking the silent spell the setting sun had cast on them.

"I thought you would," Peter said. "She likes you too, I can tell."

He gazed absently into the distance. "She's different from a lot of folks around here. I've never seen her close her mind to anything. If she had grown up in the right place, somewhere away from the mountains, and had enough education, she would have been an intellectual. I mean a real intellectual. She probably doesn't even know what an intellectual is, but that's what she is now in her own way."

"Yes, she is," Joanna agreed.

As the twilight set in and they both became lost in their own thoughts, Mrs. Tillary appeared at the front door and called them to supper. Smelling the food, HD followed them in. But Tom arrogantly turned away from their coaxing, making it plain he ate only when he choose.

"Damned cat," Peter said affectionately and walked inside, leaving Tom sitting on the top step.

As she had promised, Mrs. Tillary had topped her noontime meal. To look at the table set out with platters piled high with meat and vegetables, Joanna would have thought a dozen guests were coming. She was stuffed and stopped eating long before she had sampled all the table offered.

After they finished the second round of washing up for the day, the three of them went into the living room to spend the evening talking. As the twilight deepened into darkness and the fickle sun took away its warmth, the night grew cool. Soon they had to close the doors and windows and turn on the oil heater sitting in the corner of the living room.

A soft orange glow bathed the room from a lamp by the sofa, the only light they used as they sat and talked. The rest of the house was as black as the night outside.

As she sat with Peter and his mother, Joanna felt warm. She felt safe, the way she imagined a baby felt when it was sleeping in its mother's arms. In the three weeks she had spent on the mountain, she had been frightened – even terrified. Now she was aware of the razor's edge up which she had been sitting. It was now apparent to her just how uptight and tense she had become. Acutely aware, because for the first time since she had arrived in Sutters Hamlet, she was totally herself again. Her complete lack of fear in facing this night was in such contrast to the way she had felt the past few weeks that she couldn't help but notice the difference.

It frightened her. She hadn't known that she had strayed so far from normalcy.

The evening passed too quickly for Joanna who was enjoying sitting in the cozy room, alternately talking and sitting in silence. She watched the evening slip away, and it grew late. She knew they would soon go to bed.

The three of them had fallen into a silence when the first ominous thing occurred.

The silence grew to several minutes in duration. Joanna noticed that Mrs. Tillary's head bobbed sleepily, her eyes closed. The floorboards creaked as the rocker Peter sat in rocked forward in its pendulum like swing. The air was suddenly humid. Uncomfortable. Joanna wiped the sweat off her throat at the open V of her blouse. She looked at the heater and wondered if it was turned up too high. The quiet was more pronounced than any silence she had ever endured. Peter's eyes were closed too, and she was uneasy with the knowledge she was once again alone. She alone was awake to stand vigil in the night.

Her extra senses were working and she was uneasy for the first time that night: She didn't know why. HD lifted his head and looked intently at the door. There was only the sound of the pounding in her head as her heart pumped blood with increasing urgency to her frightened brain.

The bristles on HD's back suddenly stood on end! His lips curled up in a snarl! But he remained silent.

Suddenly, the deathly quiet was shattered! Terror gripped her for a moment, then released her! The gong that shattered the night was from the grandfather clock above the fireplace as it struck the first of twelve chimes.

"Lordy, it's midnight!" Mrs. Tillary was awake before the second chime. "It's time for bed."

Then HD howled. His hairs bristled from his neck to his tail. He jumped to his feet and faced the door. He howled again, a long wailing howl that sent shivers sliding down Joanna's spine. The only thing she had ever heard to compare with the sound that came from HD's throat was the blood-curdling howl in the movie The Hound of the Baskervilles. The chiming of the clock was lost behind the horrible sound that pierced her ears.

Peter jumped to his feet.

"What's wrong with that dog?" Mrs. Tillary snapped. She jumped from her chair and Joanna immediately followed. "Tom must have scared up a rabbit!"

Peter cast a doubting glance at his mother. "That don't sound like no rabbit!"

"Then what is it?" the older woman asked.

She stepped fearlessly to the door, threw back the bolt, and swung the door open. The dark rushed into the room, bringing with it the unknown. Peter grabbed HD by the scruff of the neck to hold him back, but the dog was suddenly whimpering, cowering behind his master's legs. He was no longer the aggressive hound, but a frightened dog.

Not a sound came from outside. HD continued whimpering at the sight of the opened door. A gnawing fear crept over Joanna. Mrs. Tillary stood like a rock against the night.

"Don't see a thing," she said closing the door. She looked down at the dog. "What's wrong with ye, ye good for nothin' hound. It ain't nothin' but a bear prowlin' around."

"I wish Tom would come in," she said, suddenly attentive to the door again. "It ain't like him to stay out after gettin' back from one of his carouses."

Though Joanna prayed that she wouldn't, Mrs. Tillary again threw open the door and called the cat. She stepped outside into the darkness and again called his name. She was silhouetted against the black of the night. Joanna saw her turn her head from side to side as she tried in vain to locate Tom. Joanna was nearly overwhelmed with an impulse to dash forward and jerk Mrs. Tillary back into the relative safety of her home. She knew there was no bear out there, but something far worse. Joanna looked past Mrs. Tillary into the black of the night. She knew it was futile. She knew she could never pinpoint black in black.

She glanced at Peter, and he was looking at her.

Reluctantly, Mrs. Tillary stepped back inside and closed the door. "Worryin' about that cat'll be the death of me yet," she said.

Peter placed his arm around her. "You never could predict what Tom would do for all these years. Don't start trying now."

"I know. I know," she said. "But there was somethin' out there. Ye saw the way HD acted."

"Yes."

Joanna saw him shoot a glance in her direction.

"Let's go to bed," Mrs. Tillary said.

"Let me get some things out of my room and you can have it, Joanna," Peter said, disappearing into the back of the house. He didn't look at her.

He was worried, she could tell. She knew he was wondering the same thing she was.

He disappeared into the darkness at the other end of the house, and when he returned he had an armload of blankets. He threw them on the couch. "That's my bed."

"Come on, honey," Mrs. Tillary said. "Let me show ye where you'll sleep. Peter can sleep out here with HD."

She led Joanna into the back room and nipped on the light. The tiny bag that Joanna had packed to bring with her was sitting on the bed.

"This will be your room whenever ye want to come and stay with us," she said. She planted a kiss on Joanna's cheek. "Ye just treat us like your own family and come visit whenever ye please. Ye oughtn't to be staying by yourself anyway."

Mrs. Tillary turned and left, closing the door behind her. Taking her time, Joanna undressed, turned out the light, and crawled under the covers. Sleep didn't come easily. It seemed hours that she remained alone listening for sounds in the night, hoping that she would hear nothing. Only the normal mountain noises greeted her alert ears. Soon HD's antics and the fright he had aroused in her began to weaken. She could hear Peter snoring. After standing her solitary vigil well into the hours, she finally fell into an uneasy sleep.

The next morning was Sunday, another bright, warm spring day. Joanna awoke late to the sound of activity in the kitchen. As she dressed and she caught the various aromas of meat and vegetables that drifted into her bedroom, it seemed that fully half the time she had spent here had found Mrs. Tillary in the kitchen. She wondered if Mrs. Tillary always prepared such lavish feasts or if it was done for her benefit.

As she emerged from her bedroom, Mrs. Tillary saw her through the open kitchen doorway.

"I thought ye was goin' to sleep the day away," she said, standing by the stove and stirring a pot. Her voice was alive and bouncy. "Do ye want any breakfast, or would ye just as soon wait for dinner? It won't be too long."

Joanna felt hungry, and the smell of roasting beef made her stomach exaggerate its need. "What time is it?"

"Nearly eleven."

"That late?" she exclaimed. "I did nearly sleep all day!"

Mrs. Tillary smiled understandingly. "Ye must have been tired."

"Yeah." She weighed her hunger against the time. "I guess I'll just wait until lunch since it's so late."

"Whatever ye want to do is fine."

Joanna looked around the kitchen, hoping to find something that needed doing, but found instead that everything was under control.

"What can I do to help?" she asked.

"Nothin'," Mrs. Tillary said. "Ye go out front and sit and make yourself comfortable."

"Nothing doing! You said to treat you like I would my own family, and if I had a mother I would expect to help her in the kitchen!"

Joanna saw an extra apron hanging from a nail beside the back door and put it on over her jeans to show her serious intent.

"Now what can I do?" she asked.

Mrs. Tillary looked at her approvingly. Those same gray strands were hanging down her cheek again. Perspiration stood on her forehead from the heat of the stove.

"If ye want to ye can keep these pots stirred while I start makin' the bread."

"All right."

Joanna took the long wooden spoon from her hand. She gave each of four pots a good stirring while Mrs. Tillary crossed the room and began mixing the flour.

"Is your mother not alive, honey?" Mrs. Tillary had stopped her bread-making and was looking at her.

"I don't know." She saw a questioning look cross the older woman's face. "You see, I'm an orphan. I never knew who my parents were."

"Oh, I'm sorry." By the tone of her voice, Joanna knew that she sincerely was sorry. "I didn't know."

Mrs. Tillary concentrated on her bread for a few moments. "I guess that's what makes ye strong enough to come up here and live by yourself. Being an orphan, I mean. You've probably had to count on yourself more than most people."

"Yes, I suppose so," Joanna said. "I never was adopted. I lived in an orphanage until I was old enough to take care of myself. I guess I never depended on anybody for anything. I never really had anybody to depend on but me."

Mrs. Tillary dug her hands into the dough and began kneading it.

"Well, you've got us now," she said. "For as long as ye want. I always wanted a daughter, but the little girl I had died when she was jest a few days old. She would've been older than ye, but ye can be my daughter for as long as ye stay."

Joanna crossed the room and placed a kiss on her cheek. "That makes you the only mother I ever knew. And if I had had a choice, I think I would have chosen you to be my real mother."

"And I'd be right proud to have ye for a daughter."

The kinship the two women had felt toward each other upon first meeting was now a strong bond. Joanna felt a strong sense of belonging. She felt a new love in her heart growing for this woman, and she knew it was a kind of love she had never before experienced. It was a daughter's love for her mother. Here, she knew, she had found more than a friend. Peter was her friend, but Mrs. Tillary was more than that. And she knew, and felt good in knowing, that Mrs. Tillary felt the same way about her.

She returned to her four pots and stirred them joyously.

"Where's Peter?" she asked when at last she realized she hadn't yet seen him.

"Oh, I don't know," Mrs. Tillary said. "He was 'round the house earlier, but HD kept kickin' up such a fuss that he went outside to see what it was. Hasn't been back."

Joanna trembled ever so slightly, but she managed to keep Mrs. Tillary from noticing. She remembered the way HD had cowered behind Peter when Mrs. Tillary opened the door. She remembered the uneasiness she had felt, even before the others were awake, while HD bristled at the door. It was her animal instincts that told her something unpleasant was outside, but hadn't told her what. Then when HD cowered, she had somehow known. And now Peter was outside, trying to find out why HD had kicked up a fuss this morning. Again her animal instincts were working. And again they told her that something unpleasant had happened, but as before they didn't tell her what. She was worried.

"If ye want to ye can start settin' the table."

Mrs. Tillary's words jerked her back into the present. She gave the four pots in her charge a final stir to insure they didn't stick, then under Mrs. Tillary's direction she began getting china and silverware from the cabinets.

The lunch, or Sunday dinner as Mrs. Tillary insisted, was splendid. Peter was quiet and avoided conversation. Mrs. Tillary didn't seem to take any notice of his mood, but Joanna did. She knew his mood was in some way related to last night's incident. Peter kept looking at her. But when she returned his gaze, he looked away. She remembered the same thing happened last night after HD howled at the door, and she wondered if he regretted inviting her to his home. He knew about the frightening incidents that had been happening to her, and she thought that he might now be having second thoughts. Particularly if by bringing her he had inadvertently introduced into this pleasant household something he hadn't bargained for.

After lunch, Mrs. Tillary decided to leave the dishes until later so the three of them could take in the early afternoon sun.

"I believe this is the warmest day we've had so far this spring," she said, as they sat on the front porch looking down the mountain. "It's too nice and warm to be inside washin' up. I'm glad we left that until later. I never liked doin' the dishes anyway."

Joanna shared her love of the day. It was beautiful. She looked at Mrs. Tillary's profile, the face and wrinkles of a woman who had worked hard all her life and she thought that some day she might like to try a portrait of her. The face was so strong; it had character. Like the woman, Joanna thought.

Peter remained moody, sitting silently staring off into space. He neither entered into nor seemed interested in the conversation the two women carried on. Joanna noticed Mrs. Tillary glance at him at times, but she said nothing. Joanna assumed it was because she didn't want to start a family argument in front of company.

Suddenly breaking off the conversation and looking around the yard as though the thought had just occurred to her, Mrs. Tillary asked, "Where's Tom? I haven't seen him all mornin'."

When Mrs. Tillary's questioning eyes came to rest on her, Joanna shrugged.

"Haven't seen him," she said.

"Have you seen him, Peter?"

Peter nodded, his eyes shifting uneasily to his mother. "Yes, I saw him."

"Oh, good." A huge sigh escaped from her bosom. "He's okay, then. I was getting a bit worried."

Peter didn't reply at first. Then looking directly at Joanna, "He's not okay. He's dead."

A stunned silence swept over them. Mrs. Tillary gasped. She opened her mouth as though to speak, but nothing came out. Joanna finally broke the silence.

"What happened?" she asked fearfully.

"Someone killed him."

"Oh my God!" Her fears of last night were true. The witches had followed her even here to the home of a friend! Would they give her no peace! She looked desperately to Mrs. Tillary and saw her slumped in her seat, her face buried in her tear-stained hands.

"My little Tom," she cried. "My little Tom."

The words sank like knives into Joanna's heart, wounding her as deeply as she had ever been hurt before. Her own heart cried as she sat and watched the woman she had come to care so much for cry unashamedly at the loss of her cat. And much of the pain to Joanna was in knowing that she was the cause.

"Have you buried him, Peter?" Mrs. Tillary asked, her face still hidden in her hands.

Peter nodded.

"Take me to his grave."

Peter led the way to the side of the house, opposite from the kitchen where his mother had been working, Joanna noted. It was a short distance into the forest. He took them to a tiny clearing that held a small patch of freshly turned earth. He stopped there, looking down.

Mrs. Tillary wept over the tiny grave. She was more in control of herself now. She straightened her shoulders and bravely turned to her son. "How did he die?"

Peter shook his head. "It doesn't matter."

"Maybe not," she said. "But I wanna know." It was the voice of maternal authority as she spoke.

Peter's eyes flooded. "They cut his head off, Mama! I looked all over for his head, but I couldn't find it!"

Mrs. Tillary sank to the ground, her trembling knees too weak to hold her. Joanna knelt beside her and embraced her shoulders. She buried her face in Joanna's breast and wept. They remained like that for several minutes, until Mrs. Tillary again regained control. Finally, with Joanna's help, the older woman struggled laboriously to her feet. Slowly, they walked back to the house.

"I think I'd better go," Joanna said. She stood at the bottom of the steps leading onto the porch.

Mrs. Tillary took her hand. "No, honey. Ye don't have to go now." She spoke through red-rimmed eyes, still moist with tears.

"I think I should." She spoke tersely. The anger in her voice was directed at no one she knew but at whoever had killed Tom. They would not stop at frightening her; now they had hurt someone she cared for. Already she could see a change in herself, in just the past few minutes. Tom's death had served as a catalyst. She was angry, angry enough to fight back. Fear had kept her from reacting before. And her determination to paint had kept her from running. But now she was angry, and her anger was far greater than her fear. She knew that any animal, no matter how docile, had its breaking point beyond which it could not be pushed – or it would turn on its attacker and fight. Before, with each push, each frightening incident, she had taken a fearful step backwards, always hoping that whoever was doing these things to her would stop.

But now she knew better. The witches had followed her, and in trying to get at her, they had hurt an innocent person. Joanna knew that she, too, was innocent. She had done nothing to warrant their torment. And now, with Tom's death and the painful involvement of a friend, she had been pushed to the breaking point.

She had taken her last backward step.

Chapter 10

Peter walked back down the mountain with her. She had wanted to make the trek alone, but both Mrs. Tillary and Peter insisted. The half-hour journey was made in virtual silence. Neither of them mentioned Tom until they reached her cabin.

Peter had been brooding since the night before. Joanna wasn't sure if he was just brooding over the events of the past day or if he were angry at her, blaming her for Tom's death. Since the killing of the cat was apparently closely related to what had been happening to her, she wanted to discuss it. During the entire trip down the mountain she had tried to bring it up but because of his sullen mood, she didn't dare. She was relieved when Peter broached the subject as they walked into the clearing in front of her cabin.

"I think losing Tom hurt Mother pretty bad," he said. He was gazing into the distance, not looking at her. They were nearly to the spot of grass where they had had their talk the day before.

"I know," she said, feeling the response had been inadequate, and afraid that she would let the chance to talk about it slip away. "Peter?"

He looked at her. For the first time that day he looked her directly in the eyes.

"What are you thinking?" she asked.

"I suppose you mean what am I thinking about the way Tom died."

She dropped her eyes before his gaze that was now steady. "Yes," she replied.

"I was thinking that maybe you're in more trouble than you realize. They followed you. How did they know where you were?"

"I don't know," she shrugged.

Peter was worried. She could tell by his deep frown. "I was wondering about that," he said. "And I was wondering about the way HD acted last night. You saw him. You saw the way he was frightened. That dog will chase any bear off this mountain. And let me tell you a bear dog is a brave dog. But he was scared to death last night. I've never in my life seen him frightened like that before. What could have been out there in the dark last night that would make him react like that?"

Joanna looked at him questioningly for a moment, unsure that they were on the same wave length.

"You know what was out there," she said accusingly.

"Yes, I know it was the witches," he said. "But they're just people. Why would HD act like that? He should have been howling his head off instead of hiding behind me."

Peter was genuinely puzzled and concerned. Had last night been her first run-in with the witches, Joanna knew that she may have been baffled at HD's actions.

"I'm not sure," she said, weighing her words. His last statement was ringing in her ears and she was disturbed at her thoughts. She was more than disturbed. She was shocked that such thoughts would come to her and that she would find herself agreeing with the strange ideas that dashed through her mind. "I'm not sure that they are just people."

He jerked attentively, suddenly coming out of the introspection that had held him for so long.

"What do you mean?" he snapped.

She was taken aback by the ferociousness of his reply. She stumbled mentally for the right words.

"Why, I don't know," she said lamely, not sure herself why she had made the statement. "The things they do. It's not human. They have some sort of power."

"That's a bunch of bull! They don't have any more power than you or me."

"Peter!" she exclaimed, her face a vessel of unmasked surprise. "Are you saying that you don't believe in the witches? I can't imagine that you grew up here and don't believe in them!"

"I believe in them," he said defensively. "But I don't think they possess any sort of special power. I believe the witches are just a bunch of people who have this mountain under their thumb, and they're rubbing it in. After all, what have they done lately?"

"What about me!" Joanna cut in. "What about the things they've done to me?"

"I'll get to that," he said impatiently. "But first listen to this." He squared his eyes on her. "They haven't done anything in years. In my lifetime, they haven't done anything . . . until now. Cows go missing and the so-called witches are blamed for it. Somebody finds some burned logs in a clearing, and we figure the witches held one of their ceremonies on the spot. But nothing's proved. No one knows for sure."

Peter spoke tersely. His voice was short, clipped, almost angry.

"The only reason there are witches here is that people want to think there are. This whole matter of witches in Sutters Hamlet began not long after the Salem witchcraft trials. Back then, people believed in many things they don't believe now. Witchcraft is one of them. If the legend of the witches hadn't begun back then, if it had just popped up all of a sudden, today, nobody around here would believe it. They would think it's a bunch of loonies. But this thing about the witches began back when people were naive, back when they would believe anything. Why they had just learned the earth was round! The people here still believe in witches because their parents believed in them, and their parents before them and their parents before them. And Sutters Hamlet is so isolated from civilization that most people here don't even know that technological progress is being made. So they still believe this dumb story."

"It's like the Bible," he said vehemently. "I don't believe in the Bible! I do believe in God. I feel there is some force that created the Earth, but that doesn't mean that I have to believe in the Bible, an ancient book written by fallible human beings back in a period when people would accept almost anything. No thinking person would believe it. If the Bible is so full of truths, why did all those miracles of God stop happening when people became more informed and scientifically aware? Because when man acquired enough knowledge to intelligently question some of these phenomena, he saw that some seemingly inexplicable events may have a scientific explanation, and it didn't necessarily have to be caused by God, up there pulling strings. Do you understand what I'm saying?"

He paused for a moment to let her question if she wanted, then continued.

"What I'm trying to say is that things that used to be mysteries are now explained away by scientific laws and formulas. But some things that still remain mysterious – like creation and the human soul and witches – are still held to be something beyond normal – supernatural. They still can't be explained, so people continue to believe in them, the same way they did centuries ago."

His lips twisted upward in a half smile. "I suppose that's what it all boils down to is that people are intelligent enough to develop a civilization of sorts, but they're not smart enough to advance along with it. If you've ever stopped to wonder why the world is in such a bad state, ecologically I mean, it's probably because we have people with medieval outlooks working with twentieth-century technology."

Peter was going to continue, but Joanna cut in.

"Well then, just who do you think the witches are?" she asked. "If you believe in them but don't believe they have any power, who do you think they are?"

"I think that whatever group has been frightening you is just trying to stir up rumors that the witches have returned," he said.

"But you don't think they're really witches?" she asked. Her voice held an edge of disagreement.

"Like I said, I don't believe they have any power. They may have formed a coven and call themselves witches, and that may make them witches. But that doesn't necessarily give them any mysterious, supernatural power. Do you understand me? I'm not saying that there aren't people here who call themselves witches. But I don't think they're any different from you or me, except that they go around frightening young women living alone."

After all that had happened to her, the things that couldn't easily be explained, Joanna knew there was something amiss. Something abnormal or supernatural was happening to her. Her inner instincts told her there was something more to this than someone trying to frighten her. There was more to it than Peter could imagine. But what? That was still the one thing, the important thing, that she still didn't know. She disagreed with Peter's explanation and thought it strange that anyone growing up on the mountain would feel that way. Particularly if the witches were as feared as Hanover said.

"I find it hard to believe that the legend of the witches has remained so strong over two hundred years if there's nothing more to it than someone perpetuating a hoax," Joanna said. "Missing cows and burnt logs aren't going to support a legend like that for all these years. It just doesn't add up."

"Look. I know there are a lot of loose ends to what I've said. But there are a lot of loose ends to try and tie together if you believe the other side, too."

Peter seemed exasperated. He seemed to be tiring of trying to convince her of the validity of his views. She supposed that he thought that with her being an outsider, she would be more open to disbelief than belief. And were it not for her occasional flashes of ESP she may have been.

"You really do believe in all this, don't you?"

"Yes." She nodded. "You didn't see that doll appear mysteriously. And you didn't discover some of your hair on its head. And you didn't wake up one morning after having a stretch of days disappear from your memory and discover that you had been raped. I get goose bumps when I think about it even now."

She looked at her cabin, sitting brown and forlorn amidst the shimmering green carpet of grass. "And I'm getting to where I'm afraid of those walls," she said softly, almost to herself. "I'm not even sure why I stay. I should leave. I'm not really getting much painting done, and that's why I came in the first place. It would make sense to get out, to get away from all this, but I don't. And the thing that worries me is that I don't know why I don't. I'm frightened and want to get away, but something holds me here." She turned to him. "Does that make sense?"

"No!" he said emphatically. "You're trying to tell me that you think the reason you don't leave is that the witches have some sort of hold on you. A spell. Is that right? Well, I thought the whole purpose of a spell was to make someone do something against their will. Without their knowledge. If you know about it, or think you know about it, why don't you just pack up and leave. That in itself should be some proof that it's nothing more than your imagination."

She turned away from him, shaking her head. "No. No – that doesn't mean anything at all. Nothing at all. Nothing really makes any sense to me right now. Especially not the fact that I'm still here. I'm not saying there's a spell over me. Maybe I'm just curious about it all in some morbid way, and maybe that's what's keeping me here. After all, I'm a Leo, and cats are curious."

She paused to collect her thoughts. "I was born August 6. And supposedly, Leos born within about four days of August 4 are very inclined toward the occult."

"Where did you hear that?" Peter asked in despair.

"I read it somewhere."

"Well it's a bunch of crap!"

"How do you know?"

"Joanna," he said in a big-brotherly tone, "you can't go around believing in every bit of hocus-pocus you hear."

"I don't," she snapped. "But when I learn something and find it to be true in my experience, I believe it."

Peter was getting angry, she could tell. But somehow it was comforting. It made her feel more secure in a way that she couldn't quite describe, to know that he cared enough to get angry at her for letting herself get caught up in whatever was going on at her cabin.

"Well, I'll tell you one thing," he said, "the witches couldn't have picked a better victim than you."

"Peter, go back up the mountain. I want to paint." She was stern, yet gentle, trying to show in the tone of her voice her appreciation, while at the same time trying to make clear that she would live her own life and take her own chances.

"If you insist on being stubborn, don't blame anyone but yourself for whatever happens. You've been warned, and I don't think you're safe around here."

"Go, Peter," she insisted.

He reached into his pocket and she watched his hand settle on an object she hadn't noticed. Something about the uneasy way he was watching her frightened her. She watched his hand slide out of his pocket, and her breathing stopped in a gulp when she saw the blue metallic sheen of a pistol pointing at her. She froze!

In a smooth motion, Peter reversed the gun and held it out to her, handle first.

"I want you to keep it," he said. "It's loaded, so be careful." He jerked his thumb toward a lever, then motioned upward. "That's the safety. Keep it down unless you intend to use it."

He thrust it into her unwilling hands.

"Peter, I don't want it!" She tried to give it back, but he had turned his back on her and was heading for the forest.

"Peter!" Her cry was urgent.

He stopped and turned.

"Peter, take it. I'm afraid of guns." She rushed to him, but he brushed her away.

"You'd better be more afraid of what's happening to you than that gun," he said. "It's a .32, so if you fire it, hold it tight with both hands."

He turned and left her pointing the gun at his back. The handle was cold, and she looked at it, the stubby nose shining ugly in the sun. She would put it away where it couldn't harm her.

Hesitantly, she walked to the cabin and unlocked the door. A shaft of light darted into the shuttered room as she swung the door open. She stood outside looking in, fearful of being alone once again and uneasy of stepping across the threshold. Even with the unpleasant incidents of last night and this morning, when it had been made clear to her that they could unnerve her even when she was not alone, she realized that she had been much more comfortable and less frightened when she was around other people. Now she was alone again. Alone against her adversaries, whoever and whatever they were. The cabin's dark interior looked foreboding. She stepped through the door, and the slivers of fear once again made her feel weak and shaky. Nothing moved. She threw open the shuttered windows and breathed easier. She went into her bedroom and did the same. It wasn't quite so eerie now that the sun reflected in the far corners of the room.

It was getting to her. These incidents that pumped her mind full of fear and pulled her delicate cords of reason too taut were beginning to make their mark on her soul. It was more evident now, even to herself. After spending just one day away from the isolation of her mountainside cabin, she could tell the difference in her state of mind. Last night she felt so safe with Peter and his mother and realized that she hadn't felt so at ease since arriving in Sutters Hamlet. The two extreme states in her mental and emotional well-being were now more apparent. It worried her. Deep down it worried her. She could feel the tension again, her confidence and peace of mind eroding... a little at a time.

Maybe this is what it's all about. To wear her down through fear and uncertainty. But to wear her down to what? For what? A floorboard creaked in the shut-off front bedroom where she kept her paintings. She looked up, alert. She went to the door and opened it. She looked around the room, but there was nothing there. She hadn't really expected to find anything. But she had become suspicious of every small sound.

She decided she must do something to occupy her mind. She must paint. Without lingering, she picked up her canvas, easel, and oils and took them outside, setting them up in the warm sunshine beside the front door. She went back in only once more for her sketch pad. She nipped through it, studying the rough pencil sketches for a simple subject that she could paint quickly, without much thought to composition or layout. She just wanted to express her feelings in paint, to let her pent-up emotions flow through her fingertips onto the canvas. She didn't want to paint a masterpiece, just a wailing wall. She chose a sketch of a stream nearby where Peter had first let her read his poetry. It was simple and it appealed to her. She roughed in the general outlines in charcoal, then from memory and her imagination, she began applying color and life.

As it always did, the act of painting soothed her troubled mind. As the picture began to grow into something real and alive, her mind forgot the world beyond the limits of that short stretch of stream with water rushing over a bed of rocks. Time slithered away from her as though daring her to catch it.

Several times she found herself thinking about the pistol that she had hidden away in the bottom drawer of her dresser. She didn't feel any safer having it there, but she knew that what Peter said was true. She should fear the pistol least of all.

She painted until the daylight faded, then took her nearly finished oil inside. She left the picture on the easel, which she set in its normal place in the middle of her painting room.

Finally, she settled down in the living room for a night of undisturbed reading by the flickering lantern light. With the approach of midnight, she tucked her book away and apprehensively prepared for bed. It was only by forcibly mustering her courage that she snuffed out the lantern, the last bastion of light in her cabin, and let herself be surrounded by the darkness. She stood by the bed until her eyes became accustomed to the black, then after a quick glance around the room she fell into bed and, with considerable effort, closed her eyes and tried to bring on an unwilling sleep. When at last sleep came, she had about given it up as a lost cause.

She awoke at midmorning. She looked at the clock sitting on the bedside table and, seeing it was after ten o'clock, sprang from bed. She had intended to get an early start, and half the day was already gone! She could have kicked herself for sleeping so late. Oversleeping was a rare occurrence. She had found that she could easily get by on six hours and not feel the least bit fatigued the next day. Normally, going to bed at midnight, as she had the night before, she should have been wide awake well before eight o'clock. Puzzled at her late awakening, though not suspecting anything amiss, she dressed quickly and went into the kitchen for a late breakfast.

Not wanting anything heavy, she settled for a half can of fruit.

She walked into the front yard and looked at the sky. Endless cobalt blue dotted with billowing white puffs of marshmallow clouds would offer ideal lighting conditions. It would be a good painting day.

She returned to the cabin for her tools. Her painting room, since it faced the cast, was the best-lit room in the cabin at this time of day. She opened the door leading to it and shafts of sunlight struck her in the face. She started for her easel, with its back facing her as she had left it, and stopped in midstride. Her foot returned to the floor with a thud.

Her nearly finished painting of yesterday was sitting in the far corner against the wall. The shallow stream rippling over the protruding rocks and the light filtering onto the scene through the trees lining the stream bed looked so real. It was so lifelike, to her the basic elements of a good landscape painting.

At the same instant that the eyes of the artist were admiring the artwork, the eyes of a frightened and bewildered girl struck realization. The painting had been moved! She looked at the painting sitting in the floor first in puzzlement, then as her cobwebbed brain began to sort out the pieces, the terror, with which she had become too familiar, returned.

She remembered, distinctly remembered, leaving the painting on the easel!

She looked at the easel. A canvas was sitting in place, its painting surface turned away from her. She looked back to the painting on the floor. She had left it on the easel. She was sure!

Her brushes were in their proper place. They were just as she had left them. Or at least as far as she could remember they were. So were her tubes of paints. Her palette was laying beside the easel. Without stepping any closer, she looked at it. There was some freshly mixed paint in the center, a darker hue than any she remembered using yesterday.

Fearfully her eyes returned to the easel and the mystery canvas. She feared what she would find on the other side. What picture or what words?

It was like finding the doll all over again. The fear was the same. The same sort of unknowing fear, the same sort of terror of knowing that something had been inside her cabin, had been there in the dead of night while she was there – asleep.

Gathering her courage she inched cautiously toward the easel. She peered around the side, dreading what she would see. There were some dark blobs on the canvas, but from her vantage point they meant nothing.

She stepped to the front of the easel and looked at the canvas head-on. The blotches took on a more definitive shape.

A wall of trees in the background, and the foreground held a large flat rock. That was all. The rest of the canvas was white, still untouched.

Her heart had returned to a more normal rhythm. She had been afraid of what picture the canvas held. She had imagined a face, a pale, livid face half-hidden by a black cape. Or a faceless doll. Or worst of all, an image of herself had flashed through her mind. Her own picture on the canvas, distorted and ugly, leering back at her from within a black hood.

When she saw nothing even remotely frightening, she breathed easier. She lost some of her apprehension. Knowing someone had been inside her cabin still frightened her, but the fear of the unknown on the other side of the canvas was gone.

She stepped closer to the painting for a better look. A sudden thought had hit her . . . almost a hope. Though unusual as it was, the picture appeared to be the beginning of a landscape painting. Could it be, she wondered, that she had painted it? Stranger things had happened. Many people walk in their sleep, even talk in their sleep without knowing it.

Once she had done even more. Once while spending a weekend with Ted, she had awakened one night to find herself in the act of making love. When she awoke, Ted was climaxing and she was already highly aroused, though she was only consciously aware of those last seconds. Ted told her afterwards she had appeared to be awake from the beginning and seemed surprised at learning that she had slept through most of it, since, he said, she had been active from the beginning.

Could it be that she painted the picture in her sleep? It was a hope, a slim thread that would ease her troubled mind by assuring her that no one had entered her cabin while she slept. It could also explain why she overslept.

She carefully examined the painting, looking at the brush strokes still evident on the painted surface. An artist's style of painting, the way he used the brush, was often as distinguishing as his handwriting or his fingerprint. It was his personal signature that, once developed, rarely changed. Many long-lost paintings of the old masters, hidden or forgotten for centuries, had been found and identified as authentic not only by the artist's actual signature, but by the brush strokes still visible in the dried paint.

It was the strokes that Joanna now studied; being a serious student of painting for years, she had become interested in the styles of various artists. From studying their techniques, she had learned that she, too, had distinctive brush strokes, strokes that she could identify as probably belonging to her had she never seen the painting before ... as unlikely a possibility as that would be.

She looked for her own style but failed to detect it.

Instead, the strokes she saw were erratic, like nothing she had ever done before. Neither a smear nor a crosshatch, but something in-between. It was as though whoever did the painting had taken a brush, a very small brush, and twirled it on the canvas to create circular brush strokes. Even to her trained eye, she couldn't see how anyone could use that stroke and maintain any degree of detail in their painting, though what there was of the unfinished painting held considerable detail.

Whoever used those strokes certainly had a completely different style from her own smooth, even strokes. The painting was not hers. Of that she was certain.

Once again she was faced with the fact that she had not been alone last night.

It made no sense to her! No sense at all! Again she was frightened and confused, mentally void of an explanation. She could make no sense from the patchwork of unexplained incidents. Why frighten her at all? But even if that could be answered, what possible answer could there be for someone entering her home at night and painting a half-finished canvas of some trees and a rock?

She looked at the picture again. The trees were too dark, a very dark hue of green. And one side of the rock was in deep shadow. As she studied the painting more closely, she came to the conclusion that it was intended to be a nighttime scene. Either that, or the artist was badly off in the choice of colors. But there was not enough of a picture to tell for sure which was the case.

She felt totally helpless. She wanted to strike out, to fight back. The same determination that had overcome her when she watched Mrs. Tillary cry over Tom's grave now returned. She was being pushed. For no reason, she was being pushed, frightened, abused. She was a Leo, stubborn, determined, the lord of her domain. And her domain was being violated by unwelcome outsiders. She would not be pushed without fighting back. She was familiar with the personality traits of those born under her sun sign, and as she applied this knowledge to her own refusal to flee at the first suggestion of fear, she could better understand her own actions. Leos traditionally were leaders. They refused to be herded. By birth she was the kingly lion and would stand and fight for what was hers. And she considered this cabin her private domain for the next year. She had invested a year of her life and considerable money on this venture, and she would not be frightened off. She would fight.

But as great as was her determination to stay, equally great was her fear. A fear of the unknown and of these mysterious events. The fear told her to leave, to run from the mountain. It told her that was what any rational person would do. But she could not – or would not. It was as though the mountain and her tiny cabin had developed some mystic hold on her. Half of her said, "Get out of here," while another side of her whispered, "Stay, Joanna . . . stay. . . ." The conflict within was driving the rational side of her nuts, creating an out-and-out fight between the two sides of her seemingly split personality. She knew by all that was reasonable, in light of all that had happened, she should not still be on Sutters Mountain. But there was that hold ... some strange hold...

She felt so helpless, so unable to explain her own actions. She was a cat – she would run until she was cornered. And now that she had turned to fight, the enemy was gone, disappeared. Like the irrational half of her that whispered remain, the half of her that she could not understand, she did not understand the enemy. It had not really disappeared, it was just unknown. That was what was so frustrating about it all, about both her enemy on the mountain and the other side of herself. Not knowing what to strike out against.

Not knowing why she seemed held here. If only she knew!

It was almost as though there were no enemy. She was half amused when she found her mind repeating the words of Pogo, the comic-strip character. "We have found the enemy and they are us." At least he found his enemy, she mused. If only she could find hers. If only there were some clue, something to give her some idea of where to start her search. She was a nation at war with a phantom army. Until she could pinpoint her enemy, she didn't even know how she would fight back. Their weapons were not so subtle, but they were terrifying. She wasn't sure what weapons she could use against an unknown. However, she was certain of one thing. If they were human, if they were flesh and blood, she had a weapon. It was in her dresser drawer.

The gun was no longer frightening. It was a friend. She was grateful Peter had left it. She would tell him.

Her thoughts returned to the picture. It didn't occur to her to destroy it. She knew it would be no use if she did. If it had happened once, it could happen again. She lifted it from the easel and placed it on the floor beside the picture that she had begun yesterday.

She wanted to finish yesterday's work, but her mind was too troubled to give her the peace she needed to begin. She decided to go down the mountain for some kerosene. She knew she was getting low. It would also give her a chance to get some exercise, to relax, and forget. After she returned, maybe this afternoon she would feel like painting.

She rambled down the mountain without caring, walking leisurely, trying to forget and unwind. Her blue-denim jeans flitted through the green patchwork of spring, hugging her hips like a lover's arms. A bulge in her front pocket where half a dozen dollar bills were folded was the only thing to mar the perfect landscape of her body.

Her first stop in town was the newspaper office to visit with Hanover. She turned the doorknob, but the door was locked. Thinking that he might still be in his living quarters in back of the office, she rattled the door fiercely, but when after several minutes he had not appeared, she gave up.

She had two other stops that would require no more than a few minutes of her time before returning to the mountain to paint. First she needed the kerosene, and she had decided that as long as she was in town, she would buy a few groceries.

She turned her back on the newspaper office and headed across the street to the hardware store. She noticed the whittler was missing from out front and wished that he were there so she could chat. She had been preoccupied. Crossing the street, she glanced to her left toward Potter's Food Store and saw Mr. Potter standing in the doorway watching her. She smiled at him, then stepped onto the creaking sidewalk in front of the hardware store.

Inside, a man not too unlike Potter in build, except he had a full head of hair, waited alone behind the counter. She was still trying to win the confidence of the locals, so she walked in with a smile on her face.

"Good morning," she greeted.

The man grunted.

"Do you have any kerosene?" she asked cheerfully, glancing around the store.

"No."

Joanna's face dropped, the smile fading away. "Oh, I do need some," she said, her eyes now sweeping the room. "I'm getting awfully low."

She turned to leave, and as she did her gaze stopped by a display of electrical sockets, extension cords, and other electrical accessories on a far wall. Her hope returned, because sitting beside the display of modern lighting fixtures were several lanterns identical to the ones at her cabin.

She strode over to them, and when she reached the section, was surprised to find a drum marked Kerosene sitting in a corner. She thumped it. It was full.

Annoyed at the man behind the counter, she stalked up to him, angry.

He watched her from behind an unfriendly mask.

"There's a full drum of kerosene over there," she said impatiently.

"I thought we were out."

His unblinking eyes told her he was lying. She saw in them hatred, but she sensed more. It was in his eyes as well as his actions. It was fear. She knew the signs well because in the past weeks she had become too familiar with fear to miss the signs in another person. Absently, she wondered what he was afraid of. But her annoyance at the man's lying to her wouldn't let her care or wonder too long at his motives. She waited while he found a small metal container and filled it, then paid and stalked angrily out of the store.

Halfway across the dusty street she looked up and saw the door to Potter's Food Store was closed. The vanilla-colored shades in the door windows were pulled, and a bright orange closed glared back at her. She crossed the street anyway. She shook the door, but it was locked. The store had been open only minutes before. Potter standing in the open doorway. She banged on the door, but there was no sound from inside.

Helplessly, she looked around for someone to ask, but the street was deserted. She alone was on the sidewalk. Not even one face peered out at her from behind the closed doors. It was as though on a signal Sutters Hamlet had closed down. It was exactly the opposite of her first drive through town when everyone had turned out from the buildings to watch her pass. Now there was no one, whether by design or coincidence, she didn't know. The total deathlike quality of the street made her feel uneasy.

She was not that low on food. She could wait. With a final glance around she stepped into the street and began her hike back up the mountain.

Chapter 11

As Joanna followed the trail up the mountain, which was becoming overgrown now with the greenery of spring, her mind kept darting back to her reception in town. How unusual it had seemed. Unusual even for Sutters Hamlet, which had shunned her from the beginning. She had expected the usual unfriendliness, the mountain reticence, but she was unprepared to have the entire town shut down in her face.

Her mind was so preoccupied with wondering, she was so self-obsessed that she did not see the whittler standing slightly off the trail halfway to her cabin.

"Girlie, ye look like ye a world away."

The sudden voice only a few feet away made her jump with a start. She spun to face it, then relaxed when she saw the whittler blending in with the foliage beside the trail. His lean face was made fuller by the two to three-day-old growth of bristles in his salt and-pepper beard.

Her heart was pounding too fast from the sudden fright.

"You startled me," she gasped.

The whittler's face creased into a smile, the additional wrinkles looking as though they would crack his leather-tough skin.

"Ye oughtta watch where ye goin'," he said, amusement showing in his eyes, "or ye gonna run smack-dab into a tree."

He stepped from the bushes and joined Joanna in the trail. His lanky frame towered over her by half a head, and again, as she had the morning he guided her back to her cabin, she marveled at his sprightly step. His actions were those of a man much younger in years.

"Ye ain't lost again, are ye?" he joked.

"No. I can stay on the trail in the daylight," she said lightly. "I was just on my way back home."

"Ye been down the mountain?"

Joanna nodded.

She noticed that he seemed about to say something else, but stopped himself.

"Where have you been?" she asked. "Down the mountain, too?"

He gave his head a negative wag. "Nope. I was down there yesterday."

"What's going on down there? Everything's closed up and shuttered."

"Oughtn't to be."

"It wasn't when I first went down," she said, then recounted their experience at the hardware and the surprise of finding everything closed when she stepped back onto the street.

When she finished her tale, the whittler stood looking solemnly at her. His lips were a tightly drawn line, and his eyes danced with excitement – or nervousness. He was silent, muscles tensed, and the sudden change in him triggered a similar change in Joanna. She became apprehensive.

"Ye know what they sayin', don't ye?" he said tersely. "That ye be the bitch's young 'un."

"The bitch!" she gasped. Her mind raced ahead with wild thoughts trying to put meaning into his words. "What do you mean?"

"The bitch had a young 'un," he said, eyes leveled at hers. "It was a baby girl that'd be about as old as ye are. When they killed the bitch, the young 'un wasn't there. Some say the witches took it and hid it, and when the young 'un grows up she's supposed to come back and take the bitch's place at the head of the witches."

Joanna's mind was reeling. The whittler stopped talking. Her green surroundings flashed yellow. She fought the dizziness. She heard his words coming again, coming as though from a great distance, coming through a swirling, dense gray fog.

"Some of 'ems sayin' that ye be the young 'un," he repeated.

"They think I'm Isadora's daughter?"

The whittler nodded his head. She saw the tautness in his face. The same apprehension in his eyes that she had seen in the man at the hardware store. It was fear, but he stood unflinching before her.

"That's why they acted like that in town today."

He nodded again. "Them folks is afraid of ye."

She stood in a daze, trying to unravel the thoughts running through her tangled mind. It made no sense. It made no sense at all.

"But why?" she finally managed. "Why do they think I'm her daughter?"

"Ye look like her," he said. She looked searchingly into his eyes, wondering if he were accusing her. "Ye look jest like the bitch. And ye be about the right age."

Stunned and speechless, she searched for words, for an explanation, but there were too many questions, too many loose ends.

"But I'm not," she finally declared. "I've never been here before last year."

"Maybe," the whittler said solemnly. "But the witches started up again after ye came. And ye look like her. So some's a sayin' that ye be the young 'un come back to take her mother's place."

"You don't believe it, do you?" she asked him pointedly.

He shook his head. "No I seen ye runnin' from 'em, jest as afraid as everybody else," he said. "But it do seem strange that they'd start actin' up again ... all of a sudden."

He gave her a hard look, and she wondered if he were being honest about his own feelings. She wondered if he had doubts and suspicions. She knew her relationship with him was tentative at best, cemented only by two wood carvings and a painting. She was grateful now for whatever good will that exchange had created.

"But a lot of people look alike," she said, almost to herself. "I can't help that they think I look like her."

The whittler gazed steadily at her, seeming to hesitate over the words she saw forming on his lips.

"She was a artist too, ye know," he said, watching her closely.

"What?"

"The bitch was an artist, too." She could almost see his mind racing back in time. "Yep. I used to see her out and 'bout the mountain painting, the same as ye do."

"My God!" she gasped, shivers sliding along her spine.

He looked at her with a quizzical stare. "It do seem strange."

She started to reply, but before the words reached her lips he was spinning away from her. "Gotta go," he said, abruptly ending the conversation. "See ye."

He pushed his way through the foliage and disappeared. She was alone, her mind filled with new revelations. She slowly continued her trek up the mountain, trying to decipher what she had just learned. But like everything else that had happened, it seemed without reason, a product of the mountain and its people who lived with their ancient superstitions.

Slowly, she continued the ascent to her cabin. There she began to paint, trying to blot out her worries with the bright applications of color.

By mid-afternoon Joanna had finished the picture of the stream that she started the day before. She placed the still-wet canvas in the front bedroom, leaning it against the wall where she had found it that morning.

She couldn't help but cast a nervous glance at the mysterious painting that had also appeared that morning. She had placed it inconspicuously in a corner when she removed it from the easel after returning from Sutters Hamlet. She looked at it, then glanced away. She realized why she had looked – to see if any new objects had been added to the picture while she painted outside. There hadn't.

She left the room, closing the door behind her. She still had most of the afternoon ahead of her. It was too late to begin another painting, so she decided to spend the remainder of the day lazing around the cabin and perhaps tidying the place up a bit.

She heard a noise outside and, heart pounding too fast, walked to the door. Hanover was walking across the clearing. He saw her and threw up his arm and waved.

"I was looking for you this morning," she said, stepping outside the cabin to meet him. "But you weren't in."

His face dropped. "If I had known you were coming I would have made a point to be there." He had crossed the clearing and stopped directly before her. "How have you been?" he asked warmly.

"All right, I guess," she shrugged.

His brow wrinkled. "Do I detect that all's not really right with your world?" He glanced past her into the cabin. "Have any more strange, weird, or bizarre things been happening?" he asked with mild concern.

She nodded.

"Do you want to tell me about them?" his tone more serious.

"You're sure you want to hear about them?" she asked lightheartedly.

"Yes."

Joanna thought back to their last meeting, trying to remember what he knew and what he didn't. She had last seen Hanover the morning the doll appeared, so she started from that point in time. With each tale his face became more grave. When she told about the morning she woke up to find herself ravaged and covered with blood, he suddenly interrupted.

"My God! And you're still here! Why?"

Joanna shuddered involuntarily, unable to answer. She only shook her head.

Looking very worried, Hanover asked, "Is that the last incident?"

She told him about Tom and the weekend she spent with Peter and his mother.

"So that's where you were!" he exclaimed. "I came by Saturday evening and was worried when I found you gone, though I thought you might still be out painting somewhere. You seem to have had more than your share of excitement."

"But that's not all!"

"It's not?" Hanover gasped in surprise. He looked stunned, his face contorted as though someone had slapped him, as though he were unable to conceive of yet another incident.

"Last night while I was asleep, someone came inside and began painting a picture. I found it sitting on the easel this morning."

She retrieved the picture and showed it to Hanover who studied it carefully.

"What is it supposed to be?" he finally asked in bewilderment.

"It looks like a rock with some trees in the background."

"And you didn't paint it?"

"No."

"Maybe in your sleep?"

"No!" she said emphatically. "I can tell my own work when I see it, and that's definitely not something I painted. The thought occurred to me, though," she said. "But it's not mine. I'm sure of that."

"Strange – it's all so incredibly strange," Hanover muttered, half to himself.

Hanover's interest had been heightened at the mention of the painting. She noticed his change, from a very intense fatherly concern to utter bewilderment and surprise over the painting. It was as though, in some way, the painting overshadowed all the other terrors she had lived through.

"Is something wrong?" she asked.

"I don't know," he said. "All the other things you've had happen are similar to the events that occurred in Sutters Hamlet before Isadora was killed. But this painting —"

He was at a loss for words, and ended up gesturing helplessly in the empty air.

"It doesn't sound like anything I've ever heard of before," he finally said. "It's uncanny. If you didn't paint it, it's extremely uncanny! This doesn't — absolutely does not — sound like something the witches would have done. At least, not anything like they've ever done in the history of Sutters Hamlet!"

"Who then?" Joanna asked, her voice quavering.

Hanover looked her directly in the eyes, his own composure now under greater control.

"I don't know." Then attempting a joke, "But I don't think it just painted itself."

Joanna felt cold. She leaned against the cabin walls for support. The mysterious painting was clutched to her breast.

"It has to be the witches," she said resolutely.

"Perhaps," Hanover said without conviction. He was staring into space, as though in a trance. But a moment later he was his normal self again, his eyes resting on Joanna who was still leaning against the cabin. "So you came to town to see me today," he said jovially.

"Umm," she replied. "But I might as well not have come in." Again she related the incident at the hardware. ". . . And then I learned that they think I'm Isadora's daughter," she concluded.

Hanover's interest again heightened. "Then you already know about that," he stated.

She nodded affirmatively and told him of meeting the whittler coming back up the mountain.

His brow wrinkled, and for a few moments he retreated into his private thoughts.

"Joanna, can we sit down somewhere?" he asked gravely. "This is what I came to see you about."

Surprised at his sudden deepening mood, she swept her arms toward a patch of grass, forgetting that he wasn't as young as she. They walked into the middle of the yard and she dropped into the grass. As Hanover began to cautiously lower himself, she realized that she should have provided a chair. He sat without complaining.

She waited on him to pick up the conversation.

"Joanna," he began, eyes gazing affectionately into hers, "I know I told you earlier that I understand your driving desire to create, and, understanding that, I would not question your insistence on remaining here alone on this mountain. Even when I made that statement I didn't agree with your decision, but it was your decision and I respected it.

"But things have changed," he said solemnly. "And if you fully realize what it means to have the people here believe you're Isadora's daughter, you can understand just how drastically different the situation is now. I felt you were in danger, before, but now with this new development I believe it even more so."

Joanna watched him as he spoke, and from his slow, serious, and deliberate manner, she knew he was being completely candid.

"I don't feel you're safe here," he said. "I would not want to even imagine that what happened to Isadora could happen again ... to you."

She opened her mouth to speak, to tell him of the internal struggle that was raging within herself. How half of her agreed with him, but the other half seemed to be under some mystic hold. How her sixth sense, her animal sense, which had always guided her in the past, told her to remain. She opened her mouth to explain these things to him, but his hand shot up and silenced her.

"I'm sure you have your reasons," he said. "Your excuses, or whatever, and I'm not interested in hearing them. I only want you to know that I think you're being a very foolish young lady."

Joanna reached across the distance separating them and affectionately touched the older man's hand.

"I appreciate your concern. And sometimes I think you're right," she said sincerely. "But then, sometimes I don't."

Suddenly her mood changed, the seriousness being swept away by a wave of curiosity that washed across her face.

"Do I really look that much like her?" she quizzed.

Hanover seemed caught off guard, uncertain for a moment what she was talking about. But then his face told her that he understood.

"You mean Isadora?"

She nodded.

"There's a dramatic resemblance," he said.

For a moment he seemed engrossed in a private debate, looking at Joanna with doubtful eyes.

"I wasn't sure I was going to show you this," he said, rumbling inside his shirt pocket and finally withdrawing a piece of a crumpled news clipping, yellowing with age. "But I suppose I really should, so that you can understand why so many people believe this thing about your being her daughter."

She took the clipping from him and saw that the reverse side contained a photograph.

She looked at the picture and gasped. The girl in the photograph was a mirror image of herself. The eyes that looked back at her were her own. The black hair, the nose, the chin, the full cheeks were all her own. Though the newspaper was old and yellowing, there could be no mistaking the uncanny resemblance.

Her eyes were fixed on the girl in the picture, a woman about Joanna's own age. For an instant, her inner convictions were dulled. There was such a striking resemblance between herself and the woman in the picture! The first sharp edges of doubt about her own identity began to cut into her mind.

"This is Isadora." It was a statement, not a question, and out the corner of her eye she saw Hanover nod affirmatively.

Under any other circumstances, had this picture been produced and she been told that the woman in the picture was her mother, the resemblance was so nearly perfect that she would have been 90 percent willing to accept the statement – the relationship – as fact. But to know that this woman – this girl – was a witch! She had been burned to death at the stake. Incredible! To think that one who had succumbed to so horrible and brutal a death could possibly be her flesh-and-blood mother! Never! She found it hard, no impossible, to accept. But yet... there was the doubt.

"Do you see now why people might wonder?" Hanover asked softly.

She nodded, understanding. When she finally tore 'her eyes from the photograph, she faced Hanover.

"You said you knew Isadora, didn't you?"

"Slightly," he acknowledged. "I met her a time or two before her death."

"And the picture," Joanna asked, nodding to the clipping she held, "did you take it?"

Hanover shook his head. "No. It was in the files when I took over the newspaper. I ran across it shortly after her death and kept it."

Joanna fell silent for several moments.

"Do you think I could be her daughter?" she asked meekly.

Hanover was taken by surprise, which showed in his eyes. "Of course not!" he snapped. "She evidently did have a child, but if it's still alive it could be anywhere in this country."

"Did you know I'm an orphan, and I don't know who my parents are ... were?"

Hanover's eyes narrowed. He shook his head. "I didn't know that." He paused. "I wouldn't advise you to spread that around; it would only add fuel to the flame."

"I don't know where I was born either," Joanna said. "But I would be out of my mind to even entertain the possibility that these people are right."

Her eyes dropped to the picture in her lap. She was suddenly overwhelmed with sadness. The poor girl! A girl her own age, and probably as innocent as she herself who died such a horrible death at the hands of these outrageously superstitious, ignorant people. She felt a great closeness to the girl in the picture. They had shared the same experience: Each had been accused of being a witch. Even though Isadora had lived a quarter century before, Joanna felt a kinship to her. A kinship of knowing, to a degree, what she must have lived through.

She looked at the picture, and the inevitable question entered her mind. The question she had been trying to keep out. Could this girl be her mother? Could these people be right, and she be the daughter of Isadora, an executed witch? Rubbish! It was too outlandish to even consider! She was from a New York orphanage and Isadora was from Sutters Hamlet. Not a chance! She resolutely denounced her own thoughts, but still the doubt, the uncertainty, the not knowing was there.

Hanover's voice brought her back from her thoughts.

"Do you remember the first day we met and I mentioned the fact that you had returned to Sutters Hamlet, and you wondered how I could remember your face after having seen it only once a year ago?"

She well remembered the incident. It was still a puzzle to her. She nodded.

He pointed to the picture of Isadora.

"That's how I knew," he said. "When I saw you last year with the young man, I thought I was seeing a ghost from the past. And then you returned. The people here aren't particularly friendly to outsiders anyway. But some of the older folks who shunned you those first days noticed the resemblance. I don't think anyone mentioned it to anyone else at first, but when the witches started up again after you came, the rumors soon began. You were the daughter of Isadora.

"So you see," he concluded, "for these people who have spent all their lives amongst these tales of witches and witchcraft, believing that you're Isadora's daughter isn't really farfetched at all. Not if you try and understand their viewpoint."

Joanna understood, readily able to see the validity of his statements, how the people could believe that she was Isadora's daughter.

"And everyone actually believed that Isadora's daughter would return?" she asked.

"Like they believe in the second coming of Christ."

"I suppose I timed it just about right," she said.

He cocked his eyebrow. "You timed it right, and you look right."

Dusk was falling when Hanover left. She watched him until he disappeared into the trees growing on the side of the mountain, then went inside and closed the door. She lit the lantern sitting on a small table in a corner and felt safer again. Something about the cabin in the dark frightened her. Too many unpleasant things had happened for her to feel safe inside surrounded by darkness. Even knowing that the witches may think her to be the daughter of their dead high priestess and meant her no harm; even knowing they probably worshipped her and wanted her to join them, it was no consolation. As much as not knowing, it frightened her.

She went to bed early, feeling tired and wanting to get an early start the next morning. Already she was planning another painting. She rested in the darkness waiting for sleep to come. The night crept by, and she, with a racing mind unwilling to surrender to the fatigue of her body, could not sleep. Several times she dozed, but at the slightest sound, she jerked awake.

Had it not been for her state of unease, they might have come and found her asleep....

Half the night had passed, and Joanna still lay awake, wrestling with her thoughts in turmoil. The brush of a craggy pine branch against the wall outside her bedroom sent shivers through her each time it scraped in a certain moaning sort of way. It kept her frayed nerves on edge, refusing to let her mind rest as it made its dying sounds in the night. Then it was quiet, and the night was still. She heard them coming. She heard movement outside her cabin. The shuffling of feet. And there was no doubt in her mind. It was the coven!

She sprang from her bed, throwing herself onto the floor lest she be seen from the window. On hands and knees, she crawled to the dresser and took the gun from the bottom drawer. Then, huddled in a corner and out of view of the window, she waited.

She heard movement behind her, outside the window. She shuddered at the thought of the hooded face that must now be looking into her bedroom. She clutched the pistol even tighter, the cold metallic handle more welcome now than any lover's arms had ever been. She squatted without moving, hardly daring to breathe, overcoming a temptation to thrust the gun into the window and pull the trigger.

Suddenly the stillness was shattered. There was a tapping at the window, the methodic rat-tat-tat of fingernails trying to draw her attention. Could they have seen her? She tried to squeeze closer to the wall.

This was the first time they had blatantly and openly approached her. Always before they had tried to remain hidden, but not now! If they had not seen her, they were deliberately trying to awaken her to let her know that they were there.

The tapping stopped. The night was still again. She listened, but could hear only her own breathing.

There was a thud at the front of the cabin. Someone had kicked the door! Then came the dull click of metal against metal. A key had been inserted in the lock! She silently prayed that she had also used the inside slide latch. She knew that she had forgotten!

She heard the key turn, then the doorknob, and the door squeaked open!

She was trapped!

She shoved aside the panic that tried to grab hold. She could not run. She could not escape. She had only one choice. To face them!

Throwing fear aside and possessed only of the will to survive and the determination to do what she must, she stepped from her hiding, ignoring the window behind her and whatever might be watching her. The pistol held tightly in both hands, she crept stealthily toward the door. Halfway to the bedroom door, she saw movement in the living room. Several black robes glided about the room, while another robe of black seemed to flow in from the outside.

She felt her thumbs tighten and heard the click as she cocked the revolver in her hands.

It sounded like a shot in the hush of the night. All movement ceased. The robes were suddenly still, seemingly on hangers in the middle of her living room.

"We mean you no harm, your highness." A soothing feminine voice came out of the darkness.

The witches held their ground, making no move to leave her living room, but making no move toward her.

The hush returned as they faced each other, the doorway their only barrier.

"We mean you no harm." The voice returned.

With trembling hands she pointed the gun into the darkness. Terror was standing at her back. She felt the rush of panic over her body. The strength that had pushed her forward to face them was leaving her, leaving her alone with herself.

"We mean you no harm." The voice came again. An image of Tom flashed through her mind.

They were waiting. She knew they were waiting to see what she intended to do. They were trying to wear her down. She remembered Mrs. Tillary, heartbroken and crying over the little cat's grave.

She tightened her finger around the trigger. Hesitated a moment, then pulled.

The darkness was suddenly shattered by the orange flash from the gun, the shot echoing through the house, amplified by the close walls. She fired again, then again

She ran into the living room, crying, ready to fire again. But they were gone.

The front door stood open to the night, testimonial to their presence. She rushed to it, slammed it shut then bolted it. She lit the lantern and searched the house. Then with the lantern still flickering in the living room, she returned to bed. With the pistol by her side she tried to sleep, but it was long in coming.

Chapter 12

The morning brought with it a preknowledge. She awakened knowing that somehow the painting was one step closer toward completion. As she had somehow instinctively sensed the morning before when the painting had mysteriously appeared on her easel, each morning would bring with it a new revelation. She knew without seeing the painting that her instincts were correct, though only seeing would erase all doubt.

The pistol was still at her side. Fear of the gun was now gone. Last night it had proved its friendship. Instead of returning it to its hiding place in the bottom drawer, she tucked it under her pillow.

Memory of the witches made her shudder as she straightened her bed, trying not to let her mind wander to the night before. A certain calmness now soothed her mind. She had faced them and they had run. She smiled inwardly, confidently. They were human like herself. Nothing supernatural about them. And like humans, they feared her gun. She flattened the wrinkles out of the single sheet that had covered her during the night. A dark-brown smudge on the otherwise spotlessly white sheet glared at her. She touched it, and her fingertips told her it was dried paint. Annoyed at her own carelessness, she tried to scrape it off, but was only partly successful.

She went directly into the front bedroom, and as she had predicted, the mysterious painting was back on the easel. She cautiously edged around it, apprehensive now that her eyes had proved her instincts right. Spots of bare, brown earth had been added around the rock and along the outer fringes at the bottom of the canvas, setting the groundwork for what appeared to be a clearing in a forest. Darker areas were spotted on one side of the rock, but Joanna couldn't tell what they were. And again there were the peculiar circular brush strokes.

Joanna studied the painting silently for a few moments, then lifted it from the easel and placed it again on the floor. This morning she was filled with fascination more than fear; last night had taught her that the witches could be driven away. More than ever before she was now convinced that the painting that seemed to paint itself was a by-product of witchcraft. For while she knew the witches to be human, she could still accept the fact they might possess some supernatural power. This she didn't question; she herself had a gift of this sort.

She gathered her painting equipment and took it into the front yard where she set it up to begin her day's work and a new painting. From a quickie sketch she had made several days before, a fast, color sketch done in an hour on a small 10-x-14-inch cardboard-backed canvas, she would produce a larger and more detailed picture on a stretched canvas. A major painting of this sort would normally take her about two days, though unusually complicated subjects requiring a lot of detail work could take her over a week to complete.

She mapped out just the roughest of outlines with a charcoal pencil, then slowly and meticulously began to add color. Her mind, which normally would become completely preoccupied by the work at hand, obliterating everything but the painting itself, began to wander. It returned to the unfinished painting sitting against the wall in her front bedroom. Something about that painting had been overlooked! Deep down inside, she had that same feeling of precognition. She knew that this morning she had seen some clue; something obvious had glared at her from that canvas. But what? She stopped her work and went into the bedroom for another look at the mysterious picture. She studied it for a full two minutes before returning it in despair to its place on the floor and went back to the new painting awaiting her brush in front of the cabin.

She painted until the sun dipped behind the mountain and the light began to fade, stopping only once at midday to make a sandwich. When the light was too dim to be able to distinguish nuances of color, she took her painting inside and put her equipment away. By now her mind had become deeply absorbed by her picture, and she was at a high pitch of excitement from watching that painting develop over the course of the day. Pleased with the work so far, she had been reluctant to put brush and easel away and wait for tomorrow. But experience had taught her she was a daytime painter and could paint well only in good, natural light.

She spent the remainder of the afternoon waiting for night, and wondering, fearfully now that it approached, what the darkness would bring.

But it brought nothing but the morning.

Her days were at last productive, as she had imagined they would be when planning her trip to the mountain. In a week she finished three full-sized canvases. And her nights were at last uneventful.

Each morning, almost as a ritual to the wakening, she went immediately into the front bedroom to see what had been added to the painting that was, stroke by stroke, painting itself. She had accepted, almost as a matter of course, that some force beyond her control was causing the picture in her front bedroom to paint itself.

Some mornings she had to carefully search for the new addition to the canvas, but it was always there. Unlike the amount of work she had found completed the first two nights, the unknown artist's work had slowed to a mere dribble of color. Some mornings she had to search for the fine, almost impossible circular brush strokes left during the night. But they were always there. Each morning, somewhere on the canvas, she found a new splotch of color.

Only once did she find enormous progress made on the picture during the night. She entered the bedroom as usual, expecting to have to search the canvas for the fresh paint, but found that the dark forest on the right side of the picture had been completed! Surprised at the sudden increase in the nightly work, she found herself ill at ease. It was as though the artist, whoever or whatever he may be, had rushed to complete that part of the picture hurriedly. But for what reason, she didn't know.

She worked on her latest painting until midday, her concentration finally broken when Hanover stumbled into the clearing carrying a bag of groceries.

"I thought you might need some of these!" he shouted as he stepped toward her. She looked up.

Joanna set down her brush and went to meet him, glad for his company. It had been nearly a week since she had seen her last human, and her last visitors had been the witches.

"What have you there?" she asked, pointing to the bag.

"It's food, my dear," he said cheerfully. "I remembered the trouble you had on your last trip down the mountain, and I thought you might be getting short of food."

She was. Her cold reception last time had kept her from making another trip for food, even though she was getting low on some items. She gratefully took the bag from Hanover, peeking inside and finding some of the items she needed.

"You're a darling!" she said, pecking his cheek.

He carried the bag inside and set it on her kitchen cabinet.

Hanover stayed for lunch, leaving with the promise that he would soon return with another gift of food to spare her the hostility of the people of Sutters Hamlet.

When he left, she returned to her painting, but was no longer able to concentrate on the half-finished picture before her. Her concentration broken, her eyes kept drifting to the patches of color on her palette. Something there distracted her, kept gnawing at her mind in an unsettling way. It was the same preknowledge that something had been overlooked she had felt the second morning she had viewed the work of the midnight painter.

Her mind drifted back to that troubled morning, and as casually as her thoughts meandered, she suddenly had the answer she had struggled so hard to discover, that morning a week ago. The clue that the painting had held! But it wasn't the painting at all!

She dashed into the house, trembling with excitement!

She ran into the bedroom and ripped the blanket off her bed that last night's chill had forced her to use. But it was gone! The splotch of paint was gone! Despondently, she dropped the blanket in a heap in the middle of her bed, remembering, now that her excitement had vanished, that she had washed the sheet with the spot of paint on it just two days before. But even without the paint as verification, she knew she was right. She knew that the paint on her sheet, and not on the canvas, was the clue she had so blatantly overlooked! And it was so obvious! Why hadn't she seen it before! She remembered the dark-brown smudge on her sheet, so thick with paint she could peel it off with her fingernails. It was the same paint, the same shade of brown that had appeared on the canvas that morning!

There were only two ways the paint could have gotten there, and either way made her feel like caving in at the knees.

She spun and left the room, heading to the front bedroom and the painting sitting against the wall, the product of an unknown and unseen hand. She picked it up and found the brown patches of earth, the color the same as the spot on her bed, she was sure.

The chilling hand played with her neck. Whoever or whatever was painting this picture had been in her bedroom, had actually touched her bed, had groped her sheets, while she slept. It had left its telltale mark! The blotch of paint on the sheet! She cast a fearful glance over her shoulder, afraid now of whatever presence, whatever nightly visitor, had the run of her house after dark.

Not since the evening she had run the witches away with the gun, the same night the spot on the sheet had appeared, had she been afraid of the painting. It now seemed to grow in the darkness on the other side of the wall. The second installment took place that very night, and every night since, a new addition. Surely the witches wouldn't have returned to face her gun again twice in one evening!

That had baffled her, believing as she did after that second night that the witches were not involved, that they would not have returned a second time to face her gun. But if not the witches, then who? That was the confusing part. But to her it had been a relief, knowing that whatever was happening, it was not the witches. She had even considered, as she had the first morning, the possibility that she painted the picture herself while sleepwalking. But that was again quickly cast aside because of the circular brush strokes. And the fact that the painting was always done in the dead of night. She could only paint well in the best of natural light. And that painting was well executed.

It had been baffling, intriguing, even frightening. But the fright to her was minimal when she allowed herself to rationalize. Equally strange phenomenon had been recorded and documented all over the world. Rocks falling from the sky. Ghosts. Apparitions. Could it be a ghost painting in her front bedroom? She chuckled uneasily at her own thought. A painting ghost!

The fear caused by the doll on her bed and blackhooded faces had been real and terrifying to her. But the realization that someone or something came into her cabin at night and added a few strokes to this mysterious canvas was somehow less frightening. Perhaps the terror created by the witches preoccupied her and kept her aloof from the painting. Though the painting sat in the room adjacent to where she slept, it was as though at a distance. Something about it benign, curious, but not so terribly frightening.

It had been that way before. She was able to accept it as a phenomenon, strange but no more to be feared than her own gift of precognition. But now it was different. It, whatever IT was, had touched her! Had touched her bed, her sheet, maybe even her body! She now knew the artist was something physical. Something that moved and walked about her house, a being to which paint would cling!

It was something to be feared, unless...

She grabbed a small canvas, one with a cardboard back of the sort that she used primarily for color sketches, before attempting a major work. She took it outside and, removing the picture she had started that morning, placed the blank canvas on her easel. Beside it she placed the mystery picture. She took her smallest stubby-haired brush and, studying the circular brush strokes carefully, tried to copy them. She rotated the brush, using the handle as an axis, trying in vain to reproduce the strokes that so mysteriously appeared every night. After half an hour of trying several means of achieving the circular stroke, she had made no headway. She could come nowhere close to making a circular stroke so small and so delicate and was even farther away from being able to create an artistic, legible pietare.

When finally she admitted defeat, she recognized if she couldn't reproduce the circular strokes, then there was no way that she could have produced the unfinished picture in some state of sleepwalk. That left open the only other possibility, the one that she feared most. It left her with the probability that something other than herself had left the paint on her sheet.

She tried to return to her painting, but was too upset to concentrate. She finally bundled her gear in her arms and deposited it in the front bedroom. She spent the remainder of the day dusting and cleaning the cabin, doing anything to keep her mind off the painting. One overriding thought kept edging its way into her mind. Destroy it! She entertained the idea, but knew that she would not do it. Destroying the painting might solve her immediate problem, but she doubted it. How could she stop the artist from beginning another? She knew instinctively that to destroy the painting would do no good. It must run its course to completion. It must serve whatever purpose it was meant to serve. For this she would leave the painting intact. And for yet another reason – curiosity. Her catlike curiosity was as great as her fear. Her feline instincts, her gift of knowledge, told her that the picture was being painted for a specific purpose. But her instincts did not tell her why, And only the answer would satisfy her curiosity.

With the coming of darkness, she began to grow nervous. Each creak of the aging floorboard sent her whirling to check out what might be behind her. Even with her chair shoved into a corner when she finally settled down to read, she still heard or imagined noises behind her. The cabin was seemingly filled with unexplained creaks and groans, the walls alive with ghostly shadows from the dancing lantern flame and she tried to soothe herself with the fantasy that it was her own imagination gone wild. But still her ears pierced the night, searching for some sound that would tell her that the midnight artist was with her. Her own reason told her that there was no more boards creaking tonight than on previous nights, that it was her knowledge that the night artist had walked and felt her, that it would return tonight to continue its work, that it may hover over her bed as it had at least once before that made her ears so keen to the sounds of the night and her eyes so aware of the eerie shadows.

But there was something that troubled her about it all. Something that distracted her as much as the frightening sounds of the night. There was something about herself that − sitting, reading, listening − she began to realize. It was a contradiction to the very fact of her sitting, huddled in fear in a corner. She realized, deep in the recesses of her subconscious mind, that there was the beginning of an understanding, but an understanding not yet grasped by her conscious self. It was the soothing voice of her inner self, the voice that gave her knowledge denied to others, that was speaking. But the wisdom it spoke of this night was wisdom she could not accept. She could not really relax when it came to thinking about the night artist, though that was the feeling she was receiving from within.

Weariness finally overcame her, and reluctantly she faced the prospect of sleep. As much tonight as ever before, she feared it.

There was no bolt on her bedroom door, but she was determined to secure it in some fashion. With a straight-backed chair from the kitchen jammed under the doorknob holding the door securely shut, she finally managed to fall into a fitful sleep.

In the morning she was out of bed as soon as her eyes opened. She dressed hurriedly, eager to see what work the night artist had done while she slept. She had to struggle with the chair. It was lodged so tightly against the door that she finally had to give it a stout kick that sent it sliding across the room.

She went into the front bedroom and found the painting once again resting on her easel, moved from the floor where she had left it the previous afternoon. The night artist had been there. The thought was not comforting. A careful examination of the picture found a new addition to the colors already on the canvas. New greenery had been added to a scrubby bush in the foreground.

She had gotten up reasonably early this morning and knew that if she worked diligently until noon she could finish the painting she was now working on. Following her set routine of the past few days, she moved her easel and paints into the front yard.

"Oh, damn!" she exclaimed as she stepped outside and cast her first glance skyward. Dark-gray rain clouds, puffed up with moisture and seemingly ready to burst, drifted across the sky from the north. She stood hesitating in the doorway for a moment, then decided to chance it. Though she was working in oils and not watercolors, the first drop of rain would send her scurrying inside shielding her unfinished canvas.

The rain held, seeming to time its arrival to suit her schedule. As she dabbed on the last touches and stepped back to scrutinize her work, she felt the first drop of rain hit her bare arm. With unpleasant memories of another rainy day in Upstate New York when she had worked in watercolors, and the ruin the rain had dealt her that day, she grabbed her easel and ran at the first drop of moisture. She had to make another trip outside for her abandoned palette and brushes, and in that half minute, the rain had developed into a steady drizzle.

After putting away her tools, she returned to the open front doorway and watched the rain, increasing now to a summer shower. As always, the new falling rain with the smell of ozone still lingering was a soothing ointment to her ragged emotions. She watched until a whirling gust of wind blew the rain in on her, then she closed the door. She parted the curtains to better light the living room, then disappeared into the kitchen to open some cans for lunch.

She was searching for the can opener when a sudden pounding at the door made her jump. Before she could gather her wits and calm herself, the pounding resumed, this time so strong it threatened to cave the door in!

She made a dash for her bedroom, grabbed the pistol hidden under her pillow, and ran to the window, her mind trying now to count the shots she had fired at the witches a week before. She had no shells to reload the pistol if it needed it, and she prayed that it was still loaded. She looked out of the window, the pounding now stopped, and saw Peter standing in the rain.

"My God, you're drenched!" she exclaimed, throwing open the door.

He stumbled inside, water pouring off his rain soaked head and falling onto his wet clothing, which clung in patches like a second skin.

"Thanks," he smiled sheepishly as Joanna closed the door behind him. He was standing in a self-created puddle.

"What in hell were you doing out in the rain?" she quizzed.

"Just trying to get in before it started," he said lightly. Then his eyes dropped to the pistol she still clutched in one hand, and he grew solemn.

"Do you always answer your door with a gun in your hands?" he asked. Then more seriously, "Has it been that bad?"

She bit her bottom lip, resisting an urge to blurt it all out right then. Alone and nearly isolated on Sutters Mountain, facing the witches by herself, and now the night artist, she seldom had a chance for emotional release through conversation and ordinary human contact. It came in spurts, on the infrequent occasions when she was with either Hanover, Peter, or the whittler. It was at those times more than others that she recognized to what extent she was suppressing her innermost emotions and how badly needed was the buffer provided by occasional, friendly human contact. And it was because of this holding back that she wanted to explode with the pouring out of her problems to Peter. But she recognized Peter's need to be more immediate than her own, so she only nodded in reply, a jerked, awkward nod of affirmation held in check by unconsciously biting her lip.

"I'll tell you about it," she said hastily. "But first we have to get you dry. Take off your clothes." She pointed toward her bedroom. "There are some blankets in the closet that you can use until we get your clothes dry."

Without protesting, he closed himself in the bedroom and reappeared a few minutes later with a gray blanket draped around him. Joanna was already poking at the wood-burning heater trying to start a flame when he brought his clothes and dropped them in a wet heap on the floor.

"It'll take a while to get them dry," he said.

"We've got all afternoon by the looks of it," she replied, casting a glance out the window.

Peter dropped into a chair, catching the flying end of the blanket as it fell off the side of his leg, threatening to expose him. Joanna couldn't help but laugh at his frantic efforts to keep himself from being uncovered, but didn't tell him that he had been too late. With the blanket finally in place, he sat huddled like a forlorn child.

"What were you doing out?" she asked again, prodding for a direct answer this time.

"I had to go down the mountain this morning for Mother. I thought I would get back before the rain started." He shrugged off his miscalculation.

Joanna had set the pistol on top of the stove while she prepared the fire. As she finally nursed a small flame, trying to fan it toward the firewood, Peter removed the gun.

"You should be more careful with firearms," he scolded. "If you had left it on top until it got hot enough, the shells could have exploded by themselves."

"I was going to take it off," she protested, but didn't make an issue of it because she knew he was right.

Peter, quiet for a moment, inspected the gun.

"I heard about your last trip into town," he said with an air of casualness that she immediately recognized as a front. He looked expectantly at her, but she didn't glance up. Instead, she vigorously fanned the fire, pretending not to notice the direct challenge in his eyes.

"Do you know what's going on down there?" he asked.

"Oh? What's that?" she said flippantly. She stopped her fanning and looked at him innocently. Their eyes met and held. Under his insistent gaze, she finally dropped her eyes. She shrugged dejectedly. "No, I don't know what's going on. But I guess I can imagine. I guess I'm the talk of the town."

"Something like that," he said. "The whole town evidently shut down the last time you went in."

She remembered the incident at the hardware, the frustration of nearly having to force the man to sell her the kerosene, and then she stepped out on the street and found the town deserted.

"If it hadn't been for Mr. Hanover, who brought me some food yesterday, I might have been starving in a few days." The memory brought her into action. She closed the heavy iron door to the heater, confident now that it would burn. She stood. "Speaking of food," she said, "I was just about to eat when you scared me out of my wits. You hungry?"

He nodded. "Starved."

"I was about to have some," she said, as she disappeared into the kitchen. "Will that be all right?"

"Fine."

She quickly began preparing a soup and salad for the two of them.

"I guess you know who they think I am," she said, speaking over her shoulder toward the living room so she would be heard. "They think I'm a witch!"

She heard Peter's chair squeak, then heard his bare feet making hollow sounds on the wooden floor as he joined her in the kitchen.

"What's more, they think I'm the daughter of their famous witch, Isadora."

"I know."

"Do you think I'm a witch?" she asked.

"Seriously?"

"Yeh. Why not?" she said lightly.

Peter's face broke into a smile. "I think you're bewitching," he said.

She looked up quickly, trying too late to catch the expression on his face as he spoke.

"What I think," Peter said, his voice leaving no doubt now that he spoke seriously, "is that the twelve people who make up the so-called coven of witches on this mountain are using you as a scapegoat. The legend that Isadora's daughter will return some day to become high priestess has been perpetuated all these years. You just happened to come here twenty-five years later and are about the right age and have the right color hair so automatically you're it!

"Nobody ever found out who the other twelve members of the coven were. After the night Isadora was burned, the coven went into hiding and has hardly been heard from since. Until recently, that is. From what I've been told about her death, the people of Sutters Hamlet turned into a lynch mob. They had been frightened and intimidated for so long, never having any idea who was behind all the horrible things that happened around here. Everyone was suspected of being a member of the coven. It was like a secret society that no one dared challenge. Then some kid said he saw Isadora turn into a fox, and that was all it took. The people had a target upon which to take out all their pent-up fears."

Peter stopped to get his breath. The words had been rushing out too fast. Joanna had stopped opening cans and stood spellbound.

"The night she was killed, a mob from down the mountain surrounded her cabin," he continued, but Joanna cut in quickly.

"Where was Isadora's cabin?" she asked unexpectedly. "I'd wondered about that."

Peter seemed shocked. "You mean you don't know?" he asked.

"Know what?" The tone in his voice frightened her.

"This was Isadora's cabin."

His words exploded in her ears. The stillness around them was more intense than any she had ever experienced.

"Oh, my God!"

"I thought you knew." His words came as a near whisper, apologetic, perplexed, frightened for her. "You knew about Isadora. I thought you knew."

Speechless, she shook her head.

"That's another reason some of the people are so convinced you're her daughter." He seemed to try to shake off the spell that had overcome them both. "But no more of this. Let's not talk about it anymore."

"Yes! Finish the story," she ordered.

"Are you sure?"

She nodded.

"I don't want to frighten you," he protested.

"I'm already frightened."

He hesitated, then agreed. His mind wandered for a moment. "Where was I?" he asked.

"They had surrounded her cabin," Joanna said shakily.

"That's right. They formed a ring around her cabin with torches, lighting up this entire area so she couldn't escape. They ordered her to come out, and when she did, she ran out the front door shouting at them, drawing their attention as she tried to run into the forest."

"Wonder why she didn't run out the back door?" Joanna injected. "It seems like she would have had a better chance of getting to the trees since they're much closer to the cabin in the back."

"And she might have gotten away," Peter said. "But she wasn't trying to escape. She was trying to draw attention away from her baby. At least that's what everyone thinks. Few knew she had a child, since she kept pretty much to herself. But after she'd been subdued, someone shouted that they'd heard a baby crying and they went in to get it too, but it was gone. They found a crib with the sheets still warm, but her baby was gone."

"What happened to the baby?" Joanna asked. , Peter shrugged. "No one knows for sure. Most people believe that Isadora sacrificed herself for her baby. She possibly could have escaped had she run out the rear since, as you mentioned, the forest is so near. But she didn't. She ran out the front-into the clearing where she was trapped. She created such a distraction that those stationed behind her cabin were drawn to the front."

"And someone sneaked the baby out the back?" Joanna asked.

"Evidently," Peter said. "Either there was someone in the cabin with her, and they took the baby and ran out the back while Isadora was raising hell out front, or a member of the coven sneaked in through the rear and got the child."

"That means Isadora could have saved herself," Joanna said softly.

Peter was pensive. "Maybe."

Joanna felt a melancholy sweep her spirits downward at the thought of a woman so young forced to make such a sacrifice. But she understood. Witch or not, Isadora had loved her child. Loved her enough to die.

Joanna shuddered away the melancholy, forcing Peter back to the story of Isadora's fate.

"Did they kill her here?" she asked fearfully.

Peter shook his head. "They took her back down the mountain and burned her . . . just outside town."

"It must have been a horrible way to die," Joanna whispered.

"Frightened people can be cruel."

Then Joanna heard herself asking something that both surprised and startled her. It was totally unexpected.

"Did she cry?"

"I don't know," Peter said. "But I can't imagine even Joan of Arc suffering that type of pain in silence."

"What a horrible ending," she said agonizingly.

"There's one other thing," Peter said. "It's one of those things that you find hard to believe, but can't help wondering about."

"What?"

"Everyone there, not just some of them, mind you, but everyone, said that before Isadora died her fingernails grew into claws."

"The fox! " she gasped.

The same familiar icy hand raised goose bumps on the back of her neck. She could well imagine Isadora's last night, alone on the mountain in this very cabin, facing the terrors of the night that Joanna was all too familiar with. She felt sympathy for Isadora, possibly the victim of the same nightly harassment. And suddenly there was a closeness, the closeness of knowing that another woman twenty-five years before had suffered much the same as she, a feeling like that of two friends who live through a dangerous experience together.

"No one knows what happened to the baby," Peter said, drawing her from her thoughts. "But shortly after that the legend started that Isadora's daughter would one day return. I think that anyone, not just you, but anyone who came here alone, any woman, would be accused of being her daughter.

"Do you see what I'm saying? It's just too convenient. I think that the members of the coven started the legend themselves, trying to take the heat off. And if we could trace it down and determine who was the first person to accuse you of being Isadora's daughter, I believe we would have found a member of the coven. They're a bunch of opportunists, and they're using you!" he said vehemently.

She had finally succeeded in getting the cans open, and she began dishing the unheated contents into two plates.

"I think there's more to it than that," she said seriously.

"But why?" he exclaimed. "You're not starting to believe that you're a witch too, are you?"

"No," she said coolly. "But too much has happened for me to believe that they're just using me as a scapegoat and nothing else. I mean, why would they keep coming here as they do if all they wanted was to convince the people in town that I'm one of them? They wouldn't have to frighten me in order to do that! In fact, it seems to me that if they were just trying to use me they wouldn't put me on my guard by coming here in the first place."

"Then just what do you think?" Peter said.

"I think the witches sincerely believe I'm Isadora's daughter," she said flatly.

"What in hell makes you think that?" he exclaimed.

"Because they were here and I've talked to them," she said with a twinkle of amusement in her eyes. She watched his shocked expression with the same mischievousness as a cat playing with a field mouse.

"You talked to them!"

"Well almost, but not quite," she said, remembering the voice that kept repeating, We mean you no harm, your highness. "Actually, one of them talked to me."

She told him about the incident and how she had driven them away with the pistol he had given her. He smiled broadly when she told how quickly they had disappeared after she started shooting.

"I noticed the gun had been fired," he said. "I'm glad you had it."

"Me too!" she said earnestly. "I'm glad you made me keep it."

She hurried away and placed their plates on the table, the two of them sitting down to eat. Peter had trouble with his blanket; several times it threatened to slide off his lap and leave him naked. He finally solved the problem by standing, twisting the blanket until the opening was at his back, and sitting on it.

During the meal Peter brought her up to date on the latest gossip in Sutters Hamlet, the continuing events that led people to believe without doubt that the witches had again come out of their hiding.

"Animals are being stolen at an alarming rate," he said. "Almost every night. And a number of places have been discovered where they are believed to have held their ceremony; there's always the remains of an animal at the spot."

"If it happens that often, can't the townspeople determine who's missing on these nights, and find out who's in the coven that way?" she asked.

"It's not that easy," Peter replied. "There's no way of knowing if some of the witches live in town or if they're scattered over the mountain. And it's getting to be the same way it was years ago – no one's sure his neighbor isn't a member of the coven. Everyone's suspicious of everyone else."

The rain continued until late afternoon, then a break in the clouds hinted a clearing. Draped across the heater, white foggy steam rising from them as they dried, Peter's clothes were soon ready to wear. Once again he disappeared into the bedroom and emerged fully dressed.

As the gray dusk settled upon the mountain, the rain stopped. An occasional mist moistened the air, but it was hardly more than a light fog. Peter stepped into the approaching darkness, dry except for his shoes, and disappeared into the rain-soaked forest. Joanna watched until he was gone, then closed herself in her cabin.

She felt not quite so safe now. The contentment, the protection, the safety of having Peter with her was gone. She was alone again with the night artist and the picture that seemingly came alive under someone's brush stroke during the night. But now there was more. Nothing to fear really, but a troublesome thought that had played on her frayed emotions, even with Peter there. Another doubt. Just one more thing to worry about. The knowledge that she was living in Isadora's cabin. The idea made her skin crawl, and she kept the cabin well-lighted with all three lanterns until she finally decided to try sleep. Again she bolted her bedroom door with the chair, praying that whatever stalked her cabin at night would be locked out.

As she lay waiting for sleep to overtake her, for the first time since arriving on the mountain, she found the idea of packing her belongings and leaving a serious possibility ... something to consider. Damned the part of her that kept whispering stay. Damned the money she had invested on this year. She had saved once, and she could work and save for another year. She could find another place, not quite so isolated, not quite so backward. Some place where witches and strange artists didn't stalk the night.

She was a solitary person, a loner. It had seemed only natural to her to seek solitude in which to work; it was when she was alone and undisturbed that she did her best painting. Solitude she had found, but she found much more than she had bargained for. To face the night alone was one thing. But to face phantoms in the night was another. She realized she was reaching her breaking point, the point beyond which she could no longer cope with anything out of the ordinary on Sutters Mountain. Only some strange inner feeling of safety gave her the courage to remain ... a feeling of being protected. "Here I am listening to that other voice again!" she nearly muttered aloud. It was puzzling, frightening, this inner feeling so contradictory to her rational ... irrational ... fear. And it was frightening to her that she should listen. But she had always listened to her innermost voice; it always knew something that she didn't. And never once did it offer false comfort or instill unwarranted fear. It had always played fairly with her. And for that voice she now listened, even though her reason told her it was irrational.

The morning, when it finally arrived, brought with it another reason to doubt, another reason to fear.

Overnight, the work of the night artist changed tempo. To the nighttime landscape around the rock, the unfinished clearing with the brooding forest behind, a new and frightening element was added. Humans!

Two figures, cast as dark silhouettes by a fire that now burned in the clearing, pranced in wild abandon, arms thrown high, heads back, both male and female clearly nude.

The third figure, a female, knelt in profile before the flat table rock. A shaft of soft light from the fire silhouetted dark strands of willowy hair falling to her shoulders. Her nude body, hardly more than a shadowy imagination shielded from the firelight by the rock, revealed the firm, upswept breasts of a young woman. Only the side of her face was caught directly by the firelight, a triangle of light illuminating her cheek and eye.

Joanna's head began to reel as she stood before the painting. She felt faint, her heart straining to pump the blood draining from her head. In an instant, she saw the painting and understood! No longer was it a mystery! She knew the intent of the artist and the painting!

The night artist was slowly, methodically painting a picture of the coven!

But it was the central figure – the girl kneeling before the rock – that made waves of nausea pass through her. The shaft of light on the face, the hair, the nude body, which was hardly more than outlined! It was her! Joanna was looking at the picture of herself!

She stumbled out of the room and, sick to her stomach, threw up on the living room floor.

Her mind was made up. She didn't have to think about it now. She knew that she would leave. Nothing, no career, no amount of money could possibly be worth the torment of staying.

Only the unforeseen could convince her to remain even one more night in Isadora's cabin. But that day brought with it the unforeseen.

Chapter 13

It was perhaps the fact that she was on edge that enabled her to hear it when it was still nearly inaudible. She had already noticed that her cabin, sitting on the mountainside, seemed to be ideally located to pick up the sounds floating upward from lower elevations. Hanover never came up the mountain without her having heard him tramping through the trees several minutes before he arrived at her clearing. The location seemed to trap the normal sounds coming from below, giving fair warning that a visitor was on the way.

Her ears, now trained to be alert to anything threatening, deceived her. To her troubled and suspicious mind, the sound was first interpreted as a high-pitched moan. A threat. Another unknown. She stopped her packing, hurriedly done and nearly half through, since she was determined to be out of Sutters Hamlet long before nightfall. She shivered, wondering what terror the merciless mountain would try to thrust on her in daylight … and listened for the sound again. It came again so faint that she found herself leaning forward trying better to hear.

She was reminded of a night spent with a lover on the rocky New England coast, and an observation that had remained with her. A light, set on a dark sea, could not be gauged for distance. It could be a strong light far away or a weak one close by. The sound was the same as it barely pierced the silence. Were it close by, and she could not determine that it wasn't, it could be coming from the front bedroom which held the painting of the night artist.

Troubled visions of the three figures on the canvas coming to life raced through her mind. Normally, such a thought would come only during dreams and be deemed ridiculous. But now she would rule out nothing.

Only as the noise grew, its pitch rising and falling, moaning then shrieking, did her fears subside and turn into curiosity. Finally it was the drone of a car fighting its way up the mountain to her cabin. She could laugh at herself and the wild imagination the mountain had given her.

In the time since she had last taken her Maverick down the mountain, the trail had grown over. She knew that whoever it was, was merciless to their car, pushing it through undergrowth that would leave it striped with scratches. Who could it be? She dropped an armload of clothes in a bundle on her bed and went to the front door to look out. The sound was louder now, as she even heard the scrape of metal as the bottom of the car dragged across a rock. When finally the combination blue and metallic nose emerged from the trees and a woolly blond-headed face peered at her from behind the windshield, she recognized Ted, last seen in New York the day before she left for Sutters Hamlet.

Joanna waved as she walked to meet the car.

"What in hell are you doing here?" she asked as she stepped up to the car door.

Ted flashed his blue-eyes and Nordic smile through the open window. "I was in the neighborhood and thought I'd drop by," he grinned.

"You lie!" She reached down and planted a kiss, and felt his lips push hard into her own. "It's a conspiracy! I'm getting ready to leave in a few hours and you drive up."

"Don't I get asked out?" he asked grinning, pushing open the door and emerging from the car. "You're leaving, you say?"

"Going to Asheville for a couple of days for art supplies," she lied. "But that can wait."

Joanna's emotions were mixed. She was glad to see Ted. But after having driven so far, she knew he intended to stay several days, and she didn't want to spend another night on the mountain.

He was slamming the car door, and in one step was before her and swept her into his arms. She didn't resist. She no longer loved him, but she knew he had never stopped loving her. She knew he was one she could trust, if not love, and in his arms she felt safe. She embraced him warmly, with relief, and knew that he would take her warmth as a sign of renewed affection and not the clinging onto the security blanket that it was. She let him kiss her again, this time passionately, and felt her lips quaver in doubt, knowing that this was another sign he would misinterpret. He crushed her loins into his own as he had done so often in the past, and she felt his passion being transferred into her and spreading throughout her body. Her doubts were gone and replaced not by love but by lust borne from abstinence. She felt a hand slide under her pullover and cup one of her breasts, and when he led her gently into the cabin she did not resist.

They made love on her bed, shoving the pile of clothes aside, and when it was over she was quietly thinking of last summer and the peace and solitude they had found here. It was as though it had returned. She was now more relaxed, content and unafraid in Ted's presence. She had released her pent-up emotions on his body, and it seemed that his thrusts had driven the fear from her. When they made love a second time it was better still, and as she again lay quietly watching the shadows of pine branches dance against the far wall, she did so without fear. Ted's hand resting on her bare belly, and occasionally creeping into her private parts, was like a shield placed between her and fear.

"Why did you come?" she finally asked.

He rolled to his side and raised up on one elbow, propping his head in his open palm. He watched her breasts rise and fall as she breathed, seemingly mesmerized by their movement.

"They're beautiful," he said. "You have a perfect body." '

She couldn't keep the grin off her face. "How many times have you told me that? A hundred?"

"Not enough."

"Why did you come?"

"For this." With his eyes he swept her body. "Hoping that this would happen." He fell silent for several moments. "And because I was worried. I've been uneasy about you lately. I can't explain it. It's just a strange feeling I had."

Her mind was alert to the implications. "What sort of strange feeling?" she prodded.

He gave one shoulder a half shrug. "I don't know. I just felt that you may be in some sort of danger all alone here in this cabin. I tried not to let it bother me, but I remember how you always used to tell me to let my inner self speak. I let it speak, and the feeling was so strong that I had to come and see if you were all right."

The tone of his voice dropped to a confessional pitch he used when wanting to give the impression of honesty. "But I guess a lot of that worry wasn't worry so much as it was that I missed you. I still love you, you know."

"I know."

"I want us to be more than just friends."

Joanna looked affectionately into his blue eyes. She had always admired his compassion and honesty. Few men she had known could be as sensitive as Ted, yet for all the warmth she felt for him, she knew that she did not feel love. Not the deep, all-encompassing love of which she knew she was capable.

"Perhaps we are more than just friends, Ted," she said, exposing her own mixed feelings.

"And what is that supposed to mean?" he asked in mock seriousness.

The question caught her off-guard, unprepared. Her reply had been intended as a pacification, but when pressed for its meaning she wasn't sure herself what she had meant, if it had any meaning at all.

"Nothing, I guess," she said flustered, feeling very naked now under his gaze. She felt his eyes piercing her, questioning. She instinctively knew what he had hoped to hear, the confession of love that she had once made him but had later withdrawn. "I guess what I meant was that we're more than just casual friends. I don't sleep around with just casual friends."

She saw one side of his face cock upward in a half smile. "I suppose I should know better than to try to pin you down," he said. "It can't be done."

It was a joke between them. An old joke from a year ago when they were close. He had tried to understand both sides of her, the dual personality that allowed her to see clearly both sides of a situation. Because she could see the right in one side, then turn around and see equal right in an opposing viewpoint, and therefore refuse to take a stand and say that either position was right, he had so often jokingly called her the world's greatest fence straddler. She could never convince him that when she refused to take a stand it wasn't because she couldn't make up her mind, but because she saw the validity in both sides, and would not say that one partial truth was more right than another partial truth.

To Joanna, the world was rarely black or white, as viewed by so many others, but instead was composed of many shades of gray. Ted had called her an elusive cat, but she knew he was wrong. It was not that she wanted to be elusive, but that the sign of Leo made her question everything. And that questioning brought with it a wider vision of truth than seen by many others who, eager to take a stand, looked only for the black or white side of an issue.

She could see the disappointment in his eyes as they watched her face, occasionally shifting to her breasts. Her willingness to undress for him had perhaps been misinterpreted. The security blanket that even their lovemaking had been to her had been misunderstood, and she could see that he was now suffering from a sudden shattering hope. She could remember many times in the past when Ted's understanding had helped her through some personal turmoil, and she now wished to help him. Perhaps her consent to lovemaking had been ill-advised, but it was over now. She could not erase the past.

"I'm glad you're here," she said, trying to ease his pain. She saw some of his hurt leave, and she smiled and knew that she really was glad he was there. "Will you be staying long?"

"I can stay a week," he replied guardedly.

"That'll be nice," she said. "Maybe we can have last year all over again, a rerun, if you will."

The decision had been made for her. She would not leave the mountain immediately – not until Ted left. The knowledge that she would spend at least another week on the mountain was met somewhat fearfully, yet with the confidence of knowing that at least for now she would not be alone.

The morning came to life like a newborn child: stormy and fresh, dew heavily coating the grass, a threat of rain that failed to materialize, instead disappearing by midmorning. They were out of bed shortly after first light, far earlier than Joanna had risen while in the cabin alone. She could see the pattern of last year repeating itself. With Ted there, it was as though the morning was her first on the mountain. She burst out of bed in excitement, looking forward to their ramblings about the mountain. It was only on special mornings that she could rise quite so early, and this morning was delightfully special. She found a joy in the day that she had forgotten existed. Only once did her confidence falter, and she found herself thinking about the night artist. With Ted frying eggs on the wood burner, in the kitchen, the sound and country aroma of sizzling bacon in the skillet, she slipped into the front bedroom to look at the picture. With relief, she found that the night artist had rested during the night. Nothing new had been added. The three nude figures still held their poses, and with a shudder, she returned to Ted and the safety of the kitchen.

He glanced up from the breakfast that he was piling onto two plates.

"What's the matter?"

"What do you mean?" she replied startled.

"You look pale. You didn't see a ghost, did you?" He laughed at his own childlike joke, then planted a kiss on her colorless cheek. "And you're cold, too. What's the matter?" He was still joking, unaware of the picture and its predictable effect on her.

"Oh, I guess I'm just not accustomed to getting up so early," she lied. "I come to life after breakfast."

After breakfast, as she knew he would, Ted wanted to forage about the mountain near the cabin, even though the morning still threatened rain. Their mutual respect for the outdoors was one thing that had drawn them together in the first place and later held them together as they made weekend trips to the outback of upstate New York. That same joy in companionship was again present, and at times Joanna found herself forgetting that she had avowed she no longer loved him.

For two days they spent every daylight hour hiking, a favorite pastime of Ted's, and eating their packed lunch by a brook a mile from the cabin. They made love on the shady edge of the sun-drenched meadow while the flock of crows circled above pinpointing them for all who cared to take notice.

In the evenings, they returned to the cabin to spend a quiet night talking, sitting Indian-style in the middle of the living room floor. Or they would bring two chairs into the clearing out front and sit under the stars talking about the past and sometimes the future. Joanna found that once again they were drawing closer to one another, becoming emotionally attached as she had thought could never again happen between them. From their talks and now frequent lovemaking, Joanna found Ted reverting to his self-assured self. Assured, she supposed, of his position in her life. The thought was not so unsettling as it had been only a few days before. But even so, she was still uncertain if she was again in love with him, or if he was still little more than a security blanket.

She enjoyed the evenings most. Returning to the cabin after a day's exhausting climb over the mountain seemed a stimulant to her mind. Never were they at a loss for interesting topics to discuss, and on the occasions when a lull did develop, the bed was close by. At first she thought that she simply enjoyed the sex and companionship. It was almost by accident that she realized that her evenings were now spent without fear. She hadn't thought of the night artist or the witches since their first morning when she sneaked a look at the painting. Somehow it was no longer important. With Ted always present, there was no danger, nothing to fear. During one of their first evenings she considered telling him about the witches, but decided that would spoil their week together. Anyway, she would be leaving soon after Ted, and the witches of Sutters Hamlet and the mysterious night artist would be only memories from her past.

Halfway through the week, her serenity was abruptly ended.

It was another early morning. As was his habit, Ted had commandeered the kitchen. Joanna had long ago accepted a reverse male-female role, acknowledging Ted's culinary superiority, and staying clear of the kitchen while a meal was being prepared unless she was asked to help. She had never objected to this reversal, since she knew that she was far from a perfect cook. Her few attempts at originality had ended in disaster. Any meal that could he easily burnt was. It was her distaste for scorched meals that drove her to a high rate of consumption of canned goods. This she augmented with the simplest preparation of meat or fresh vegetables. To have Ted, a master in the kitchen, prepare the meals was a delight.

They had finished breakfast and were debating how to spend the day when a call came from the front of the cabin.

"Joanna!"

Recognizing Peter's voice, she pushed away from the table and, followed by Ted, entered the living room. Through the front door, opened earlier to let in the morning sun, she saw Peter standing outside. He was hardly more than a dark silhouette with the sun directly behind him reflecting off the dew, the glare nearly blinding Joanna as she approached him.

"Come on in," she said uneasily, uncertain as to how Ted and Peter would react to each other. Ted was in love with her, and she knew Peter was attracted to her, so she assumed that alone would make the two men rivals.

Peter stepped inside out of the glare and was a three-dimensional person again. He saw Ted and stopped in midstride. He started to speak and his jaw dropped open, gawking. Ted, more sophisticated, flashed a friendly smile.

Trying to save the situation, Joanna introduced them.

"This is Ted, a friend of mine from New York. He had a premonition that something was wrong and drove down to see if I was all right."

She saw Peter's face relax slightly, then he forced a smile.

"And this is Peter," she said, as Ted extended his hand.

"Glad to meet you," Ted said. "Joanna told me that you've been looking after her." Again he flashed his Nordic smile, and as designed, it eased the tension. "We've just had breakfast. Would you care for any?"

"No thanks," Peter replied. "I just dropped by to see Joanna for a few minutes."

"Fine," Ted said, moving past him toward the door. "Why don't you two visit while I bring the rest of my things in out of the car?"

Joanna breathed in relief as she saw Peter nearly back to normal, the accusation in his eyes now gone. Ted's brilliant lie had worked. She didn't want to alienate Peter, and Ted, sensing that, had performed beautifully. After being here for half a week, she knew that he had nothing in his car to bring in.

She led Peter outside, to the side of the cabin away from Ted's car, and positioned herself so that he had his back to the cabin and could not see that Ted returned empty-handed. She was the one surprised when, over Peter's shoulder she saw Ted return to the cabin carrying an overnight bag.

"Ted is the one that helped me rent this place," Joanna said breaking the silence. "Then he started getting premonitions that something was wrong and drove down to check on me."

"Does he know about the witches?" Peter asked, his interest aroused at mention of the premonitions.

Joanna shook her head. "I haven't told him anything. If he knew what's been happening, he would insist that I leave today."

"You probably should."

"I am leaving. Soon. When Ted leaves." She shrugged despondently. "It's just got to be too much, Peter. I can't take it anymore."

"Has something else happened?"

"Yes."

"What?"

"Oh, it doesn't matter," she said, trying to remember if she had told him about the night artist. "It's just all getting to me, so I've decided to leave."

"I'm glad," Peter said. "I'll miss you, but I think you should go."

She detected an urgency in his voice that had never before existed.

"Why? What's the matter?"

"The people in town are getting all stirred up. There's all sorts of rumors going around, and you don't know what to believe. At least a dozen people claim to have seen the witches in the past few nights. All at once several animals have been reported missing.

"Some of the old folks say this is the way it used to be when the witches were preparing for an important ceremony ... before Isadora died. Everybody in town is frightened, and there's talk of trying to stop the witches before they get a foothold again."

There was a thud behind him, and Peter turned and watched Ted close his car. After he disappeared into the cabin, he returned to Joanna.

"With the old-timers saying it looks like they're preparing for a ceremony of some sort, everybody started wondering what sort of ceremony. Somehow, the rumor got started that they're getting ready to crown a new high priestess."

The words stopped Joanna cold. He didn't have to explain. She knew what the rumor was supposed to mean. With a shudder, she remembered the night artist's painting. The ghostly figures dancing nude around the fire, and an image of herself kneeling before the flat rock − an altar! She knew! Suddenly, she understood the full implication of the painting! It was a picture of her being accepted . . . initiated . . . into the coven, being crowned high priestess. With each swirl of paint on the canvas, the night artist clarified her future. Showed her, visually, the coven's intent.

As the sight of herself on the night artist's canvas had been the final factor in her decision to leave, it was again the canvas that told her that all the rumors the mountain whispered were not rumors at all, but truths. The coven wanted her. She no longer doubted. She no longer wondered why. They wanted her. They thought she was Isadora's daughter, and they wanted her.

She believed Peter had been right. Any woman who had turned up at this point in time would have been selected by the coven as the daughter of their slain priestess. It was her timing that had cast her into this starring role, and nothing more.

Trying to hide her newfound fear, and able to do so with the knowledge she would leave the mountain before the night artist's prophecy had time to come true, she returned her attention to Peter.

"How did the rumor get started?"

"Who knows?" Peter shrugged. "Just gossip, probably. But those people in town are in such a high-pitched state they'll believe anything. They think the witches started the rumor themselves."

"Do you?"

"Like I said, I think the rumor was started by some frightened townspeople. Unless . . ." He paused and lifted his eyes to meet hers. "If a member of the coven started the rumor, it could be another way of trying to get at you."

"But how!"

"By turning everyone against you so you have no one to turn to."

"Wait a minute!" she said adamantly. "The last time you were here, you didn't even believe in the witches."

"I said there may be a group calling themselves a coven of witches, but that they don't have any sort of power. Their only weapon is fear. If they really are trying to make you their priestess, can't you see what might be happening? They couldn't bring you into their circle by frightening you. So they may be trying to drive you in by turning everyone else against you."

"It doesn't make sense," she said. "If they really want me, why would they let the whole town know it? Particularly in light of what happened to the coven after Isadora was killed."

Peter shrugged, admitting defeat. "Some of the mountains around here are pretty isolated. Maybe they think you can hide. Or maybe they don't care what happens to you. I don't know!" The words burst from him. "But I think it's a good thing you're leaving. And I don't think you ought to go into town anymore. Just drive through it as fast as you can and keep going."

"You think the townspeople might harm me, don't you?"

"They killed Isadora. And some of them are talking about trying to stop the witches now. If they believe the coven is about to crown a new high priestess, and they think you're Isadora's daughter, who knows what might happen?"

His words had an ominous ring to them. They held warning of another threat, a threat she had seen but not fully recognized. Not only were the witches of Sutters Hamlet to be feared, but also the ordinary townspeople. She was glad she had resolved to leave, that the decision was made. She only regretted the lost year, the year that now seemed so out of reach. In searching for an isolated place, she had become the one isolated. She had chosen too well in selecting a place out of touch with civilization. If it were true that civilization devoured all in its path, it seemed equally true that the uncivilized would devour the civilized ... if it could.

She sensed Peter looking at her, and it drew her back from her thoughts and to the situation at hand.

"You think I'm in danger from more than just the witches, don't you?"

Peter released a deep breath, dramatic in its despair.

"Yes, I do," he said emphatically. "I think your life's in danger."

"It's not," she said, startling herself.

"How do you know?"

She could see the surprise in his eyes, the shock of hearing her quietly deny danger after she had just admitted she planned to leave the mountain out of fear. After his own vivid warning of the rumored witches' ceremony.

She forced a smile. "I'm leaving, aren't I?"

"But maybe not soon enough," he said. "If there's anything to the rumor about their crowning a high priestess, you have to be gone before Saturday night."

She wrinkled her forehead inquisitively.

"Why Saturday night?" she asked confused.

"That's Midsummer Night."

"Midsummer Night?" She tried to pull from her memory where she had heard mention of Midsummer Night recently. It was only a fuzzy memory, and the riddle was finally solved when Peter explained.

"Midsummer Night is sort of New Year's Eve for the witches. Supposedly, for all witches. Legend has it that they always hold important ceremonies on that night."

Now she remembered Hanover's story.

"And the people around here still hold lookouts for the witches on Midsummer Night to keep them from stealing livestock, don't they?" Joanna asked.

Peter nodded. "If they're going to crown a new high priestess, it'll be then. I'm not as worried, about what the witches might do on Saturday as what the people might do to you, since most of them think you're Isadora's daughter."

"I'll be gone by then," she said assuredly. "Ted's leaving Saturday morning I think, and I'll leave then too."

Peter seemed to breathe easier. "I'll be sorry to see you go," he said regretfully. "I know how bad you wanted to spend a year here painting."

"Can't be helped, I guess." Her mind moved to the few paintings she had completed, only a fraction of what she had hoped to do. She regretfully pictured each one, wishing there could have been more.

Their talk was ended when Ted emerged from the cabin again and, in long strides, approached them.

"Am I butting in?" he asked, plopping himself down on the ground.

Peter grinned, appearing not so ill at ease around Ted as he had been a few moments earlier. "No. I was just bringing Joanna the latest news from town."

He winked openly at Joanna, and she smiled in return. She knew he would make no mention of the witches and the new warning he had brought. Independence was her nature, and she still saw no need in involving Ted. She realized that her views might have been different had he arrived before she decided to leave. As long as Ted was in the cabin with her, she knew she was safe. The witches would not visit her; the townspeople would not bother her. Irritated at first at Ted's inopportune arrival, she was now glad that he had come. As she had hoped, his visit had become a repeat of last summer. It was like a holiday before having to return to New York.

Suddenly, Peter was saying good-bye. He shook Ted's hand, then waved casually to Joanna, promising to visit her again soon. His eyes penetrated deeply, saying their final farewell. But outwardly he kept her secret, treating it as only a temporary parting, and sparing her the need of explaining to Ted beforehand why she would leave with him when he returned to New York. She watched Peter's back disappear into the forest. She wanted to call out to him, to tell him she appreciated his friendship, but she remained silent.

His parting saddened her. She descended into her blue depths of moodiness, and Ted, sensing her changed mood, spent a low-key day lazing about the cabin, making no suggestion that they roam the mountain as she knew he had planned. Her foul mood lasted most of the day. By evening she was not feeling so down and eagerly joined into a discussion that developed from one of Ted's chance remarks. When they closed the cabin doors to go to bed, she was eager to fall into his reassuring arms and be told she was loved. Afterwards, she fell into an easy sleep, her hand held protectively in his.

In the morning she awoke tired. Ted's tossing beside her as he emerged from sleep in stages woke her earlier than she normally would have. When she finally forced her sleepy eyes apart, Ted was on his side looking at her.

"Good morning," he said.

She answered with a smile, and forced a sleepy acknowledgement from her lips.

"Where were you last night?" he asked, fully awake.

Still partly asleep she mumbled a muffled, "Right here."

"You got up in the middle of the night and stayed away for ages. I thought you must have fallen in the toilet."

"I didn't get up," she said defensively, his accusation shaking her awake.

"I was pretty sleepy, but I didn't dream it," he replied. "You woke me when you got out of bed. I think I fell asleep a couple of times before you came back, but I know you were gone quite a while."

"I didn't even get up to go to the bathroom," she objected, her voice stilted from his accusation.

"Then you must walk in your sleep."

"I do not!"

"Well, you went somewhere," he declared.

"Well, goddamn! What's the matter with you this morning? You sound like an old woman with the pip!"

Angrily she threw the covers back, sprang out of bed, grabbed her clothes thrown across a chair, and stalked out of the bedroom to dress. Five minutes later Ted emerged, fully clothed, and like a tribal ritual went straight to the kitchen to begin breakfast. He made no more mention of her absence, apparently convinced that to question her further would serve no purpose, since she obviously had no recollection of the incident.

After she was out of reach of his persistent questions that she had no answer for, her anger quickly left. But her curiosity did not, nor did her concern for what might have happened during her absence from bed. Too much had occurred in the cabin for her to call Ted a liar. With an uneasiness, she realized that perhaps she was not as safe in Ted's presence as she had thought. Something had happened last night. But what? It was a slight consolation to realize that she had only one more day in the cabin. Tomorrow was Friday. Then Saturday, when Ted left, she would pack and leave with him.

She apologized for her burst of temper, hoping to patch up the day that was already cut and bleeding.

With their relationship more normal than the day before, her moodiness from Peter's speculations and farewell gone with the morning sun, Ted proposed they spend the day roaming the mountain. They chose a new direction of exploration, directly behind the cabin, an area Joanna had left largely unexplored in previous trips. Packing a picnic lunch, they set out shortly after breakfast, keeping to the cabin's same approximate elevation on the mountainside.

As was their custom when exploring the mountain together, they walked aimlessly, going wherever the mountain seemed to lead them. Occasionally, when part of nature's picture book caught her attention, Joanna longed for her sketch pad. But it was back in the cabin, in the front bedroom with her other painting equipment, all untouched during Ted's visit. The door into the room had not been opened since their first morning when she sneaked a peek at the night artist's painting and later that same day when she showed Ted the paintings she had completed, careful to divert his attention from the night artist's work. As they ambled about the mountain, the scenes passed her by, their very abundance pricking her side like a thorn, reminding her of her own forgetfulness, and of the fact that her year on the mountain, cut back to only a few short weeks, was nearly up.

"I'm getting hungry," Ted said, a full hour before noon. "Must be the fresh air and exercise."

He snatched the paper bag filled with sandwiches from her clutched fist.

"What do we have for lunch?" He peered inside, wrinkled his nose questioningly, then looked at her, waiting for an answer. Gallantly, he had suggested that she pack their lunch, pointing out that he always did the cooking and was entitled to a change. She accepted his attempt at humor good-naturedly, though she knew what he actually meant was that no one, not even she, could foul up fixing sandwiches

"Sliced ham and cheese on stale bread."

"How stale?" he asked, poking a finger at one of the sandwiches in the bag.

"Stale stale."

He wrinkled his nose again. "Joanna," he said reproachfully.

"Well, you were the last one in town," she accused. "You should have remembered the hard bread we had last year. It's not so easy to go all the way down there just for a fresh loaf of bread."

She turned her back on him and started to walk away.

"Well let's eat anyway," he said resignedly. "I'm starving."

"We have to find a place." She tossed the words back over her shoulder.

He caught up with her in half a dozen giant strides and fell in step beside her. They walked in silence for half a minute, then he veered off, dragging her along by the arm. "Over there," he said, pointing to a boulder standing alone in the middle of a small clearing.

They made a table of the rock's flat surface, setting out their food and quart thermos of iced water and sat on the boulder's edge. Ted made another remark about the stale bread, saw that Joanna was not particularly amused, so dropped the subject and ate his sandwiches without further complaint.

Joanna noticed him looking around the clearing, craning his neck between bites as he peered first one way, then another. She turned to follow his wandering gaze when it seemed to settle on something behind her, but she saw nothing, only the wall of trees at the edge of the clearing.

"What on earth are you looking at?" she finally asked when she could find nothing worthy of such notice.

He returned his attention to her.

"At first I couldn't figure out what this place was," he said, some undercurrent in his voice making her curious, yet uneasy. "This is your clearing, isn't it?"

"My clearing?" There was no attempt to mask her bewilderment.

"The clearing in your painting," he said with certainty.

A nauseating feeling crept into the pit of her stomach. She looked around her, the clearing suddenly somewhat familiar, yet there was no immediate recognition. No recognition because she knew, without doubt, that she had never before been on this part of the mountain, never before seen the clearing. Yet there was something about it, some uncommon likeness to something she had seen.

"Which painting?" But she knew.

"The weird one that you seem intent on keeping hidden."

Her eyes looked blankly into his face.

"The one with you kneeling naked by this rock," he said, tapping the empty lunch bag sitting between them. The crackling of the paper as he tapped the bag, like sharp, staccato shots, drove his message permanently into her brain. "And those two nude figures dancing around you. What in hell is that picture supposed to represent?" he asked good-naturedly, unaware of the blow she had just been dealt.

She realized, somewhat sickeningly, that this was the clearing in the night artist's painting. Though the painting was a night scene, and the trees behind her were in deep shadow in the picture, she could see that they were one and the same. Without replying she strode halfway across the clearing, slightly down the mountain to the artist's vantage point, then turned and looked back upon the rock. Ted sat on the rock watching her, like a solitary sentinel standing guard over the scene. A gust of wind caught the paper bag and blew it away, but Ted made no attempt to catch it, so intently was he watching Joanna.

From twenty feet away she looked at the rock and knew that there could be no mistake. It was the same rock, the same clearing. She remembered Peter's warning of the imminent ceremony, and with a shudder she knew that this was where it was supposed to take place. She was standing in the clearing where the witches intended to crown her their high priestess.

"Are you all right?"

The words, hardly reached her ears, coming as though from a great distance and unable to penetrate her trancelike state. Suddenly she was being shaken. Something grabbed her roughly by the shoulders and shook her until she thought her head would be jerked off. She pulled away and looked into Ted's frightened eyes.

"What in hell's going on around here!" he demanded.

She shook her head, trying to shake away the feeling.

"I'm all right," she said unconvincingly. "It was just such a shock finding this clearing when I thought it was just a place I made up in my mind."

She lied and she hated herself for it. Inside, something was crying out to her, telling her to tell Ted about the witches. Telling her to run, to collect her belongings, and leave the mountain today. It was her inner voice that had so often guided her. But now there was another, a voice, just as strong counteracting every warning the first voice issued. Reassuringly, it told her that she was in no danger, that she should remain silent and not involve Ted.

The feeling of being torn from within, one part of her crying out in terror to leave and the other convincing her to stay, reminded her of the morning she awoke covered in blood and with no memory of the previous days. She had wanted to leave then. But something would not let her. Something inside her had seemed determined that morning to have her remain. It seemed to hold her there, determined not to lose its grip on her. She had questioned this mood as being unlike herself, but had not feared it. She had put it down to her own leonine stubbornness, her catlike refusal to allow herself to be pushed about.

Looking at the real-life scene of the night artist's painting, which grew mysteriously in the dark of Isadora's cabin, she was once again torn from within. Something inside her told her that her only safety existed away from Sutters Hamlet, but another side of her laughed at the notion. It told her that she would be leaving Saturday morning with Ted, that she would be safe then, and there was no point in getting panicky.

She found herself once again being persuaded by the second voice, convinced that Saturday was soon enough, that she need not tell Ted and spoil their one remaining day together. But even so, fleetingly, a dark question was thrown in by the first voice, like a handful of sand thrown into the delicate gears of a fine watch. The white flecks at her door that morning. Could the witches have cast a spell on her? Could the second reassuring voice be coming from the witches? But Saturday was soon enough.

"I'm all right," she repeated.

"Are you sure?" He put his arm around her, and she felt comforted by the security he offered.

She nodded, her head jerking awkwardly, yet affirmatively. "Yes."

"You looked like you'd seen a ghost," he said, leading her gently back to the boulder to finish their lunch.

"I did, in a way," she said. Stronger than ever was her urge to confess to Ted the events that had transpired at her cabin, but the consoling voice from within told her that it was the one who had warned her of Betty Susan Henderson's death, and that it would certainly warn her of any danger to herself. She believed it. It had always been truthful in the past.

The remainder of the day passed sluggishly for Joanna. The shock of stumbling onto the night artist's scene, a possibility she had never even considered, had a telling affect on her mood. Even Ted, normally considerate of her various whims, complained of her sudden tendency toward moodiness the past two days. When they returned to the cabin in late afternoon, she was glad to be home, having hardly spoken, except in reply to a direct question, since stumbling onto the clearing.

She suggested that she fix supper, though she did so only to keep her mind occupied. Ted, who normally would have vetoed the idea, consented. Joanna noted with relief, since she was in no mood for communication, that Ted seemed withdrawn. Though somewhat remorsefully, she knew that his darkening mood was a direct reflection of her own, that since Peter's visit the day before and her subsequent sulking, Ted's usual good humor had deteriorated. Their relationship was strained, and he must be wondering why.

As she prepared their meal, he left her alone in the kitchen, another uncharacteristic move, since like a typical Cancerian he was normally beside her whenever possible. All was quiet in the house as she cooked. She could not hear him moving about, and she wondered why. After she dished out the meal out of a can, tasteless and nearly odorless, compared to Ted's more exotic creations, she started to call him to the table, but instead stepped into the living room. He wasn't there.

The door to the front bedroom was cracked open, a yellow shaft of flickering lantern light escaping and cutting into the twilight of the unlit living room. She knew he was in there, knew he was looking at the painting, and immediately she was angry. Like a wave washing over the beach sands, the anger swept over her body, surprising her by its very fierceness. Behind her back, or so it seemed to her, Ted had sneaked a look at the night artist's painting, a picture that he had even acknowledged knowing that she didn't want him to see. She didn't know why it should be so important to her, but suddenly it was. Through embarrassment, fear or whatever, she felt compelled to keep it from prying eyes.

Just as she started for the door, her eyes ablaze, it opened and Ted stepped out.

"What in hell do you think you're doing!" she screamed, the ferociousness a surprise to them both. The cabin walls seemed to tremble from her blast.

Stunned, Ted stopped abruptly. He reeled backward, nearly stepping back through the door. Fear flickered through his eyes, instantly disappeared and was replaced by disbelief. His jaw dropped open, but he remained speechless.

"I said, what in hell do you think you're doing in there!"

"I just wanted to have another look at the picture," he said uncertainly.

"'Another look'." Just how many times have you sneaked in there like that?" she demanded.

"I didn't sneak in, Joanna! I walked in quite openly."

"Shit!"

"What's wrong with you?" he asked, anger creeping into his voice.

"You, by God! I don't like people sneaking around my house!"

He took a menacing step toward her. "You're sick!" he said vehemently. "You've gone off your Goddamn rocker! You walk in your sleep, you paint sick pictures, and go crazy when someone looks at it, and you pretend you've never seen the scene in the picture before!"

She stormed past him and slammed the door shut.

"Don't ever go in there again!"

He looked at her quizzically, both love and bewilderment clearly on his face. Without a word he turned and walked into the kitchen. She heard his fork strike the plate a metallic click as he began to eat. It was over. As quickly as the anger had come, it was gone. Already she was sorry for her outburst, and puzzled.

She joined him at the table, and tried to eat but found that she wasn't hungry.' His eating was mechanical, robot like bites shoved in, one after another. His eyes never wandered to her. Repentantly, she reached for his hand. She felt his muscles grow taut, repulsing her overture. She withdrew her hand and they finished the meal and most of the night in silence.

There was no lovemaking that night, though Joanna wanted it. Not so much from physical need as from wanting to put their relationship back on the even keel the past two days had destroyed. But as soon as he fell into bed, Ted turned away, and in a few minutes his deep breathing indicated that he was asleep.

She faced the night alone awake for an hour listening to the night sounds of the mountain. Some pine branches scraped the bedroom window when an occasional gust of wind tossed them about. Not far away an owl hooted, its cry so soft that, had she not known better, she would have sworn it was halfway down the mountain.

Then she heard the cry of the fox and it made her shiver. She imagined Isadora in the moments before her death, her fingernails growing into claws before the terrified eyes of her murderers. She lay in the dark thinking, remembering all she had learned from the mountain, and she wondered if it were really possible that Isadora and her ancestors could turn themselves into foxes? Without her willing it, her mind went from the past into the future. If she and her ancestors could, then Isadora's daughter should be able to change into a fox, too. She shoved the subject from her uneasy mind. But she could not push aside the fact that she was in Isadora's cabin.

Sometimes it even seemed that she could sense Isadora's maternal presence. Just a feeling, an uncanny feeling that she could not explain. Yet not uncomfortable, not once she had accepted it. Frightened at first at learning this was Isadora's cabin, she was no longer. She was frightened of the witches, of the events they had caused to happen. She was frightened of the picture that grew on the other side of her bedroom wall. But she realized, with Ted's comforting presence sleeping at her side, that she was not frightened of Isadora. Perhaps because she knew the dead could do her no harm.

She didn't know when her consciousness left her and she fell asleep. She didn't know because when her conscious thought ceased, her dreams began. She was thinking of Isadora, pitying her the way she had died. And so young. She was drowsy and drifted into a fitful sleep, awakened for a few moments wondering if she had actually slept. Then again into her half-sleep, her mind still alert, she thought, but not certain if she were awake or just dreaming that she was. Then the witches were there. Twelve of them. She counted them. Black robed and hooded they stood in a circle around her bed. She dreamed they did. They were not menacing. They were nothing. Just there.

One of them spoke. A woman's voice. The same voice she had driven way with her gun.

"We will visit you no more."

She could feel Ted's lifeless body beside her. She dreamed that she felt him breathe, his chest expanding against her as he inhaled.

"When you next see us, it will be because you seek us out."

She dreamed that the fox barked three times beneath her window.

Then they were gone. It was morning and she was awake. She remembered the dream, somewhat uneasy at its clarity. Ted was already up. She heard him moving about the kitchen.

She got up and dressed, then went into the kitchen, expecting to see Ted preparing breakfast. But the stove and table were bare. Ted stood by the wash pan, wiping dry a saucepan in his hand. A pile of freshly washed dishes were stacked on the cabinet beside him.

She quickly surveyed the situation, remembered that there were few unwashed dishes left over from the night before, and realized that he had already had breakfast. She had expected to find him preparing breakfast for them both, a habit she had grown to expect from Ted. Her stomach, more than the rest of her, complained.

"I guess it's every man for himself this morning." She had intended to say it lightly. To say something that he would laugh at. But when the words emerged, she heard them come from her with a cutting edge. Ted looked at her with resignation, as though he had expected to find her in another foul mood.

"I don't know why I said that. I didn't mean for it to sound that way," she said. But she knew the damage was done. It must seem as though she were trying to continue her flare-up of the night before. "It's just that I heard you in here and thought you were fixing breakfast," she continued ineffectually.

"It's a bit late for breakfast," he said curtly. He arrogantly turned his back and placed the clean saucepan on the cabinet with the other dishes. "I ate two hours ago when it seemed that you were going to spend the day in bed. It's nearly noon."

Her mouth dropped open, aghast. Disbelieving, she stepped back into the living room so she could see the clock sitting by her bed. Eleven o'clock!

"Ted, I'm sorry! I didn't know it was so late."

"Evidently." He looked uncaringly at her. "Do you want breakfast?"

Relieved, and in her tenderest voice, she gasped, "Yes, if you don't mind."

"I don't mind," he said, throwing down the dish towel he had used to dry the saucepan. "The kitchen's yours."

He shoved past her into the living room, clearly leaving her to do as she pleased. She put two pieces of hard bread on the wood burner and had toast for breakfast. She couldn't blame Ted for his actions. It seemed that everything she said or did managed to come out wrong. From his vantage point, she could see that it must seem that she was purposely trying to find fault and argue. But she wasn't. She was sometimes as surprised as he must be at her outbursts. She didn't plan them, they just happened. Out of control, she lost her temper, or spoke with an acid voice, and she didn't even know why. As she considered her mental state over two pieces of burnt toast, it was as big a mystery to her as was her presence on the mountain. Both actions were out of character.

Yet another step out of character was that she realized this and was not unduly concerned. She realized, but did not act. Knew, but was unconcerned. Only half of her was frightened at what was happening. The first voice was frightened. The other half was not. The second voice said that all was as it should be. Any warning that the first voice offered, the second overruled. Whenever she thought she realized what was happening, the second voice convinced her otherwise. She guessed the truth, but was powerless to fight it. Because to fight it, she must overcome herself.

For the second time on the mountain she thought of Pogo's remark: "We have found the enemy, and they are us." But she wondered which side of her was the enemy? Which side was real? Was the side that was frightened the real Joanna? Or was it the other side, the side that seemed unconcerned with the witches? What was that side? Or who? Why was one side of her not frightened by the barking of the fox, and the other side terrified?

One thing she did know. She knew which side was stronger. She did not know why. But in the back of her mind, a suspicion was beginning to grow, like the picture in the other room.

After breakfast she found Ted resting peacefully in the grass in front of the cabin. His eyes were closed to the fluffy white clouds floating silently past overhead. They remained closed when she dropped into the grass beside him. A crusty silence set in, and she knew that he had no intention of breaking it.

Gathering her courage with a deep breath, she finally spoke. "We're not doing too good, are we?"

His eyelids flickered, and beneath their surface she saw his eyes move about, rolling as she had read they did when a person dreams. She wondered if he were asleep, but before she spoke again his eyes cracked open and he looked at her through the slits, the sun making shadows of pine needles dance out of focus across his face.

He seemed to study her intently, making no effort to reply. His lips finally parted as though he were going to speak, but his words hung there silently, unspoken for a dozen seconds before their sounds finally emerged.

"Maybe I was wrong in coming here."

She bit her lip, trying to hold back the tears that suddenly wanted to rush into her eyes.

"No, you weren't wrong. I'm glad you came," she said honestly. "All this is my fault. Not yours."

He silently considered her reply.

"There's something wrong, isn't there?"

It was a challenge. Phrased as a question, yet a statement just the same. His way of saying he knew there was something out of place on the mountain. She flinched, quickly covered her surprise, and wondered if he had noticed.

"No, there's nothing wrong," she heard herself say, both lying and telling the truth at once. Satisfied with her evasion, yet sickeningly aware that it was just that.

"I had an odd dream last night," he said, closing his eyes again. "I dreamed that there were some people in the bedroom talking to you. It was just a dream, but it seemed so real and spooky that I can't get it off my mind."

This time she knew that, had he been looking, she could not have disguised the look on her face. No soothing second voice could have consoled her, nor erased the look of terror that gripped her. No amount of rationalization could have eliminated the suspicion that permanently embedded itself in her mind. And the suspicion grew until it was the full knowledge that the dream had been no dream at all. She wondered if he too had heard the fox bark three times beneath the window, but she didn't ask.

"That was an odd dream, don't you think?" he asked. He kept his eyes closed, as though he didn't care if she answered or not.

"Yes," she mumbled.

Several seconds passed in silence before he spoke again. When he finally did, he sat up and faced her, seeming not to notice her pallid face.

"I'm leaving for New York today," he stated.

"Today!" she gasped.

He nodded. "There's no point in trying to salvage something that can't be salvaged. We've gotten back to the same point we were last time. Always arguing. And without cause."

"Can't you stay the night?" she asked.

He shook his head, shaking off her hopes, her plans, her belief that Saturday was soon enough. "That's what I'd planned, but I don't see any point in it. Not now. I just want to get away."

"Please stay," she begged.

He looked at her with surprise, uncertain at the pleading in her voice. Then his eyes frosted over, and they were hard. There was no love or understanding in them, just a shield put there to protect himself from his own emotions.

"So you can go into one of your rages?" he said half mockingly. He shook his head. "No. I don't want any more of that, Joanna. You've always been like that, you know. Like there were two separate people inside you. One sweet and lovable, a girl I could love more than life itself. And the other with a heart like a shark."

She felt the corners of her eyes grow moist. Her lips trembled at the thought of being left alone again on the mountain. She started to blurt out an explanation, to tell him about the witches, but she found in his eyes no willingness to listen. They looked at her unflinchingly, void of compassion, crusted over for self-protection like the hard shell of the cancer crab. She knew Ted was emotionally vulnerable to her moods, and this was his way of protecting himself from what he must consider a heartless love.

"Then when will you be leaving?" she asked bravely.

"In a little while. I have to pack."

"You don't have much to pack."

"Is that an invitation to get started?"

"Yes," she said coldly, purposely, hoping that her tone would speed him along. She would not spend another night alone on the mountain, no matter how strong the voice. She had decided that before Ted came, and the knowledge that she would be alone again made her not so brave. As soon as Ted left, she would pack her belongings and follow.

Without another word, he pushed himself from the ground and disappeared into the cabin. Several moments later he emerged with an armload of clothes and tossed them in a heap into his car. He made several trips until his back seat was piled with his belongings. She watched from a distance as he made his last trip, then turned to face her again.

"See you in New York sometime," he called out.

She forced herself to cross the distance between them. She searched his eyes for any change, but there was none. They looked at her without caring.

She wanted to cry out and apologize, to relieve some of the pain she had caused him, but she dared not. If he were determined to leave today, she couldn't risk having him remain so late that she would have to stay the night.

"See you," she said.

He paused, as though to speak, then turned and climbed into his car and disappeared down the rutted trail that weaved its way down the mountain. She heard the whine of his engine long after he had disappeared. And when she heard it no longer she went inside to begin packing.

Mid-afternoon found her packed. Her remaining food was boxed and ready to take to the car. Her luggage was full and sitting on her bed, left open for any last minute additions she might find. All that remained was to gather her painting equipment and the handful of finished canvases, load everything into the Maverick, and be off.

It was when she first stepped into the front bedroom, which she had so diligently avoided during Ted's visit, that she got her first hint that all might not go as planned. Something about the room was different. Something subtle. Something that her eyes could not pinpoint. Not at first. It was only after a searching, visual sweep of the room that she saw it. The fresh paint! Her palette, cleaned the last time she had used it, had thick globs of paint heaped in piles on its surface. Her skin tingled as she saw the signs. The night artist had been there!

Drawn more by some inexplicable fascination than by any ordinary curiosity, she fearfully peeked around the edge of the night artist's canvas, dreading what she might find. She was unprepared for the scene before her. A nearly finished canvas. Thirteen nude figures instead of the three she had last seen.

All the naked players on the canvas were finished in minute detail, except for one. A solitary male, a dominant figure in the scene, stood faceless by the rock, his hands extended to Joanna, as she knelt amidst the witches. Around them danced eleven nudes, all of them jumping, cavorting, dancing in absolute abandon. Either the night cast deep shadows across their faces, or their heads were turned away, or the flying hair of the women hid their identity. The night artist had drawn them so that they were all anonymous. Only Joanna, and the unfinished figure standing beside her, were drawn so they could be identified. But he had no face.

She stood spellbound in front of the picture, the circular, snowflake like brush strokes creating a delicate pattern of mystery. She placed her fingertip on the unfinished figure standing beside her in the foreground. The paint was dry. She saw the flesh-toned dab of paint on her palette. As an afterthought she touched it, and recoiled like a spring when she felt it yield. A firm crust had formed as it had begun to harden into a rubberlike heap, not yet fully dry. She knew from. its softness that it had been mixed during the night, evidence that the night artist had worked even in Ted's presence.

From the dark recesses of her mind, a fear began to push its way forward, demanding recognition, demanding the right to be removed from the exile she had imposed upon it, demanding to be heard. And though she tried to keep it shoved out of her mind's grasp, she found its demands too strong to overcome. It reminded her of Ted's accusation that she had disappeared from his side during the night and of the paint spot found off' her sheet one morning.

It made her reconsider what she had refused to accept, what she had so convincingly proved to herself could not be. It cast suspicion on another of the inhabitants of Sutters Mountain. Only this time the object of suspicion was a trusted friend. She suspected herself.

Chapter 14

Without lingering over the picture, she scraped the drying dabs of paint off her palette, then washed it. She packed her tubes of paint away in their wooden carrying case, stuffed her brushes in their compartment in front of the paints, then closed the lid. Done. Now she could begin loading her belongings into the car. Her paints and canvases would go in last, saved for the relative security of the cushioned back seat

Wanting to load the heavier things first, she began with the three boxes of canned food sitting packed on the kitchen table. She stashed them in the Maverick's trunk, then returned to her bedroom, closed and locked her luggage, then carried it to the car. She struggled for space, trying to make it all fit, and finally after rearranging the food, she managed to close the trunk.

She leaned against the car for a rest. Shifting the heavy boxes and luggage had caused her to break out in a sweat. Her breath came in gulps, her lungs trying to supply her oxygen-starved body. She rested limply against the car for several minutes, in no hurry now that all she had to do was load her painting equipment in the back seat.

She surveyed the mountain, so serene appearing in the sun's afternoon blaze. The shadows were beginning to lengthen, bringing that time of day that produced the most interesting lighting and subjects for her canvas. Even the cabin seemed totally benign, its walls giving no hint of the terrors they had held. Down the mountain, she saw the crows again engaged in their aerial games, making a fuss over something below.

She pushed away from the car and went inside to complete her packing, emerging a few moments later with a load of empty canvases under each arm. She made a neat stack of them in the back seat, their white untouched surfaces reminding her of the year's work barely begun.

The crows, closer now than before, were creating such a fuss that she stopped to watch them for a few moments. The sun reflected like a signal flare as one dipped its black wings and dived toward the ground, then pulled out at treetop level and climbed back to the flock. Another followed as, one by one and sometimes in pairs, they nose-dived toward the treetops, pulling out only at the last instant. Above the divers, the flock kept up their incessant cawing. The pranksters of the air had evidently spotted a predator below, perhaps a bobcat or fox, and were pinpointing his position for all to see. She remembered the day the flock had pinpointed their location as she and Ted lay naked on the forest floor, alone in their lovemaking, except for the crows that tattled on them from above.

With a backward glance at the air games, she returned to the cabin for the remainder of the empty canvases, leaving only the handful of paintings she had completed, and the night artist's work, to pack carefully for the trip. Her paint box and easel she could shove in anywhere there was room.

When she brought the last of the bare canvases to the car, the crows were closer still. Uncomfortably closer. From the point she had originally noticed them, halfway down the mountain, they had continued their aerial game and moved slowly toward her cabin. She quickly shoved the canvases on top of the pile on the back seat and gently closed the door. She stopped again to watch the crows, now no more than one hundred yards away, and heeded the inner warning she was receiving. She felt the accustomed quickening of her heartbeat, so familiar to her since arriving on the mountain, the chill running down that worn path of her neck, and the voice, only one now, or two speaking in unison, which warned her as it had warned her of Betty Susan Henderson. The crows were stalking a predator – and the predator was stalking her!

Her entire body was alert. Her ears, attuned to the forest, picked up the first sound of twigs being crunched underfoot. Grateful for the warning the crows had given, and the acoustics of the mountain that carried sound upward to her cabin, she lost no time in reacting. She leaped to the car's front door and closed it gently so as not to give the appearance of a hasty departure. She cast a wistful backward glance at the Maverick, sitting like a red beacon in the clearing, and knew that with danger so near it offered no escape. Not down the rutted trail that could be traveled twice as fast on foot as by car.

With a glance over her shoulder as another twig snapped, this time barely inside the forest wall, she disappeared around the side of the cabin and slipped quietly into the forest. She found herself circling the clearing to the same thick cluster of bushes in which she had hidden the first night the witches arrived in their black robes. On hands and knees, she crawled into the thickest part of the tangle, found a place where she could sit crouched in the midst, and waited. Through the maze of leaves and branches, she could see the clearing reasonably well, finding a peephole here that gave her a view of the cabin and another there that gave a tunnel – view of her red Maverick.

The noise of her intruders had stopped, and she sensed that they were surveying the clearing from the safety of the trees. With a sinking heart she wondered if they had heard her frantic efforts to crawl into hiding. Certainly, they may have been close enough. She heard the crows overhead, but she dared not move to look at them.

She sat totally still, refusing to even scratch her face when a leaf brushed against it and caused it to start itching. The silence, except for the prankster crows, had turned the ordeal into a game of nerves. A game of waiting. She knowing they were there, they hopefully not knowing that she was hidden in the forest the same as they. And gnawing away at her frayed nerves was the possibility that they had heard her flight into the forest and knew she hid nearby. She weighed the possibility of breaking cover and running for her life. She considered it, then discarded it as being too risky, deciding to take her chances hidden in the bushes.

She heard a movement to her right, then heard a harsh whisper. The muffled rustling of leaves told her that they were nearing her, coming directly toward her hiding place! She braced herself, ready to spring out of the bushes and run. The rustling was now so close that she could hear each footfall as it was placed gingerly on the ground. It reached her hiding place and suddenly stopped. Like a granite monument she sat rigidly without moving. She heard several muffled whispers only a scant two yards away. One of them was breathing heavily from the climb, his breath wheezing as he tried to keep it under check.

She tried to control her pounding heart, afraid that it was banging so hard that it might give her away. She controlled her own breathing, regulating each slow mouthful of air so that not a sound came from her lungs. She desperately wanted to turn her head, just slightly, to get a glimpse of the intruders, but she dared not. She feared any movement, refusing even to raise her eyes to check the density of the bush between her and her hunters. A sudden gust of wind brought her a sickening whiff of heavy body odor. She instinctively twitched her nose, then sat frozen and afraid that even that tiny motion might be detected.

"Come on!" a disgruntled voice whispered with unmasked urgency. "We've got to get to the back door!"

One set of feet moved, then two other pairs followed. Joanna's hopes soared as they moved away, though she still sat like a stone. She heard them circling the forest's edge to the rear of her cabin, taking the same route, only in reverse, which she had just followed. When it reached a point directly opposite the cabin's rear door, the sound stopped. She waited, and again the mountain fell into a deathly silence.

Several minutes of waiting, knowing that something was about to happen, brought her nerves to a frazzled, nearly uncontrollable edge. She felt every inch of skin on her body pulled taut by the tense muscles beneath. Her eyes, trying to see into the foliage where she knew the men waited, began to ache from the unaccustomed strains put on them. But still she sat unmoving, afraid that even the tiniest motion would draw attention to her hiding place.

Then suddenly the waiting was over. As though on cue, the men burst from the forest. At the same time, another group of three men, hidden without her knowledge at the front of the cabin, trotted across the clearing to the front door. Several yards away they stopped. From her obscured view through the bushes, she saw a burly man in the front clearing step forward, asserting his leadership.

"We know you're in there, so come on out!" he shouted hoarsely, his words carried away by the wind. When there was no reply, she saw him fidget, look over his shoulder at the two men behind him, then repeat his challenge like a villain in a western movie. One of the men behind him stepped forward, giving Joanna her first clear view of anyone other than the speaker. She immediately recognized his face! He was the owner of the hardware store.

When his challenge again went unanswered, the third man stepped forward, who like the leader was a stranger to her. The three conferred, were joined by another unknown but familiar face from the rear, and after a few moments in a huddle, they appeared to reach agreement. The fourth man disappeared out of her vision to the back of the cabin, then hardware man and the leader stepped to the door. Without knocking, they threw open the door and ducked inside. The single sentry in the front looked nervously around the clearing, his gaze sweeping past her hiding place without stopping. Even from a distance, and with the branches partially blocking her vision, she could see the strain on the man's face, and couldn't help but giggle inwardly that anyone could think her so fearsome. The man was obviously relieved when one of the men from the rear came to support him in his solitary vigil.

The hardware man and the leader were still inside, and the nervous one was beginning to worry.

"Will, is everything all right?" he called out uncertainly.

A muffled reply came from within the cabin, and the two in front seemed satisfied and were immediately less tense. The hardware man and the leader soon stepped out, shaking their heads in defeat.

"She ain't there," the leader declared. Then he raised his voice and called to the two in the rear. "Ya'll come on around. She's gone."

"Has she cleared out for good?" the nervous one asked.

"Naw," the hardware man replied. He walked over to the Maverick and looked at the packed back seat. Hey, lookey here!"

The others gathered around the car. The leader turned back toward the cabin, the veins on his face swelled red with anger. He nudged his buddy.

"Go in and check her dresser drawers. See if she's packed all her stuff."

Half a minute later, the hardware man was "back, excitement showing in his face. "All her clothes are gone, and there's not a bite of food in the house."

"Goddamn!" The leader looked angrily around the clearing, and Joanna thought she saw his eyes hesitate when they swept past her clump of bushes. She was prepared to dash into the forest and run for her life, but his eyes kept moving, and soon he was looking at the other side of the clearing, and a half-hidden trail that led up the mountain.

"That's what I was afraid of," the leader said, tapping his knuckles on the side of the Maverick. "She must have heard us coming and made a run for it. Up the mountain," he said, indicating the trail leading into the denser forest above the cabin. "But that witch'll be back," he said vehemently. "And when she does, she's gonna get the same thing her mother got!"

Slivers of cold fear pricked Joanna like icicles stabbing her in the dark. As Peter had warned they might, the townspeople were moved by a contagious fear. Their terror had snowballed into a lynch mob that wanted to take her life! She was on the run and they knew it! She could only wait and see what they would do. Her only chance was the Maverick, the red beacon that now seemed so far away. If she could somehow get to it and get off the mountain, she could make a dash for safety. But if she had to try and hide from them on Slitters Mountain, then she was doomed. These men knew the mountain like the back of their hands, she imagined, and would find her sooner or later.

The leader gave the car hood an angry jerk and threw it open. Then he reached inside and a moment, later triumphantly held out part of the little car's innards for the others to inspect. She had to stifle a cry.

"The bitch won't go nowhere without this," he said. Out of his throat rolled a raspy chuckle.

She stared in disbelief at the dangling wires and the black object in the leader's hand. It was as though he had just triggered a coiled trap; she could feel its steel jaws closing around her. A fleeting moment of panic coursed its way through her body, and it was only by asserting her will power that she remained immobile and hidden. If she were to escape now, it would have to be on foot. She must outwit them on their mountain. As the odds began to turn against her, she knew that she must maintain her equilibrium, use every cunningness of the Leo cat to outwit them and remain alive.

The leader's fat face had lost its anger, replaced instead by a leering half-smile as he took obvious delight in the blow he had dealt her. He held the distributor cap before him like a crown. His beady pig-eyes danced viciously in pleasure. Her self-doubt began to set in, prompted by the wicked pleasure she saw in the leader's face. His initial anger in finding her gone was now replaced by something even more fearsome-the joy of the hunt. The obvious pleasure he would take in tracking her down ... and in killing her.

She knew how it must feel to be a participant in a fox hunt ... only she was the hunted. Unless the fox could outwit the hounds, it was doomed to be torn to shreds. She knew the feeling of the hunted. She wondered if Isadora had felt it too?

"We'll wait for her," the leader declared. He closed the open car hood. "You three go out back and hide. We'll cover the front. When she comes, let her get inside before you make your move."

He waved them off, then called after them. "If she don't come, stay hid till I tell you. Even if it's all night, y'hear?"

He motioned to the hardware man, and the three of them took their positions at the edge of the forest, just outside the front clearing. She heard them shoving leaves aside and breaking branches as they tried to make themselves comfortable. Then when the noise stopped, she knew the waiting period had begun.

The afternoon turned sluggishly into evening, the evening into night. Hidden in the very midst of her hunters, Joanna welcomed the night. It offered relative safety, though still no escape. With her pursuers so nearby, she dared not chance it. She dared not give her position away, and she knew that she could not remove herself from her hiding and slip into the night in silence. She napped, though never fell into a deep sleep for fear of making some tiny noise that would tell them of her presence. In her short-sleeved blouse, the night air was cold, and she sat huddled and shivering from the chill that ran like a current through her body. With the first gray shafts of dawn she was wide awake, her ears alert and waiting, every muscle in her body tense, hung on the suspense of what the morning would bring.

The orange face of the sun burned its way through the early-morning mist, driving away the chill that hung over the ground. She could hear them somewhere down the mountain, her friends, the crows, as they dived and screamed through their playground in the air. The dew-covered grass in the clearing glistened emerald green, reflecting the sun's light into her eyes. And from her right came the first alien noise of the day.

The leader stepped out of hiding into the edge of the clearing and surveyed the cabin. His face looked even more piggish from a distance, his burly frame more sinister, more threatening than the night before. He lumbered into the middle of the clearing, with the hardware man and the other one following.

He raised his voice and belched to the others, "Come on around here."

The three in the rear stumbled sleepily into view. "Colder 'n hell last night," one of them growled, rubbing his arms to warm them.

"Let's go home." the leader commanded.

"Don't you think she's coming back?" the cold one asked, still rubbing his arms.

"She'll be back, all right," the leader said, "but so will we. She ain't going nowhere long as I got her distributor cap. Now let's go get some breakfast."

He turned and tramped away, with the others following in single file. They left in their wake a spider web pattern in the grass. It was evidence of their having plowed through the grass, knocking off the dew; the telltale grass turned dull without the dew to catch the sun's light. One of them turned and looked back, surveying the scene for a moment, then hurried to catch up with the others.

Joanna remained hidden long after their sound of movement in the underbrush disappeared with them down the mountain. She was afraid of the clearing now, afraid of the cabin and the car that wouldn't run, afraid of being seen and trapped. But, she thought with resolve, she was trapped anyway. The little red Maverick couldn't get her off the mountain now.

When she emerged from her hiding, careful to exit on the forest side and not the clearing side, she did so with a plan. There was only one person who could possibly help her now – 0. T. Hanover. Like Joanna, Hanover was an outsider who made occasional trips to the world outside the city limits of Sutters Hamlet.

Joanna needed an escape, and Hanover was the only one who might help her who had immediate access to a way out. And there was yet another reason. If she could reach safely Hanover's newspaper office, she would be off the mountain where she was now being hunted. And that was the most important reason of all.

Cautiously, measuring each move from one hiding place to the next, stepping lightly in silence, she began to inch her way down the mountain. She stopped often to wait and listen, to check her bearings, to make certain of her safety. Foot by foot, she descended the mountain, careful not to follow any well-traveled paths. She swung a wide arc around the town, following a route that would bring her in from the rear, bring her in, yet avoid the main street through town. She would use the mountain for cover, let it bring her nearly to the back door of the newspaper, let it hide her the way it hid the witches and the men who tracked her. She would be stealthy like a Leo cat, silent, unseen, cunning. With a silence surprising even to herself, she crept through the forest hardly aware of her own presence.

Halfway down the mountain, and still in familiar territory, she heard voices. Faint, yet as she listened, they grew louder. Like a caged animal, she looked around for a hiding place. Ignoring larger bushes, she ran to a rock outcropping farther away, surrounded by a flimsy screen of briars and weeds. The voices were gaining on her, and though they didn't seem threatening, she knew she couldn't risk being seen. In dismay she looked at the rocks she had chosen, cursing herself for her selection. They would never hide her! She started to run to one of the bushes she had bypassed when she saw it! Just the edge of it visible behind the weeds and the scrubby little bushes growing amidst the rocks. A hole! She pulled aside the bush and saw the entrance to a small cave tunneled beneath a rock. The smooth, brown, packed earth told her she had found the den of some animal. But it was large, large enough for her to squeeze into. She scooted in, rear first, and when she let the bush fall back in place it covered her completely!

The sun was approaching its zenith, its blaze and the sudden excitement drawing sweat, causing her clothes to cling to her body like matted animal fur. But she was safe. She heard the voices come and pass nearby, with her presence never known. She lingered in the den, the earth and rock around her so strong, comforting, offering the protection of a home. She wondered at her luck, or fate, in finding it. Long after the voices had disappeared, when she was certain that she was again alone, she crawled out and continued her creep into town.

Another two hours of carefully descending the mountain found her approaching her goal. The backside of town was half a mile away, a straight shot down the mountain and nearly to the back doors of the stores lining one side of the main street. Most of the farms were spread out along the valley, off the road that had brought her into Sutters Hamlet that first day. Only a few hardier souls, like the whittler and Peter and his mother, actually lived on the craggy mountainside. For the community of farmers, the fertile soil was in the valley. And where there was fertile soil, there were farms, and humans, now a threat to her very existence.

Only once while descending the mountain did she encounter inhabitants. Sitting low on the mountain slope behind town, and in new territory to her, causing her nearly to stumble into the clearing before seeing the human signs, the little house, much like her own cabin, had come as a surprise. As she tried to ease quietly away, the farm dog barked. She heard it bounding across the clearing and into the foliage headed straight for her, setting up a fuss that she knew could not go unnoticed by the people.

And it didn't.

She heard a man's voice shouting, "What you got there, boy?". By the way he talked, she knew the owner was running after his dog, no doubt expecting to find a coon or possum, or some other game animal of the mountain.

The undergrowth before her came crashing open and the dog, a big brown and white spotted hound, ran to her, its tail wagging. Behind the dog, and only a few bushes away, she heard the man crashing toward her. She turned in panic to run, but when she did, the dog, its tail still wagging excitedly, began to follow. Biting her lip, and apologizing to it under her breath, she slapped the dog smartly across the nose. It let out a yelp, then turned and ran headlong back into the bushes. Instantly, Joanna disappeared into the undergrowth in the opposite direction. Behind her, she heard the man cussing, demanding that the dog, as though it were a human, tell him about its encounter and retreat.

She ran without caution, and only when she was certain that she wasn't being followed did she stop to catch her breath and regain her bearings. Behind her the mountain jutted upward like a green giant into the sky. A thin swirl of gray cooking smoke climbed above the trees and was swallowed by the air. She noted its location, wanting to swing wide around it should she have to retrace her route back up the mountain. Should there be a next encounter with the dog and man, she may not be so lucky.

She cautiously edged her way the last few hundred yards before the mountain gave way to the ramshackle, stick built stores of Sutters Hamlet. Never having entered from the rear of town, she didn't know what to expect, how easy or how difficult would be the flight through the open space from the base of the mountain to the rear of Hanover's newspaper. She only knew that with its freshly painted, white clapboard sides, the newspaper would be easily recognized from the rear.

Stopping often to let her ears tell her all was well, she crept silently forward until she could see the buildings, stretched before her like a scene from the nineteenth century. Few New Yorkers would believe such a place existed, a wooden replica of the past. Only a cloud of dust crawling up the valley off to her left and the black metallic bug that rolled along without the aid of horses, ruined the time machine effect.

The town was alive as she had rarely seen it. But then she realized that on her other visits it had been alive until she was recognized and the inhabitants went inside. Now she watched it unseen, and she knew that until some of the activity subsided, visible to her through the alleys between some of the buildings, she would have to remain hidden. When late afternoon approached and the people left the street, she would run for the back door to the newspaper. It sat like a great white light before her, less than two hundred feet away, but the nervousness in her stomach told her it would be the longest journey of all.

Growing more accustomed to bushes as the day passed, she found a thick clump of shrubs overlooking town and settled down amongst them, an unobstructed view of Sutters Hamlet spread out below her. A glance at the sun and she guessed that it was nearly three o'clock, several hours before the stores would begin to close for the night.

She sat idly in the bushes as the afternoon dragged slowly past, watching the movement below as people would pass the alleyway, then disappear from her vision farther down the street. Safely hidden, and no longer needing to remain so acutely alert, she was able to let her mind thumb slowly over the events of the past twenty-four hours.

Though Peter had warned her, she actually had never looked upon the ordinary folks of Sutters Hamlet as posing a danger to her. True, they were unfriendly, and had turned into a mob twenty-five years before when they killed Isadora. But she had never imagined that she could be in any danger from them, and only halfway so after Peter's warning. To her, ever since that first night when she thought she had dreamed seeing the hooded face peering at her through the window, the witches had been the villains. The witches had been the sinister ones that lurked in the night, which frightened her, that erased her memory for four days. It had been the witches that she feared, though she had bravely stayed on and defied their will.

But it was the night artist who had eventually planted the seed of fear, which grew so large she could no longer fight it. The night artist, with his unexplained picture that grew in the night, which had forced her into the decision to leave. The night artist, who drew her as a witch, heightened her fear of the witches and their ceremony, a ritual that the canvas brought to life.

But neither had banned her. Not the night artist.

Not the witches. Only the ordinary people had attempted physical harm. It was they, people not too unlike herself, who now hunted her. It was from them that she hid.

She had been lucky in eluding the leader and the hardware man and the others. Lucky in finding the den on the mountain and in evading the man with the dog. She wondered how long she would remain so lucky?

But something about her flight down the mountain troubled her. As she had time to retrace each step, she found it puzzling that she had found the den, that she had passed by such obvious hideaways as the large clumps of heavy foliage scattered around her. Passed those by to run to the rocks, a far inferior place to hide had it not been for the den hidden away in the ground. It was as though she had known about the den, though she knew that was impossible. It was her sixth sense again, the sense that failed to save Betty Susan Henderson, which had guided her to the den. Either that or some uncanny twist of fate.

Her mental games were abruptly ended by movement in a nearby alley, a movement that made her spine grow icy cold.

The leader stood silhouetted in the alley, the walls of two buildings towering over his husky, white. T-shirted frame. Even though he stood in shadow, that shape was unmistakable. He dipped his head toward his cupped hands and put an orange glow to the end of the cigarette dangling from his mouth. A cloud of blue gray smoke poured out of his nose and the corners of his mouth as he puffed nervously on the weed. He glanced around irritably, as though he were waiting on a late arrival. Curiously, for the first time since his intrusion into her world the day before, Joanna wondered about his name. As she watched, he seemed to grow more settled, more relaxed, as he propped his back against a wall and waited.

His wait was short. The hardware man scooted around the corner and slithered down the alley to join the leader. By their clandestine, guarded manner, Joanna wondered if that was indication that the majority of Sutters Hamlet was unaware of their hunt? They conferred, their heads shoved together immodestly close, their very intimacy advertising the secrecy of their meeting. The leader did most of the talking, his mouth a mere inch from the hardware man's ear whose attention was complete. He nodded in solemn agreement to the leader's words, his head cocked slightly toward the other man.

As suddenly as it had begun, the conference ended. The two men stood feet apart, talking normally. The leader turned to face the mountain. When he raised his hand and pointed toward the slope where she hid, Joanna froze. She half expected them to dash toward her, but it was evidently a false alarm. The two men laughed, then turned together and walked back to the street, disappearing from her view.

Uneventfully, the rest of the afternoon slid past with hardly a notice. The sun dipped to its five o'clock spot in the sky, and Joanna saw fewer shoppers passing the alleys. With a tightening in her stomach, she realized that she must soon make her way to the ivory white building that stood before her. The open field was flooded by the golden glow of late afternoon sunlight. Metallic flashes of light dotted the ground where cans and glasses, thrown as garbage from the stores' rear doors, reflected the sun's light, nearly blinding her when the sun hit them just right.

She steeled herself for the last leg of her journey, trying to will away the nervousness she now felt, telling herself without conviction that with no one there to see her she had nothing to fear. The number of people passing the alleys dwindled to nothingness, the sun sank lower, and from the back of her mind came a nudging that told her it was time to move.

With an air of casualness that surprised her, she sauntered from her hiding and walked confidently into the open. She had to resist the urge to dash across the open space, and forced herself instead to continue her stroll to the newspaper. A dash would be quicker, but it might also draw the attention of some random observer who would take no notice of a girl walking across the field. With her throat tight and dry, heart pounding, and resisting the fire burning at her heels, she walked openly across the field and onto the back stoop of the whitest building in town.

She gave the door several quick raps. Waited. No Hanover. Doubling her fist again, she banged loudly, enough to bring Hanover should he be at the front of the building. She looked in through a slit in the curtains and saw not a trace of life. No hint of an inside light burning left the buildings innards to the mercy of the fading sun. With a sinking heart, she realized Hanover was not there.

In desperation she tried the door and found it locked. Grabbing the doorknob, she shook the door. It felt flimsy, loose and weak in the frame that held it. She looked around to see if anyone were watching, then without hesitation or guilt, slammed her shoulder against the rickety door. The lock snapped and the door swung open. Quickly she stepped inside and shut the door behind her.

She looked around her at Hanover's living quarters, a combination living room and dining room that somehow seemed not too inviting in the murky light. Something she couldn't pinpoint made her uneasy, something about the depth of darkness in the room. It was as though she had stumbled upon a mourning widow's quarters, where every ornament, every decoration, even the walls bespoke their sadness through their dark colors, totally void of gaiety. The fading sunlight only added to the effect.

She passed by a closed door along a narrow hallway that led into the front half of the building. The newspaper office was empty, the front shades closed tight, casting the office in even more darkness than the living quarters behind her. Only in the front corner, beside Hanover's desk, did a shaft of light penetrate the gloom as it cast its telltale beam on the old Underwood.

"Mr. Hanover!" she whispered.

She knew there would be no reply, but wanted to hear some sound for reassurance, even the sound of her own futile cry. She retraced her steps along the hall and into the living room, pausing momentarily at the closed door which she assumed was his bedroom, but decided that she had already violated his privacy enough by bursting in the back door. His closed bedroom door indicated to her that it was his private inner sanctum, a place where he retreated in private moments, and not to be violated without cause or invitation.

She settled herself into a chair shoved away in a corner, out of sight line of any peeping tom and therefore safe. She wished for a flood of light to wash away the uneasiness she felt, but she dared not risk giving away her presence. So she reconciled herself to waiting for Hanover amidst the creeping darkness.

The afternoon seemed in a state of suspended animation. Ages seemed to crawl by with every five minutes that passed. She had no wristwatch with which to check the time, and there was no sign of a clock in the living room. But a low-pitched methodical tick floated toward her from the hallway, and she knew that behind the closed door Hanover had an alarm clock. She threw the thought aside, for some reason apprehensive of that room. Some inner voice, though not a voice of fear, made her apprehensive about what was behind the closed door. And with the apprehension, with the knowledge that something inside that room had touched off her sixth sense, came fear. Not a fear for her own safety, but a fear born from experience of the mountain's strange ways that warned her of something. Something akin to her fear of her own cabin when she knew the night artist had been there. Not tangible, not physically harmful, but unnerving just the same. And most unnerving of all came her curiosity, the one emotion she knew from experience she could never conquer.

She tried to overcome it by shoving aside a curtain for a quick glance outside, to judge by the daylight the time of day, and therefore to eliminate any need to venture into that room. The outside seemed the same. Even brighter, though she knew it to be an illusion created by her own darkened surroundings. She could only guess at the time, but a guess would not satisfy her curiosity.

Periodically, she peeked outside to watch the afternoon slowly fade away into twilight, and then in the accustomed swiftness of the mountain, darkness engulfed the valley. An uneasiness penetrated even the tiniest recesses of her being, an uneasiness that reminded her that this was the night of June 21st. This was Midsummer Night!

She prayed for Hanover to return, but with a certainty entrenched with each passing minute, she knew that he would not. Not this night.

The ticking was the only sound on her earth.

She knew that she could not spend the night here. Not Midsummer Night. Not in Sutters Hamlet or on the mountain. But it seemed now that she had no way out, not unless she were to try and leave the valley on foot. Her alternatives were few, and none of them palatable. Remembering Peter's warning about Midsummer Night put her in a turmoil. Perhaps Hanover's place could offer her safe-hiding through the night. Perhaps it could not. Perhaps she should attempt the twenty-mile hike to the paved road and get the help of the authorities in removing her belongings from the mountain. She was undecided. Confused. If she were to try hiking out, valuable time was slipping away.

In one swift catlike move, she rose and crossed the room, heading for the ticking behind the door.

The cold metal of the doorknob was a shock to her sweating palm, causing her to recoil involuntarily. She eased open the door, and the ticking seemed like crashing thunder to her nervously alert ears. She intended to flick on the light switch, glance at the clock and shut the door, to shun the room except for that. Since corning to the mountain, she had grown too accustomed to this feeling of foreboding to want to know its cause. The feeling was overriding even her leonine curiosity.

She fumbled in the darkness until she found the switch, then bracing herself, she shoved it upward. The sudden light partially blinded her, and she spent a moment accustomizing her eyes to the brightness. The clock, sitting directly in front of her on a small table beside Hanover's bed, spelled out the time. Eight thirty. She had started to shut the door, her brain bleeping the signal to her fingertips to flip off the light, when something on the wall made her stop.

A painting of a girl hung on the wall beside Hanover's bed, the ends of her mouth cocked upward in amusement, penetrating brown eyes holding the room in their innocence, and a long mane of black hair falling loosely at her shoulders. The eyes seemed to be watching her. Joanna stood spellbound, staring at the painting that could be a portrait of herself. But she knew it wasn't. She remembered the photograph Hanover had shown her, and she knew the painting was a portrait of Isadora. A self-portrait, no doubt. She remembered her conversations with the whittler when he drew analogies between Isadora and her. Besides their appearing to be twins, spaced twenty-five years apart, the whittler had said that Isadora also painted.

She strained her eyes to see the artist's signature, but could not distinguish it from her vantage point across the room. She stepped into the room, filled with fascination now, and not fear or foreboding, to search the painting for the signature. Two yards away she saw it – and more. She stopped, chilled. The room seemed suddenly cold. She shivered, clasping her arms about herself as though holding an infant. Isadora. The name was scrawled in the picture's bottom right-hand corner. Below it the year. 1949. The year before her birth.

She stood dazed before the portrait, cold to the bone, trembling with excitement, struck by a sudden comprehension.

The canvas was covered with hundreds of tiny, circular, snowflake like brush strokes. The intricate pattern, that she had failed to duplicate in her own attempts, spun a beautiful web of color in the self-portrait of her mother.

With her fingertips she gently caressed her mother's face, rejoicing in the knowledge that the creation before her came from the hands of her own kin. Her own kin! An expression that she had never before been entitled to use. She, an orphan facing the world alone, was at last in touch with her past.

She felt the strokes of the night artist beneath her fingers, and there was no fear. She no longer feared that which had grown in the front bedroom. She knew and understood.

The drop of paint on her sheet, Ted's accusation that she had disappeared during the night, all had a meaning now. A meaning that she had seen before but feared, and refused to let herself believe. Her own hands had been the hands of the night artist, her body the night artist's body. Her mother had come nightly and directed her, possessed her in the night. Possessed her body, and with the strokes of Isadora, had painted the scene that had seemingly grown on the canvas.

Now, standing in the presence of her mother, and finally accepting the fact that Isadora was her mother, she had full understanding. Using her own feeble deductive process, she had determined what the night artist's painting depicted. But until now she had no hint of the painting's true meaning.

Her mother, now at one with the past, present, and future, could see the future as well as Joanna could see the past. She had foreseen the hunt on Midsummer Night and the death it was intended to bring, but she could not change the future. She could only warn her daughter in a medium they both understood, in an attempt to save Joanna from a repeat of her own horrible death at the hands of Sutters Hamlet.

The painting and its one unfinished face held the key! It held the identity of the one person her mother knew she could trust.

Joanna stood numbly before the picture. Surprised, relieved, calmed by the thoughts that had swept her mind. But her inner self told her that she was right. The unfinished face on the night artist's painting, a member of the coven, offered her passage to safety. It was a macabre twist, she realized, that would have her find her safety in the coven. But then she remembered the dream as she lay half awake by Ted's side, which had been no dream at all since he had heard the voice too, which had told her they would bother her no more. That she would seek them out if there were another encounter.

With the knowledge now of what she must do, she quickly left the room, turning out the light and shutting the door behind her. She eased out the back door and into the night. And under the cover of darkness, she headed for her cabin, this time taking the most direct route to the end of town and along the rutted trail that would lead her to the clearing.

She heard noises in the night, noises that told her that she was not alone on the mountain. Halfway up the slope came the first sign of pursuit. A voice, distant, muffled on the breeze, somewhere behind her. The pace of her heartbeat quickened, as she wondered if she had been seen and recognized leaving town. But the voice was faint, and she knew the mountain's strange ways of amplifying sound. She quickened her pace, but not so much that she could not glide noiselessly over the ground. Her feet seemed in unaccustomed oneness with the terrain, guiding her blindly and in silence over the brittle foliage beneath them. Not a twig snapped, not a limb pricked her as she slid past, though in the darkness they were all unseen. She glided silent as a fox through the night, while behind her the hunters combed the mountain like a fan, their sounds occasionally reaching her ears.

She hesitated at the edge of the clearing. The red top of her Maverick glistened with the moon's dull glow. The shadowy hulk of the cabin sat behind it like a dark whale on the side of the mountain, its windows shuttered, the front door still standing open from the leader's visit. But there was no sign of danger. No sign that some of the leader's men lurked away in the darkness awaiting her arrival. But then there would be no sign. They would simply pounce on her from the darkness. She could not be certain. She could not be certain that they were there, nor certain that they weren't. But she must gamble that they weren't; in that clearing was her only way to safety, the only hand that could deliver her from her pursuers. The picture.

A spine-tingling howl rolled up through the trees, shattering the stillness like rock waves on a quiet pond. She glanced over her shoulder and looked into the black face of darkness. Hounds! Hounds had been brought in to trail her! Another deep-throated howl echoing through the trees shoved her into action; it was the howl of a dog on a scent.

She burst into the clearing, trusting her fate. She ran into the cabin, pulling the door shut behind her. She could feel the cabin's emptiness, its lack of dwelling. Its walls seemed to engulf a coldness she had never before encountered there. It was alien to her, inhospitable, but no longer unknown and frightening.

In the bedroom, she found the painting still propped on the easel. Grabbing one of the legs of the easel, she spun it around facing her. Her hands were reaching instinctively for a brush and paints. She fumbled in the darkness. But she had already packed her paints in the car. One of the hounds struck a higher note, its voice a repetition of excited yelps. She reached for the lantern, then stopped herself. It wasn't to be she who painted. She needed no light.

Calming herself, she stood before the canvas, a camel-hair brush clasped tightly in her hand. She found a brush – now the paint. Her paints were here spread out in confusion beside her, unrecognizable in the darkness. She lifted her head, her eyes closed. She felt her body tremble. The room was warm again.

"Mother," she whispered into the night. "Help me. Please."

A warmth brushed her lips, caressed her face, and a touch of moisture was planted like a kiss on her cheek. Her body quavered as the warmth slid like a gentle rod into her body, and she felt lifeless, yet alive.

Her hands began to move, but she did not will them to do so. In the darkness, and without the aid of her eyes, she felt them lift a tube of paint and deposit a drop onto her palette, then another tube, then another. Deftly they mixed the paint. Then, like a hand doing automatic writing, her right hand began to paint. Small, delicate strokes. Unaccustomed strokes to her. Her fingers swirled the tip of the brush in a pixie way, and she knew that on the canvas, the night artist unveiled the mystery to her work.

She heard noises outside, near the forest's edge. The hounds had been quieted, so they must know she was inside. But still the night artist painted. She heard a voice now, a whisper that was meant for someone else.

It stopped. Her hands stopped moving. They dropped to her side and were hers once again. Her body, her being, all were hers. She peered through the darkness at the face, but her eyes were not as adept as the night artist's hands, and the identity of the last figure remained a mystery,

She fumbled in the darkness for a match. Outside, there was the sound of feet shuffling in the grass. Many feet. They were in the clearing! She flicked the match and it was a pinprick of light in the night. From outside there came a shout. She glanced at the canvas for only a second before snuffing out the flame, but she saw the face and knew. It was so logical, so plain. She should have known, should have guessed after finding her mother's portrait.

The room was in darkness again, but for only a moment. Through a crack in the window she saw a light outside, a dancing, living light. Firelight. Then there was another, then another as a ring of torches were lit encircling the cabin. She saw the clearing aglow with shadowy figures, silhouetted against the fires they carried, fires that were intended for her.

"Come on out! We know you're in there!" It was the leader's voice, the voice she had come to know and dread. The cabin's interior was bathed in a gentle light from the flames. Stealthily, she crept from the bedroom, through the living room, and into the kitchen. Emotionlessly, she gazed out the rear window. The flames from half a dozen torches licked at the darkness, blocking her escape from the rear. Yet she knew that the forest's nearness to the rear of the cabin offered her the only chance of escape. She stood before the window and peered out. Outside, a hand pointed at her, followed by a shout, and she ducked away, aware that she had been seen.

She felt no fear. Felt only the calming presence of another, a guiding hand. The kiss of moisture again brushed her cheek and she was reassured.

Behind her, the leader's voice rang out again, cursing her. A heavy foot smashed against the bolted front door, and she knew it was his. Turning her back on the window, she approached the back door. She paused. The crash came again at the cabin's front, and with it the splintering of wood. She reached for the rear door latch, listening for any movement. There was none. The crash came again.

The same warmth again entered her body.

She fumbled with the latch. Couldn't make her fingers grasp it properly. Couldn't make them close around it. Couldn't make them move nimbly. As she tried, now frantically with the sounds of splintering wood behind her, to shove back the hand latch, her nails scraped the wood of the door.

The scratching of her nails. Then she knew! She knew what was happening. She knew why her fingers were no longer nimble. Knew how she had fled up the mountain in such silence; how she had found the den in the rocks, uncannily, as she crept down the mountain in search of the faceless one.

The metamorphosis had begun.

She heard her scratching sounds in the night, and she knew the change had started, would be complete in moments. She felt her claws digging deeper into the wood, biting into it, eating away at it until one was behind it and she could flip the bolt up and shove back the latch.

The door cracked open and she pushed herself away, but could no longer stand erect. Instinctively, she dropped onto her front feet. She pranced nervously on the wooded floor, her claws clicking like a tap dancer's shoe on the wood each time she shunted her feet.

She looked through the cracked door with her night vision and saw the ring of hunters still waiting. But they were not waiting for her. They waited for Joanna.

ABOUT THE AUTHOR

Youngblood Hawke has been writing since the 1970's and a published novelist since 1978. Writing and running a business has kept him busy for two decades. With the publishing of THE COVEN CONSPIRACY he now writes full time. His next novel, a paranormal suspense thriller, is ANCIENT MEMORIES.